ROD

CW00402494

The Year 1072
~Retribution~

The Harrying of the North Series
Book Three

Hindrelag Books

The Year 1072
~Retribution~

This is a work of fiction. Names, characters, organisations, places, events and incidents are either a product of the author's imagination or are used fictitiously.

Text Copyright © Rod Flint 2019.

The right of Rod Flint to be identified as the author of this work has been asserted by him in accordance with the Copyright, Designs and Patents Act 1988.

All Rights reserved.

No part of this book may be reproduced or stored in a retrieval system or transmitted in any form, or by any means, electronic, mechanical, photocopying, recording or otherwise without express permission of the author.

For Earl Gospatric

*~My many times great grandfather
and the inspiration behind my
Harrying of the North stories~*

To Anne,

The 'Comma Queen',

Thank you for all your

hard work and assistance.

All my love

Rod

Contents

Author's Note

My motivation for writing the tale of Hravn and Ealdgith and their experience of the Harrying of the North, was a desire to leave something for my family's future generations that brings to life an early and easily forgotten period in our past. My parents' families, the Flints, Martins, Wilsons, Mattinsons, Pattinsons, Curwens et al can trace their lineage through 1000 years of life in Cumbria and the Borders, as far back as the nobility of the pre-Norman north, and through Gospatric to Earl Uhtred of Northumberland, King Ethelred 2nd of England and King Malcolm 2nd of Scotland.

Modern Western societies are increasingly equal and diverse in their social attitudes. The Anglo-Saxon and Norse societies of pre-Norman England had evolved from pre-Roman Germanic cultures and followed an Orthodox English Christianity. They were more equal in their attitude to women and their legal status, than the strongly Catholic, constraining and more misogynistic society that developed under the Normans. I wanted my two heroes to reflect all that is good about today's society whilst remaining true to their own time.

Whilst writing, I have tried to use words that are authentic and made a deliberate effort to avoid those that have a French or post-invasion origin. That is why 'stake-wall' is used instead of the French word: palisade.

I now live in Richmondshire, but spent many childhood holidays in the Eden Valley and the fells of the Lake District, where I chose to use the traumatic time of the Harrying of the North as a vehicle for this tale. The geography speaks for itself. These are places I have known and loved all my life.

I would like to thank all those who have supported and encouraged me, not least in the laborious task of proof reading and for helping to ensure that the story is understandable to all. In particular, my wife Judith for her support and encouragement; my mother Clarissa, herself a true Cumbrian and incredible font of family history; my daughter Lara, always full of enthusiasm for the tale and in some little way a role-model for Ealdgith and my brother Paul and good friend Anne Wicks for their attention to my grammar.

My thanks are also due to Andy Thursfield for his graphic design and art work, and to Kathleen Herbert whose book, 'Spellcraft – Old English Heroic Legends,' recounts the tale of Hildegyd and Waldere, from which I drew in Book 1, and helped inspire the characters of Ealdgith and Hravn.

Map

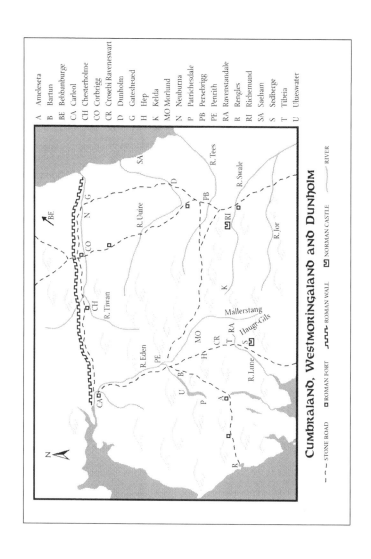

A Ameleseta
B Bartun
BE Bebbanburge
CA Carleol
CH Chesterholme
CO Corbrigg
CR Croseti Raveneswart
D Dunholm
G Gateshefued
H Hep
K Kelda
MO Morlund
N Neuburna
P Patrichesdale
PB Persebrigg
PE Penrith
RA Ravenstandale
R Renges
RI Richemund
SA Sachan
T Tibeia
U Ulueswater

Cumbraland, Westmoringaland and Dunholm

- - - STONE ROAD   ⊡ ROMAN FORT   ⊓⊓⊓ ROMAN WALL   ⊡ NORMAN CASTLE   ~~~ RIVER

Place Names

Place names are those shown in the Oxford Dictionary of English Place-Names. I have used the name for the date nearest to 1072. Where a similar name has several spellings, I have chosen a common one in order to avoid confusion. Places that existed in 1072, but aren't listed, retain their present names.

Alnewich. Alnwick. Dwelling on the River Aln.
Ameleseta. Ambleside. Shieling or summer pasture by the river sandbank.
Amounderness. A hundred in Lancashire. The land between the Rivers Lune and Ribble. It extended from the coast to Yorkshire, and contained the modern towns of Fleetwood, Garstang, Lytham, and parts of Lancaster and Ribchester.
Aplebi. Appleby in Westmoreland. Village where apple trees grow.
Askum. Askham. Place at the Ash trees.
Bartun. Bartun. Barley farm.
Beaurepayre. Bearpark.
Bebbanburge. Bamburgh. Stronghold of a Queen called Bebbe.
Brethstrett. The ancient Roman route that runs north-south across Lakeland's eastern fells, now known as High Street.
Carleol. Carlisle. Celtic; fortified town at a place belonging to Luguvalos.
Cattun. Cowton. Cow farm.
Corbricg. Corbridge. Bridge near Corchester.
Corburne. Colburn. Cool stream.
Crosebi Raveneswart. Crosby Ravensworth. Manor with a cross owned by a man called Rafnsvatr.

Crokesteil. Croxdale. Projecting piece of land of a man named Krokr.

Cumbraland. Cumberland. Region of the Cumbrian Britons.

Culewen. Colvend. A small village on the mouth of the River Urr in Kircudbrightshire, Scotland, from where the family name Culwen (or Curwen) originates. In the spelling of Curwen and its derivatives, the surname is English and Cumbrian but is believed also to originate from Scotland. The place name meaning and hence the surname is obscure, but is probably a development of the Old English pre 7th century 'col wincel': the cold place.

Defena. Derwent, or River Derwent. From the Brythonic Derventio, meaning valley thick with oaks.

Doolish. Douglas, on the Isle of Man.

Dune. Downholme. Place in the hills.

Dunholm. Durham. Island with a hill.

Dyflin. Dublin. Norse, derived from Gaelic 'Dubh Linn', meaning 'black pool'.

Efenwuda. Evenwood. Level woodland.

Eithr's Lake. Hayeswater. The lake by the enclosure.

Ellintone. Ellington. Farmstead at a place where eels are caught.

Elreton. Ellerton. Farmstead by the alders.

Ériúland. Eire / Ireland.

Esebi. Easby. Village of a man named Esi.

Euruic. York. From Celtic; probably meaning yew tree estate.

Gatesheued. Gateshead. Goats' headland or hill.

Gegenforda. Gainford. Ford on a direct route.

Ghellinges. Gilling West. Capital of the Wapentake of Ghelliges-scir.

Ghellinges-scir. Approximates to Richmondshire. North Yorkshire local government district embracing Swaledale, Arkengarthdale and Wensleydale.

Hagustaldes-ham. Hexham. The warrior's homestead.

Haugr-Gils. Howgills. Hills and narrow valleys.

Hēg Denu. Haydon Bridge. OE. Valley where hay is made.

Helton. Hylton. Farmstead on a slope or hill.

Hep. Shap. Heap of stones.

Hindrelag. Richmond. English name before 1070. Origin not known.

Horedene. Horden. Dirty or muddy valley.

Hudreswelle. Hudswell. Place at a spring of a man named Hud.

Hunstanwortha. Hunstanworth. Enclosure of a man called Hunstan.

Hurdewurda. Hurworth. Enclosure made with hurdles.

Jor. River Ure. Origin not known.

Kelda. Keld. The spring by the apple tree.

Kircabi Lauenesdale. Kirkby Lonsdale. Village with a church in the valley of the Lune.

Kircabi Stephan. Kirkby Stephen. Village with the church of St. Stephen.

Kircabi Thore. Kirkby Thore. Village with a church in the manor of Thore.

Kirkstein. Kirkstone. Old Norse: Kirk, church; Stein, stone. A high pass over which a Roman road connected Patterdale and Ambleside.

Langelye. Langley Park. Long wood or clearing.

Langecestr. Lanchester. Old Roman fort.

Loncastre. Lancaster. Fort on the River Lune.

Lundenburh. London. Celtic; place belonging to Londinos.

Lune. The River Lune derives its name from the Old English word Lon which has its origins in an Irish Celtic word meaning health giving.

Middeltun. Middleton-Tyas. Farmstead in the middle.

Morlund. Morland. Grove in the moor.

Mortun. Moreton on Swale. Farmstead on marshy ground.

Muclingwic. Muggleswick. Farmstead of a man called Mucel.

Neuburna. Newburn. New stream, i.e. a stream that has changed course.

Nieweburc. Newbrough. New fortification.

Ofertun. Orton. Higher farmstead.

Patrichesdale. Patterdale. Valley of a man called Patric.

Penrith. Penrith. Chief ford.

Persebricg. Piercebridge. Bridge where the osiers grow.

Ravenstandale. Ravenstonedale. Valley of the raven stone.

Rengles. Ravenglass. Either derived from words equivalent to Welsh *yr afon glas*, meaning "the greenish or blueish river", or the name may be of Norse-Irish origin containing the Irish personal name *Glas* and meaning "Glas's part or share".

Richemund. Richmond. Norman name after 1070; meaning strong hill.

Rie. Reeth. Place at the stream.

Routhebiria. Rothbury. Stronghold of a man called Hrotha.

Saeham. Seaham. Homestead or village by the sea.

Schirebi. Skeeby. Village of a man called Skithi.

Sedberge. Sedburgh. Flat topped hill.

Shaldeford. Shadforth. Shallow ford.

Simundeburn. Simonburn. Stream of a man called Sigemund.

Stanhopa. Stanhope. Stony valley.

Stanmoir. Stainmore. Rocky or stony moor.

Swale. River Swale. Old English 'Sualuae', meaning rapid and liable to deluge.

Tibeia. Tebay. Island of a man named Tiba.

Tinan. River Tyne. Celtic or pre-Celtic meaning river.

Tirnetofte. Thrintoft. Thyrnir's homestead.

Twisla. Haltwhistle. Junction of two streams. The old French, 'Haut', was added latter.

Ulueswater. Ullswater. Lake of a man called Ulfr.

Uuire. River Wear. Celtic or pre-Celtic meaning river or water.

Westmoringaland. Westmorland. District of the people living west of the moors (Pennines).

Wlsingham. Wolsingham. Homestead of a man called Wulfsige.

Principal Characters

*Historical character

Lady Ealdgith. Orphaned and dispossessed heiress to lands in Richmondshire. Second cousin to Earl Gospatric.
Sir Hravn. Ealdgith's husband.

Their Family:

Earl Gospatric*. Earl of Northumbria 1067-69 and 1070-72. Ruler of Cumberland and descendant of the House of Bamburgh.
Lord Gospatric*. Ealdgith's uncle. Brother of her father, Thor. Thegn of nine manors.
Aethelreda*. Earl Gospatric's second wife.

Their Household:

Ulf. Housecarl and master-at-arms.
Orme. Steward for Hravn and Ealdgith.
Cyneburg. Ulf's wife.
Frida. Ealdgith's friend and maid. Orme's wife.
Ole. Hravn's servant.
Ada. Ealdgith's maid.
Eadwulf. Earl Gospatric's master-at-arms before joining Hravn.
Godric. A man-at-arms, then Ealdgith's housecarl.

Others:

Lord Elftred* Earl Gospatric's man in Cumberland and Westmorland. A common ancestor of the De Lancaster and Curwen families.

The Harrying of the North

The Year 1072
~Retribution~

Winter 1071

Chapter 1

Ealdgith focused on the brown, blood-shot eyes of the soldier in front of her, striving to read his intentions and dominate his mind, yet very aware that the cold intensity of his stare was beginning to freeze her ability to think. Her senses were alive, the tips of her toes and her fingers tingled with the need to move as she balanced on the balls of her feet, swaying gently, ready to spin and twist to avoid the next swing of his sword.

As they rotated slowly around the centre of the marked square of ground that formed their arena, the low early-morning sun caught the soldier's eyes and Ealdgith suddenly saw her own reflection within them. A tan-coloured leather helmet with eye and cheek guards framed her head, capped her long fair hair tucked underneath, and her green eyes glinted behind the eye guards. She realised that despite her opponent's domineering presence, she still presented a very physical challenge.

In the periphery of her vision Ealdgith saw the tension increase in his right hand and the marginal transfer of weight onto his right leg. His next move was imminent. She breathed deeply. Speed and timing were everything.

Ealdgith exhaled explosively. The rapid expulsion of air from her lungs assisted the force and speed with which she twisted backwards to her left just as the soldier's right arm thrust his sword point towards her chest. As Ealdgith's body rotated she danced past the soldier's right shoulder and thrust her long seax into his right midriff, the sudden pressure of its wooden tip causing him to gasp. The first blow, physical and psychological, was hers.

Ealdgith continued to move to her left, to force the soldier to shift his stance. He was sweating, she could smell it, and she could tell from the flush of blood in his face that her speed and attack had unsettled him. This was only the start. She had to rile him further, and quickly, before he could regain the initiative. His anger was her advantage. If she forced a rash, ill-judged move against her she could use his aggression against him.

"So? Women can't fight? I'm only good for controlling women in my household, but not men in battle? Is that what you think? Then think again! I've just spent a year taking revenge against the Normans, and the year before fighting with Cumbric outlaws." Ealdgith spoke quietly and deliberately, to force him to concentrate on listening. "In your eyes, I may just be a girl of sixteen, but in the two years since my people were slain, I have killed, and killed again. I've killed to protect my virtue, I've killed in cold-blooded revenge for my slain family, and I've killed in the heat of battle; don't forget that." As she spoke, her mind flitted back to the previous morning's training and the argument that had followed. This was a fight that she did not want, but now had to win.

*****

2

A lot had happened since Ealdgith and her husband, Hravn, had arrived at her uncle's fortified manor at Bebbanburge. Having fled from the Norman attack on their sanctuary in the wooded hills above Richemund they had led their band of resistance fighters, women and children, who formed their disparate household, across the border lands into Northumberland and the safety of Gospatric's Earldom. Their service to the Earl, during which they led a year-long resistance against the burgeoning Norman strong-hold of Richemund, had been rewarded surprisingly with a knighthood for Hravn and a mission to reclaim, and then hold, the Earl's lands on his southern border in Westmoringaland. Ealdgith, too, had been granted lands in her own right. An honour that, as the orphaned and dispossessed daughter of an English thegn, she had never expected. But before they could leave for Westmoringaland her uncle wanted them to represent him to his cousin, the Scot's king, share the intelligence that Hravn had gathered about the Norman king's intentions, and lead a short campaign of harassment into Norman lands in the extensive shire of Dunholm. Her uncle had granted them a troop of his men-at-arms for the task; hence the early morning training session that had sparked her clash with Eadwulf.

The previous day had started well. Unseasonal late-autumn sun cast a warm glow over the small group of men-at-arms and resistance fighters mustered on the firm sand below the craggy outcrop of the Bebbanburge fortress. Hravn, now taller than most men, black-haired with dark eyes and a close-trimmed beard, looked older than his seventeen years. His mail hauberk shone as it reflected the light of the low sun. Its torn and abraded metal links signified his experience of combat and contrasted with the perfect mail of the men he addressed. He spoke with a natural authority that belied his age, as he introduced his deputy and housecarl to the Earl's men.

Ulf was an ox of a man in his mid-twenties. Taller than all around him, his short-cropped yellow hair and beard framed a ruddy, blue-eyed, face. A thick-set frame evidenced his strength. Six years earlier Ulf had served his master, Ealdgith's father, in the shield-wall that faced the Danes at Fulford, where he had saved the thegn's life and been appointed to his household guard. Ulf had been away from Thegn Thor's manor of Hindrelag when the Normans harried the Ghellinges-scir lands in the early Aefter-Yule of 1070 and, deeply shamed that he had not died alongside his lord, and his own wife and daughter, he had fled to seek sanctuary in the wild woodland hills bordering the Swale. Ealdgith had grown up knowing Ulf. Their respect and affection were mutual and had developed into a deep friendship. When Hravn and Ealdgith had chanced upon him in the woods a year later, he had joined their resistance, sworn immediate and total fealty to Ealdgith, and promised to serve her as he had her father.

That morning, Hravn had welcomed Eadwulf, the Earl's master-at-arms, and introduced him to his own small band of fighters. They called themselves the 'green men', though the Normans knew them as 'silvatici', or men of the woods. Hravn and Ulf had trained them in the use of the crossbow and swift, quiet, movement. Hravn had then addressed the dozen men-at-arms that Eadwulf commanded, welcoming their skill as soldiers and swordsmen, and embracing them as future comrades and green men.

Deferring to Ulf, Hravn had nodded his approval as his housecarl's deep voice echoed from the cliffs behind. Ulf gripped the men's attention as he explained how they must now move on from their traditional way of war, fighting on foot in the shield-wall, and learn to fight whilst mounted, using spear and

4

sword. Hravn would soon lead them against Normans and whilst their tactics would be to hit and run, to destroy Norman property, they must be prepared to fight the Normans on their terms. Warfare had changed and they must learn new ways if they were to survive and serve their new lord. Those who could not adapt would be replaced; the Earl would see to that.

The morning had culminated in a demonstration. Hravn signalled to Edric, who sent four men with eight man-sized wicker targets onto the firm sand, to place them at close intervals in two rows, fifty paces in front of Eadwulf's men, and fifty paces apart.

Ealdgith and Orme, their second housecarl, had then ridden forward leading Ulf's black stallion and Hravn's roan. Then, mounted, helmed and with spears drawn from their saddle holsters, the foursome had cantered down the beach before turning to gallop, line abreast, towards the double row of targets. Their two wolfhounds following close behind the hooves of Hravn and Ealdgith's horses. Ole, their servant, had told Ealdgith afterwards that it was at this moment that the jocular scepticism of the watching men ceased suddenly as the sound of pounding hooves hung in the air and reverberated through the firm sand. The ground trembled and Ole had found it hard to focus as the four riders, crouched forward over their mounts with spears lowered, closed rapidly on the targets.

Gulls roosting on the cliffs exploded skywards with a cacophony of startled angry cries as the spears ripped through the wicker targets, shattered the fern stuffing into green clouds, before being impaled in the sand behind. The closest rider, the only one not wearing mail and with long fair hair that flowed from under her leather helmet, peeled off to her left, leaving the three mail-clad riders to draw their swords and in one fluid movement lower them to slash through three of the targets in the second row.

As Ealdgith continued past the second row at the gallop, she unslung the bow from her shoulder, drew three arrows from her quiver and, holding them between her teeth, turned her horse to return at a canter. She guided her mount with her knees, raised her bow and fired three arrows rapidly into the back of the fourth target.

Hravn then signalled for the riders to close in on him and trot back to the silent, awe-struck, men-at-arms. They halted and paused, as Hravn held the gaze of the group in front of him. "That, men, is how you will all learn to fight. My men will train with you, for they are still in need of your instruction in the art of the sword, just as they will teach you the use of the crossbow. You have two months to master the skills we have shown you. Ulf will teach you, as will Lady Ealdgith and I. Remember, she and I lead as one, and Ulf speaks for us both. Some of you may want to master the bow and learn how to fight unarmed. Lady Ealdgith will teach you. I have yet to see a man better her at either." He paused, "Thank you. Now, prepare your equipment. We will meet here again, an hour after first light tomorrow."

Ealdgith spoke as Hravn finished, her voice clear, authoritative, enchanting. "Before you leave, meet Hati and Sköll. They fight alongside Hravn and me and have saved our lives more than once. Be confident around them and get to know them, they will respond, but please don't feed them. Hravn says they are worth ten men to us. I wonder if he is right?" She teased, with a challenging smile.

As the men-at-arms left, inspired and joking at the prospect of unarmed combat against a woman, albeit their new lord's wife, Eadwulf stepped forward and took Hravn by the arm. "My Lord, this new way of fighting is truly different, and challenging. I can assure you that my men will follow you and not let you down, but..." He hesitated, suddenly uncertain, "My men will not take orders from a woman, no matter how well-born."

Ealdgith gasped at Hravn's reaction as he stared, open mouthed, his fists clenched, stunned momentarily by this unforeseen challenge to his authority. She stepped forward, placed herself between the two men, and faced the master-at-arms, aware suddenly that although he was not much taller than her, he was very stocky and doubtless immensely powerful.

"What you mean, Eadwulf, is that you won't take my orders. Your men take their orders from you, and it is through you that I will speak to them." Ealdgith spoke quietly in forceful measured words, not willing to be overheard. The matter had to be resolved quickly, without loss of face and with their authority intact.

"I challenge you to a holmganga, to stand against me, here, tomorrow. I will show you how a woman can fight and inspire her men. I will beat you, and you will take my orders."

She turned on her heel. "Come Hravn, this matter will be resolved. Ulf can teach Eadwulf the rules of the holmganga."

*****

The tip of Eadwulf's wooden sword blade flashed past Ealdgith's eyes and the sudden waft of air refocused her attention. She jumped back, very aware that she was treading close to the edge of the ten pace-wide square that marked their holmganga, or place of trial by combat. If she stepped outside she would lose.

Hravn bit his lip as he watched. Ealdgith's movements were fast and fluid, she almost danced around Eadwulf. She was lithe and light whilst his weight and bulk told against him. Hravn could see that Eadwulf was tiring, but it was obvious that he was not holding back. He wielded the wooden training sword with a power that would doubtless hurt Ealdgith if it caught her. Hravn glanced at the faces of Eadwulf's men. Several were openly encouraging Ealdgith, impressed by her ability, awed that a woman could fight like this. He was sure that whatever the outcome there would be volunteers for her training sessions. Others, though, frowned and shook their heads in disapproval of a woman who had the better of their master. He held his breath, willing only one outcome, as his hand gripped Hati's collar. If Ealdgith was knocked down he knew how the wolfhound would react.

"Did I not tell you that the hermit monk who taught me to fight once served in King Cnut's household guard, and then, later, in that of the Byzantine emperor? He showed Hravn and me the ways of the East. Oh, you have so much to learn." Ealdgith goaded Eadwulf. She moved quickly, always holding Eadwulf's stare, conscious of the movement of his hands and sword on the edge of her vision. His eyes were the key, she could read his intentions. She sensed the lunge just before it came. As Eadwulf drove forward, his anger took over. Ealdgith dropped her long seax, flicked the small seax from her left hand to her right, and dived through the gap between Eadwulf's legs, twisting to slash at his hamstrings and trip his forward movement with her foot. It was her master move, it always worked; but this time it didn't. She knew before she had completed her roll that she had missed her chance and that Eadwulf must still be standing. As she gained her feet she crouched and twisted to face him. The crouch saved her. Eadwulf's sword glanced off the top of her helmet. A hand's width lower and she would have been knocked unconscious. They were even on blows. The next would be the decider.

The climax was sudden. Ealdgith, still crouching, feinted to her left as Eadwulf stepped forward for his final blow. As his sword swung wide to his right to counter her, Ealdgith pounced. Eadwulf's step forward had brought her within his sword circle. There was little he could do as Ealdgith landed on his chest like a leaping cat, wrapping her legs and left arm around him whilst her right hand thrust the short seax against his neck. He staggered backwards and collapsed. Ealdgith straddled his chest, the seax tip pressed hard against his throat.

Eadwulf gasped, his face flushed red. Ealdgith wasn't sure whether it was from lack of air, embarrassment or fury, she didn't care. Victory was hers, and she had proved her point. The crowd were silent, stunned. Ulf moved first and stepped forward to offer Ealdgith his hand. "My Lady." Ealdgith read the pride and relief in his eyes as she grinned and stood up.

"Thank you, Ulf. You too, Hati." She patted the wolfhound's great head as he nuzzled against her hip.

Ulf broke the tension, stooped again to offer Eadwulf a hand up, and laughed, "Edie beat me once too, Eadwulf. You're in good company. Did we not tell you that we know her as 'the wildcat'?"

Eadwulf laughed, grateful for the face-saving joke. "Wildcat indeed, My Lady. I was wrong. Our men will, I am sure, follow anyone with the skill to topple me."

Ealdgith nodded and smiled, acknowledging the master-at-arms' acceptance of her status, but still unsure of him as a man.

As Hravn stepped forward to embrace Ealdgith he whispered "Well done Valkyrie" in her ear as he kissed her, then turned to clasp Eadwulf on the shoulder in recognition of a soldierly fight. The men around them cheered. Hravn winked to Ealdgith and led Eadwulf by the arm to one side, to quietly reinforce their authority. Ealdgith turned at a gentle touch on her shoulder. A squat thick-set man in early middle-age looked at her. His warm good-humoured smile, framed by greying red hair and thick beard reassured her instantly. "I'm Cenhelm, My Lady. Your uncle's armourer. You fight with a rare skill, I can see why the Earl has such faith in you." He paused, "He's often talked to me of you," and added quietly, "and you put Eadwulf in his place just now. He's a good soldier, but one whose ego is perhaps too big at times."

Ealdgith smiled back into Cenhelm's grey eyes, as a sense of joy and relief surged through her. He continued, "If you don't mind me saying, My Lady, your agility is your strength, but you are very vulnerable to a sword blow."

"I know," she nodded, "but I fear the weight of mail would slow me too much. It's a risk I have to take."

Cenhelm shook his head. "Not necessarily, come to my armoury later. I have a suit of mail designed for a lady. It is old, very old, but skilfully made. It is lighter than you might think."

"Thank you. I will."

*****

Ealdgith had a skip in her step as she walked with Hravn from their household's quarters in the fortress's upper ward down to the armoury above the main gate. Bebbanburge was built in wood, save for the three-storey stone tower that dominated the middle of the outcrop. It reminded Hravn of the derelict Roman tower in which he and Ealdgith had sheltered on the top of Stanmoir.

The great hall and several lesser halls clustered around the base of the tower, all surrounded by a high stake-wall. A small wooden tower guarded the entrance to the lower ward that wrapped around the upper ward.

The fortress was bounded by a tall stake-wall above the crags. A series of towers guarded its length whilst a miscellany of thatched, turf or shingle-roofed buildings huddled close to it, leaving the inner area clear for movement and marshalling troops. The lower ward was a hive of activity as Earl Gospatric's craftsmen and women followed their daily routines. Sounds, smells and smoke from the blacksmith, bakery, butcher and laundry mingled in the still autumn air.

This was a different world. The freedom and security they enjoyed within the fortress contrasted starkly with their last two years, living wild in caves, under make-shift shelters or in the Pendragons' stables. Her heart sang, full of light; the clash with Eadwulf cast the only shadow. She turned to Hravn.

"What did you say to him afterwards? Was he contrite? He deserved to be."

Hravn stopped and turned towards Ealdgith and gently tugged his beard. "Yes, in his own way. I'm coming to understand him. He's a good soldier, a firm leader; one that demands loyalty from those who serve him. He didn't take part in the Earl's campaigns that led to the harrying, and I sense that irks him. We challenge his understanding of the order of things. He's old school and I'm young, very young in his eyes, yet I have experience of fighting the Normans that he lacks and, of course, he serves me – us," he added cheekily. "I, we, Ulf and Orme too, are beginning to understand the new ways of fighting. We are the ones that have resisted and taken revenge against the Normans. He knows that, and he is on the back-foot. As a soldier, he doesn't like that."

Ealdgith nodded, as Hravn continued. "You don't fit into his order of things at all, and you really challenge him. Although the Earl made it clear what you have done, he simply couldn't believe it. Hravn laughed and pulled Ealdgith to him. "He does now."

Ealdgith smiled as she lay back in Hravn's arms, looking up at him. "Good. I had to beat him this morning, and it was hard. When I fought Ulf, I knew that he was holding back and I had to really goad him to make him come at me. Eadwulf really went for me. There was real anger in his eyes and behind his sword. It made me realise how vulnerable I am."

Hravn nodded. "I know, Edie. It was a lesson that he had to learn, but we must make sure that he doesn't feel as if he has lost face in front of his men. Work with him. Charm him, no matter how much he might irritate you, and make him appreciate your other skills. You are the only one in our household who can read and write. You understand herbs and healing too. You're unique. Once he understands that, I rather think that he will accept your word and command." He laughed drily, "Not that he would accept any other woman's word. I don't like him either, but we have him, and we will make it work. Now, here's the armoury. Introduce me to Cenhelm."

*****

The armoury emitted a warm smell of oil, leather and wood smoke, and was lit by weak sunshine that filtered hazily through an opening in the shingle roof. It was frosty outside and Hravn and Ealdgith were attracted initially by logs blazing in a brazier in the central hearth. On the walls the glint of oil lamps reflected from racks of spears and swords. Round shields were suspended from the rafters. Whilst Hravn was soon distracted by the swords, several with ornate pommels, Ealdgith's attention focussed quickly on a long trestle table. She gasped on seeing a glimmering mail tunic stretched across the scratched and pitted surface. A sword, with scabbard and belt, lay alongside.

Cenhelm stood up from poking the brazier and turned. "My Lord Hravn, Lady Ealdgith. Welcome. My Lord, the Earl, bids me offer you my services."

Hravn stepped around the table and held out his hand to Cenhelm. "Thank you, that's an offer you can be sure I'll take up. I fear you may be busy in the weeks to come."

"Cenhelm, this is beautiful. There is no other word for it." Ealdgith ran her fingers lightly across the oiled mail, marvelling at the intricacy of the small, finely interwoven, metal rings. They shimmered as she did so, muted colours of silver, gold and brown flowed across the metal surface. "How is it made?" Hravn gave a low whistle of surprise.

"It's made of iron, steel and alloys of copper and bronze, My Lady. There's no pattern, just a random mix throughout the tunic. You'll see that as you move the colours change; it's sometimes difficult for an opponent to focus on you properly." He stepped forward and lifted the tunic. "Feel it, it's like fabric. The links are so fine that the weight is maybe half that of a man's mail. It lacks some of the strength, but it helps blunt a blow and trap a dagger point, especially when worn over a leather jacket and breeks."

Ealdgith took the tunic and held it to her shoulders. "You're right Cenhelm, it is so much lighter than I expected, and longer. It comes to my knees."

Cenhelm grinned, he took great pride in his work and felt it an honour to serve a woman so imbued with a warrior's spirit. "Try it on My Lady, it holds a few more surprises yet."

Hravn watched, fascinated, as Cenhelm held the tunic open for Ealdgith to step into. It was different to those she was used to and tailored for a lady. A series of leather straps and buckles secured the tunic from her neck to the base of her spine. It was split front and back from the groin to the hem, and further straps and buckles allowed it to be secured around the legs when riding. The front was shaped to fit around the breast without constraint, whilst slits and straps down the sides of the waist served to fit a variety of shapes. The

13

top, at the front, hung open in a shallow collared V, which could be fastened across to protect the neck.

Ealdgith couldn't stop grinning whilst Cenhelm fitted the tunic. It was perfect. As Cenhelm stepped back, Ealdgith rolled her shoulders, stretched her arms, twisted, turned and bent to touch her feet. "Oh Cenhelm! You're right. It is light and I can move. What a work of art. Who made it? Who on earth could pay for it? You said it was old, when ..."

Cenhelm interrupted Ealdgith's constant questions. "I can't answer you with any certainty. There is a tale that it was commissioned by Queen Aethelflaed of the Mercians, but you must ask your uncle. If it is true then it must be eight or nine generations old, or more. All I can say is that it is ageless, if looked after and kept oiled. I have replaced the leather over the years, that is all that will perish with time."

Hravn interjected. "My servant, Ole, looks after our armour. He is a good worker, and keen to learn. Can I send him to you when I don't need him? I rather think Ole will be in need of all the skills that you can teach if he is to look after Edie's wardrobe. Oh, and Aelf too. He will be my armourer when we move on. He's a woodcutter and carpenter, but can turn his hand to most tasks. He's been keeping me supplied with arrow shafts and bolts." Hravn chuckled, "He's as old as Ole is young. I'm sure he will share the burden of supporting my demands upon you."

"Of course, my Lord. A willing apprentice is always welcome and, if you permit, I will equip him with his own mail and sword. A sound eye and hand are even more helpful. Aelf will be most welcome."

Cenhelm lifted the scabbard. "Now, My Lady, I overheard Hravn call you his Valkyrie, though I fancy you are more than just a shield-maiden. This came with the tunic. It too is timeless and crafted by the swordsmiths of old." The scabbard was of dark polished wood, inset with alternating ivory crosses and wolves' heads, and bound with silver wire. Cenhelm drew the sword from it. It slid easily, silently, from its lining of oiled lamb's wool.

Ealdgith stared, slack-jawed. Hravn's eyes widened in surprise. "Now, that is a sword. I've never seen one so fine."

"Aye, My Lord, it is that. A Valkyrie's sword. Look, the blade is slightly shorter than the norm, but is better suited to a lady's height. The steel is exceptionally strong and flexible. It must be from the East; their forges are more skilled than ours. And, see how narrow and tapered the blade is, its strength permits this and, of course, it's even lighter because of it." He passed the sword to Ealdgith, hilt first. "Take it, My Lady, feel how well it is balanced. I think the weight of the amber jewel in the pommel is the key. I am sure it was chosen so that its size is perfect to balance the blade."

Almost hesitantly, Ealdgith took the sword. She felt the weight of history in her hand, yet the sword had no weight at all. It was so much lighter than her long seax. She knew instinctively that she would be able to use it with incredible speed. The lack of patterning in the blade surprised Ealdgith but, as she moved the sword, she saw that there was a depth to the burnished metal. Greys, purples and blues swirled and moved within the blade, giving an ethereal beauty that complemented the mail tunic.

Cenhelm stilled Ealdgith's hand with his. "See, My Lady, the blade's beauty is within. It needs no marks other than this." He pointed to a word engraved in the base of the blade: '*Ulfberht*'. Ealdgith raised a quizzical eye. "A Flemish master swordsmith, My Lady. Again, from the past. Sadly, much copied now. But, this is doubtless his work, or one of his craftsmen. He was the best in Carolingia in his day."

Ealdgith beamed, her green eyes alive. "How can I thank you, Cenhelm?"

He laughed, touched by her girlish enthusiasm. "Not me, your uncle. Ask him about Queen Aethelflaed too. Now, before you go, let me measure you for a new padded jerkin. I'll have another made without padding, it will be lighter in warm weather; and some breeks too.'

Hravn laughed, "You're becoming an expensive woman to keep, I'm glad your uncle is paying. Don't forget that you need to start wearing dresses too." Cenhelm smiled, enjoying the repartee, as Ealdgith poked her tongue at her husband. Hravn turned as they left, "We're in your debt Cenhelm. I'll send Ole to you now, he can collect Edie's mail and sword as his first task." He hesitated. "I'll talk to you about making shields for all my men in a day or two. With your guidance, it will be a good task for Aelf."

Hravn took Ealdgith's hand as they walked back to the upper ward. "You're a Valkyrie indeed now. I doubt any man would stand against you in that tunic, wielding that sword. Today's fight with Eadwulf may have been the last time you need to fight unarmed."

"Mmm...mayhap." Ealdgith wasn't convinced. A woman wearing mail and openly setting herself up to fight, was just the challenge some men might relish.

Chapter 2

"Oh, Edie! It's you. I thought you were Aethelreda."

Ealdgith laughed, "Well you might, Uncle. She gave me some of her gowns and dresses. She insisted that I only dress as Hravn's Valkyrie when I'm training with the men or out hunting. She's right, but it'll take some getting used to." Her laugh gave way to a frown.

Earl Gospatric and Hravn each pulled a face. The Earl spoke, "I trust that won't stop you thinking like a Valkyrie. Come, we need to discuss what I want you to do in Dunholm and how to represent me to my cousin, Canmore." He gestured for them to sit with him at a trestle table in the great hall as he unscrolled a parchment map and placed oil lamps at either end to hold it flat and add light.

Hravn was fascinated. He had an instinctive understanding for the lie of the land and his ability to describe it as if viewed by a bird always amazed Ealdgith, but he had never seen a drawn map.

"It's just like the models that you scrape in the dirt, only better," Ealdgith teased her husband. "Look, even the manors are named." She pointed, reading the italic script: Gatesheued, Dunholm.

Ealdgith glanced at Gospatric and waited for him to speak. Although she called him 'uncle', he was a cousin at a remove. Tall and well-built with the deeply tanned face of one who spent most of his time outside, he was balding and had entered middle age. A neatly trimmed brown beard framed his jaw and complemented the rounded shape of his face. It was, however, his warm, dark brown eyes that invariably drew her attention. She felt that they always saw deep within her. She loved him unreservedly, unlike her dead father, who had always been distant and unable or unwilling to accept her boyish way of life.

"Before we look at the map, I want to talk through the situation across the shire of Dunholm. Hravn, the secrets that you stole from Count Alan confirmed what I suspected."

Hravn nodded. "Do you mean the King coming north to take on the Scots? I think he'll wait until the haerfest is just in and he's yet to settle the rebellion in the Anglian fenlands. I would plan on him arriving on Hlafmaesse Day, just in time to take the bread from our people's mouths."

Gospatric laughed. "Well put, my thoughts too. Let's see if we can make him a little hungrier on his way north. Now, the changes across Dunholm are key to our plan. Unlike Gellinghes-scir, which is in Count Alan's firm grip, Dunholm has been given to the Church to control. It's not the Church as we know it, but the Church of the Roman Pope. He who claims to be Christ's vicar." Gospatric referred to the schism that, two decades earlier, had split the Roman church from the Orthodox church, changing the relationship between Church and people.

He continued, "Serfdom has been imposed harshly, thegns and freemen dispossessed, the people oppressed by both the Church's own knights and mercenaries. William Walcher was made Bishop earlier this year. He's a Lotharingian and too saintly for his own good. He has no thought for the people and leaves his knights to take what they want in his name. It's a nightmare, made worse by the involvement of my cousin, Walthoef. He's the King's man now, by all accounts."

"Earl Walthoef? Surely not!" Ealdgith's exclamation caused both men to jump. "He rebelled alongside you. He visited my fader's hall. He ..."

"Well he might have, Edie, well he might." Gospatric lent across the table and squeezed her arm. "He bought himself back into the King's favour, as did I, doubtless paying him an equally large sum, but things have changed. He's taken William's niece, Judith of Lens, for his wife. He's close to Walcher too. My spies tell me that he is in Dunholm at the moment."

"Spies, Uncle? They must be well placed."

"They are, Edie. Many in the Church resent Lotharingian teaching and they resent the new Bishop even more. Just as I needed Hravn's military mind to infiltrate Count Alan's fold, I need a religious mind in Dunholm. You remember Earl Ealdred of Bernicia?"

Ealdgith nodded, a hazy recollection of an old man's face in the back of her mind.

"His daughter married Ligulf of Lumley, a man of the church. Although he is a Lotharingian, he resents Norman repression more than he loves the new Church. He's close to Walcher and at the hub of my network of priests."

Hravn smiled, then grinned slowly, understanding. "Like Brother Patrick and Father Oda?"

As Gospatric nodded in affirmation Hravn's face froze, as another thought formed. He hesitated before speaking, the implication of Walthoef's questionable allegiance was suddenly obvious. "We know from Count Alan that the King questions your loyalty and your closeness to King Malcolm. Walthoef is of the House of Bebbanburge too. He's in the King's favour and is befriending Walcher ..."

Gospatric interrupted, "I know. I fear my Earldom may be vulnerable. I've yet to consider the options. It's one reason I want you both well into Westmoringaland before the King comes north. I may need to send some of my children to Carleol too," he added sombrely, then pulled himself back to the present. "I digress, that's for another day. Tell me, how do we make life more difficult for Walthoef and, by implication, that bastard, William?"

Ealdgith smiled, used to the familiar derogatory reference to the King's birth.

"Where are the lowest crossings of the Tinan?" Hravn gently touched the map and traced the line of the river that formed the border between Northumberland and Dunholm. "If we can cross near the coast we could quickly get to the River Uuire and then raid along its length. See how it winds its way south through the heartland of the shire, past Dunholm itself and then turns north. We could join the stone-road and return quickly back north, cross the Tinan at Corbricg and then be back over the border."

Ealdgith nodded. "Uncle, it makes sense and if we did so, we could perhaps establish a base in the old fort we passed through on our way here. It's just to the west on the Stanegate."

"Which would mean that you would need to clear the outlaws from that area first." Gospatric appreciated the logic of the idea. "It's remote and would give you a base right by the back door into Dunholm. We could provision it from here but you would need to keep it secure once we do so. There are stone-roads between here and there and they've been maintained from time to time. Ox carts could haul what you need."

"Hravn nodded in acknowledgement, his mind thinking ahead, mulling options. He sucked his lips in thought. "I think we should raid into Gellinghes-scir too, before we raid Dunholm. That way we could damage the Count's ability to support the King. We know where his granaries are and we know that they have been rebuilt since we destroyed them a year ago; new thatch will burn very well. If we destroy his winter reserves and seed grain it will be harder for him to sustain his garrison and grow next year's haerfest. He certainly won't have the reserves that the King expects him to feed his army with when he comes north."

"Go on." Gospatric was intrigued by the scope of Hravn's plan. It was ambitious, but risky.

"We'll only have one opportunity. Once we raid Dunholm we can't risk another raid further south. We could take the stone-road from Corbricg all the way south to the Tees. I doubt the Normans will use it much; it's too far to the west for their needs. If we cross the Tees at Persebricg we can keep the river behind us and attack manors to the north of the Swale using the corridors of wasted land and half-deserted vills left after the harrying. I think we should travel fast and light. I intend to train the men to work and fight in small groups that can come together when I need them to. That way we can cover a much larger area and have a lot more flexibility. I'll call them sections and will need to choose the best of Eadwulf's men to lead them. For this raid, it will be Edie and I, Ulf of course, and then Eadwulf and two section leaders I've asked him to appoint. We can make our way in at night, lie up near the waste vill of Cattun, destroy the granaries at Mortun and Elreton, here and here, on the next night," he tapped the map. "Then be clear across the Tees by daylight. It would also be a good opportunity for Eadwulf to practise raiding before he goes into Dunholm."

"Yes!" Ealdgith tapped the table enthusiastically with her forefinger. "And it also means that I can revenge myself against my uncle again." She referred to the other Gospatric, her father's brother, who had forsaken his people, but saved his lands by siding with the Normans. It was his granaries that they had burned the previous winter. She took a deep breath, then hesitated, unsure if she was being too enthusiastic. "We could do more. Last year, we only torched the granaries. There is a mill by the Swale at Elreton. If we attack both at once we can destroy my uncle's reserves and his means of production."

Hravn chuckled, "I don't see why not Edie, he deserves it." He continued to study the map, frowning; the others watched, waiting. Ealdgith smiled, knowing how quickly her husband's mind was considering options, opportunities and constraints. "Lord?" he turned to Gospatric after a few minutes. "Can you arrange for us to meet one of your spies? Before I raid along the Uuire I need to know where the key granaries are, those that support Walcher and his collaborators, bridges and fords, any castles and fortified manors and mills too. Destroying his mills would really hurt his ability to make good the grain we burn." He paused for breath. "And the state of the tide and the moon in the month of Hrēðmonath. We should be ready to go by then, once we've met the Scots' king, cleared the outlaws and warmed your cousin's toes again."

Gospatric leant across the table to clap Hravn on the shoulder, and chuckled. "I'm glad I knighted you; you've a soldier's mind for certain. I'll do more than you ask. I'll have two of my spies, as you call them, meet you here to guide you over the river and then stay with you throughout the raid. Is there anything else you need at the moment?"

Hravn nodded, "Yes, I think we'll need a crossbow for every man. Ambushes are the key to success in the fighting I envisage, particularly against cavalry. We need to be able to punch arrow heads through mail. Crossbows can do that, but I doubt Cenhelm has the skill to make them, not in the numbers we need and in time."

"Agreed. I have a ship leaving for Flanders in a couple of days. That is the place to buy them and the bolts and arrow heads. I'll have a man fetch them and more cloth for green waterproof cloaks like the ones I had made for you last year. Let me know numbers by tomorrow. Now, we'll discuss how to handle my cousin, Canmore, when you see him. I want you to sail within the week and be back by Yuletide."

Hravn glanced at Ealdgith then spoke to the Earl, "There's one more thing and we're probably asking a lot." Gospatric raised an eyebrow and nodded.

Hravn continued. "Horses. We've a mixed herd: mainly bays and chestnuts, but there's Ulf's black stallion and several greys. Once we're back in Norman lands we need to be inconspicuous and blend with the woodland. The greys stand out too much and will draw attention when we least want it."

Gospatric continued to nod. "It's a valid point. Choose those you need and swap them with those that you don't. Just remember that temperament is as important as colour. Speak to my head groom. Oh, and plan on taking remounts and baggage ponies. I suggest you'll need one per armed man to carry their mail and spare weapons. Think about grain and feed too. You'll need to cart it to your base in the old fort on the Stanegate. You'll have a lot on your hands looking after that as well as raiding into the south."

Hravn nodded sombrely. "I know. Edie and I were talking about it last night. Orme has a sharp mind and was trained as her father's groom. Rather than have him as our second huscarle, we'll appoint him as our steward. Edie will help him get to grips with learning his letters and sums. We'll take him to the Scots' Court for the experience but thereafter, can he perhaps work alongside your steward whilst we're away?"

Ealdgith smiled to herself. She was sure Orme would grasp the opportunity. It would also keep him close to Frida in the latter stages of her confinement.

"Uncle?" Ealdgith turned to Gospatric as he rolled up the map and pushed back his chair on concluding their meeting. "Can you tell me about Queen Aethelflaed? Cenhelm thought that the mail and sword you've given me might once have been hers. But who was she?"

Gospatric settled back into his chair and a smile played around the edges of his mouth as he looked at Ealdgith. "I wondered if you might ask, Edie. Our family has a very long history, not just here in

Northumbria where we once ruled as the Lords of the North but also in the great ancient kingdoms of Wessex and Mercia too."

Hravn nodded, pleased secretly that Ealdgith was at last showing real interest in her family's history; a history that he knew more about than she did. "Through Edie's great grandfather, Earl Uhtred the Bold, and his third wife, your grandmother, Aelgifu, perhaps?" He interrupted, giving Ealdgith an 'I told you so' smile.

"Exactly." Gospatric continued, unfazed by the interruption. "Aelgifu was King Ethelred's daughter and of the direct line of King Alfred. Aethelflaed was Alfred's eldest daughter and Queen of the Mercians during the Danish wars. After her husband died she ruled in her own right and led her armies from the front, regaining much lost land south of the Humbre and the Mǣresēa. It is even said that she led an army of Scots and Northumbrians against Ragnall the Viking at the battle of Corbricg."

Gospatric paused, and ticked names off against his fingers. "She would have been my aunt, six generations back I think. Some of her blood might be in your veins, Edie."

Ealdgith gazed at her uncle, wide-eyed, wondering.

"Now, I can't say that the mail and sword were hers, but I do know that they came here as part of my grandmother's dowry. I can't think of anyone more deserving of them than you, Edie." Her uncle paused before adding, his voice serious, "Respect them, Edie, remember how Aethelflaed led and cared for her people. Let her inspire you."

Ealdgith reached across the table to take her uncle's hand in hers, "I will, Uncle. I will. Thank you."

*****

"Listen! What's that?" Hravn touched Ealdgith's arm, to stop her as they stepped out of Gospatric's hall. They paused, music, carried by the wind, came from around the corner.

"It's a harp, or at least one of the instruments is...and a flute, I think." Ealdgith cocked her head, "It's beautiful, it sounds like the call of birds flying over the sea and the moors." She tugged Hravn's hand, "Come."

They stopped as they walked around the corner of the hall. Lady Aethelreda sat with two of her ladies, who paused at the interruption. Ealdgith hesitated. She wasn't quite sure what Gospatric's second wife really thought of her. "I'm sorry, Aunt, but the sound drew me; it's so...so haunting, evocative; like the curlew calling as she flies from the moor to the sea."

Aethelreda smiled, impressed by Ealdgith's appreciation, surprised at the contrast to the martial character she presented. Maybe she didn't know her as well as she thought. "Yes, we play together, the harp, lyre and flute, trying to capture nature's sounds. Do you play?"

Ealdgith gave a low laugh, "Sadly no, Aunt. Nor do I sing." She paused, seized by a sudden thought. "One of my ladies does though. Cyneburg, Ulf's wife. Her voice is as clear and fresh as running water. Could she perhaps sing with you? Hravn and I will soon be claiming Ulf's time and she would doubtless welcome the company." Ealdgith omitted to say that Cyneburg was the daughter of a lowly Dales farmer, estranged from her family after being gang-raped by Norman men-at-arms. Ealdgith had helped her give birth to Adelind and Ulf had saved Adelind from being cast out onto the fellside by Cyneburg's parents. He had taken mother and child as his wife and daughter. Ealdgith had always been sceptical about love at first sight; Ulf and Cyneburg had proven her wrong.

"Of course, Edie, of course. Introduce Cyneburg to me before you leave to visit the Scots. I'm intrigued."

Ealdgith hoped the meeting would work. Aethelreda, a daughter of the House of Wessex, spoke with the harder Saxon accent and could be intimidating but, if Cyneburg was accepted by her, it would boost her friend's self-confidence.

"And Frida, my other companion too, Aunt? She is Orme's wife and is with child. Mayhap she can just sit with Cyneburg and listen. They will both need companionship whilst I am away. Would that be alright?" Ealdgith knew that her household of disparate refugees from Norman oppression would find it hard to adapt to their new life in a house that was the scion of North English nobility.

Aethelreda understood her step-niece's dilemma; the need to lead and care for her people was a great burden for such young shoulders. "Of course, Edie, your household is mine too. We are one now. Don't ever forget that."

Hravn touched Ealdgith's hand gently. "Come, Edie, we need to talk to Ulf before the day is out." He smiled at Aethelreda, and mouthed 'thank you,' before turning to lead Ealdgith through the series of gates that led to the shore.

"The days are shortening, see how the shadows are lengthening quickly." Hravn pointed to the beach and the long, distorted, shadow of the fortress. "It's cold too, here." He wrapped his cloak over Ealdgith's shoulders, remembering that she wore only a thin linen shift under the borrowed blue gown, then called, "Hey! Ulf!"

Ulf turned and broke away from his lesson on the fundamentals of the crossbow. His eyebrows twitched and his glance became a stare as he saw Ealdgith. "You look different, Edie, but I'm not sure why?" A broad smile creased the big man's ruddy face.

Ealdgith blushed, then poked the tip of her tongue at her friend and bodyguard and laughed. "Your lady has to look the part from time to time, Ulf. Wildcat one day, lady of the manor the next. It's the new 'me'."

Hravn shook his head in mock bemusement as they waited for Ulf to reach them. "We'll leave for the land of the Scots in a couple of days. I want you to run the training, Eadwulf knows that he has to work with you. I'll take Orme and Ole with us, Ada too. It will be good for her to get to know Edie better. You should have the extra crossbows we talked about by the time we get back. The Earl is sending to Flanders for them. Can you have the men ready by Yuletide? I've agreed with the Earl that we'll start by securing the old border fort as the base from which to raid into Dunholm."

Ulf nodded, smiling. It was just as they had previously discussed. "What about shields? Have you spoken to Cenhelm?"

"That I have." Hravn was enthusiastic. "Aelfric is helping him. I've given a lot of thought to their design too. Look." Hravn drew his sword and began to sketch an outline in the firm sand.

"We're agreed that the Norman kite-shield is too long to fight with on foot and in woods, but it is what is wanted on horseback, whereas round shields are only good on foot. We need a compromise - and this is what I want." Hravn stood back and revealed the outline he had drawn.

Ulf stroked his beard and gave Hravn a long expressionless stare. As Hravn's confidence dipped Ulf burst out laughing. "Of course it's a good design. I like it, though I've never seen one before. A shortened kite shape will work well, give more protection on foot and when mounted. It will be heavier though," he cautioned.

"I know, I've asked Cenhelm to see what he can do about that. He'll fit Norman-style straps behind the boss, as well as a bar, so that we can hold it on the fore-arm when riding, and he'll make smaller, lighter ones for Edie and Ole. Edie's got her own ideas about the design too."

Ealdgith drew her smaller seax and knelt down, careful not to smudge the sketch. She drew a line across the middle of the shield. "We've decided to colour the shields. Red above the line and black below. Above, we'll have a soaring raven, painted black, watching all below before it swoops to take its prey." She etched an outline carefully. "Then below the line, a screaming wildcat, all in red." She glanced up, inviting Ulf's approval. This was the symbol that they would fight behind; it had to hold meaning for them all.

"I love it Edie. The men will too."

Chapter 3

Hravn retched and lunged to grab the gunwale at the bow of the longship. He stared at foam-streaked grey water only a few feet below, only half focussing as his long-empty stomach churned and light-headedness muddled his thoughts. He feared that his first time at sea would be his last. Suddenly weightless, as the bow dipped into another trough, he flinched as cold salt spray lashed his vomit-streaked face and washed his short black beard clean. His head cleared as the icy water froze his skin. Suddenly sheepish, his stomach calmer, he turned around.

Orme shook his head slowly, a faint smile teasing his lips though his green hued cheeks belied his real feelings. "We'll be there afore dusk, My Lord, it's a grand day to sail, is it not?" The confidence of his words masked his real emotion. He too had never sailed before.

Ealdgith laughed. "I'll credit that you are acting Orme, you mask your sickness better than my husband." Both men stared. Ealdgith's radiance belittled them as she sat cross-legged on a sea chest wedged against the base of the mast, arms braced behind her to counter the roll of the long sleek snekkja as it sliced through the cold northern sea. Clad in leather breeches and jerkin, her long fair hair flew behind her and her green eyes caught the sunlight. Ealdgith was enraptured by her first experience of the sea.

"I'd say that you were more Rán than Valkyrie today, my love." Hravn teased, likening her to the Norse goddess of the sea rather than the shield-maiden who fought habitually by his side.

Orme chuckled. "Aye, Lady Edie, he's right, you shame us all." The snekkja lurched suddenly, rolling and plunging into another trough, sending the two men back to the gunwale together.

Ealdgith sighed and shook her head in sympathy, before she turned to look back towards the rest of her household. Ole and Ada, their two young servants, were sitting on the deck boards in the stern, their backs to the hull. The boy and the girl were asleep, heads and shoulders together. Sköll and Hati lay close by, sharing bodily warmth, eyes watchful. Most of the forty-man crew lay on the flat deck by their sea chests and slept too. Those that didn't either watched the broad square sail that caught the wind and swept the boat onward, confident in their helmsman's steady hand and sharp eye, or glanced surreptitiously towards Ealdgith awed by her reputation, puzzled by her clothing, cautious of her status and impressed by her looks. She relaxed and looked over her left shoulder to the coastline of Lothian behind, across to the wide estuary, source of troublesome cross-currents and swell, and then ahead to the unknown high ground of the Scots' lands. As she shielded her gaze she reflected on the chaos and change in all their lives over the past few months and the challenges and opportunities to come.

*****

"I see it. Look!" Ole turned, wide-eyed. His breaking voice, unusually high pitched, made Ealdgith laugh at his excitement, and his youthful puppy-like enthusiasm always amused her. "There, across the fields, just up from the river, behind the vill. You can see stone walls and smoke from the hall." He pulled Ada close to him and pointed, laughing as her thick brown hair blew across his face. Neither could say with any certainty how old they were.

Ole was probably fourteen and Ada possibly thirteen. Ole was Frida's young brother. Both had been

30

orphaned suddenly the previous Lencten when a Norman hunting party had chanced upon their forest shelter, snatched Frida and slain their parents. Hravn, guessing that Frida would be held in Richemund garrison's whorehouse, had taken Ulf, Ealdgith and Ole and raided the building that night. They had freed Frida and found Ada. She too had been orphaned and dragged there, days before. The trauma of their experiences bound them together. Ada only smiled when she was with Ole or Cyneburg. Ealdgith knew that the two girls, who now spent most of their time together, had confided in each other and shared experiences that they could not describe to others. Ealdgith wanted an opportunity to get to know Ada better, as she would become her maid once Frida gave birth. Ealdgith hoped also that, with Ole's encouragement, she might teach Ada the skills of self-defence as she desperately needed the confidence to stand up to men.

"Thank Thor! We'd best get dressed for the occasion. Ole, can you fetch our mail please?" Hravn stood and stretched, having become more accustomed to the roll of the snekkja under his feet. "It's been a long day. I pity the oarsmen," he said as he watched forty sweating men sitting on their sea chests, heaving on the oars as they rowed up the river.

"I fancy they're used to it." Ealdgith was only half listening as she squinted towards her distant kinsman's palace. "The trip up the river is much longer than I thought." She turned to Hravn, then glanced towards the rows of straining bodies and lined faces, "You're right, I still find it hard to appreciate that we are the reason for their efforts."

Hravn squeezed Ealdgith's shoulder in acknowledgement, then turned to speak to the oarsman. "Osgar, when we come alongside, I want to say a few words to your men. Their stamina and your skill is much appreciated. I'm impressed and...", he paused, adding sheepishly, "...I hope to be a better sailor on our return."

Osgar laughed openly, for once taking his eyes off the line that his vessel followed and glanced sideways. He appreciated Hravn's easy familiarity and concern for his men, "I've seen many worse, Lord. The young ones did well. Lady Ealdgith is a rare sailor too."

Hravn chuckled under his breath, "Don't tell her, Osgar. I'll never hear the last of this trip as it is."

*****

"My Lord King, I am Lady Ealdgith of Hep and Ulueswater." Ealdgith knelt down onto her right knee, bowing her head, before standing and turning to Hravn who stood by her right side, "My husband, Sir Hravn of Ravenstandale." Hravn knelt, "My Lord, King."

King Malcolm, the third king of the Scots with that name, sat astride a black stallion at the edge of the landing stage, his face impassive as he assessed the scene. Earl Gospatric's messenger had told him to expect a young woman who was his distant kin and that she had, with her husband, spent a year resisting Norman rule in the south of the Earl's land. She was not what he had expected. His eyes had at first been drawn to the very young woman standing behind her holding a large wolfhound on a short leash. He had mistakenly taken the slim, long-haired person in shimmering mail to be the young knight's attendant. He briefly studied her more closely. Tall for a woman and naturally confident in her stance, he could see that she had the upper-arm physique of one who practised regularly with sword and bow. Swinging down from his horse, he turned and offered Ealdgith his hand to kiss. "Ealdgith, come walk with me, I've yet to meet a woman with something of a warrior's reputation."

Hravn fell in beside Ealdgith for the short walk to the royal palace of Forteviot. Orme was left to oversee the movement of their luggage along the paved track that led past the royal vill towards a gate in the high stake-wall surrounding the hall and other buildings.

Whilst they walked, Hravn studied the king as he monopolised his wife's attention. Heavy-framed, but of average height, his head was the size of a taller man's. Coils of thick red hair and a bushy beard enhanced it further; it dominated not only his body but those around him. Hravn understood the double meaning behind the Earl's epithet of 'Canmore', or big head; the head dominated the man whilst the man dominated the people he headed. He smiled to himself, aware that the Pictish-Scots name, 'Ceann Mór', was the same in his native Cumbric.

Two guards at the entrance stood rigidly to attention, their eyes watching the royal party closely as Canmore strode through the gate without an acknowledgment. A third trumpeted a salute from the tower above the gate. It was as much an acknowledgement of the King as a warning to the many people within the outer bailey who paused and bowed briefly before resuming their labour. Hravn sensed an atmosphere of formality very different to that of Bebbanburge.

The main hall was within an inner bailey behind another stake-wall. Hravn turned to Canmore, impressed. "My Lord, I have never seen a stone building such as this. The Normans are building a stone castle at Richemund, but it is far from complete and there is a church tower in stone in the Vale of Eden, but nothing like this." He was awe-struck by the two storeys of finely shaped red sandstone capped by a roof of wooden shingles. Groups of narrow arched slits pierced the walls, which he assumed admitted light through the massive walls.

Canmore's large head nodded, the smile hidden within the red beard was evident in his eyes. "There're more buildings in stone than you might think and my forebears have had their palace here for ten generations. We've had time to work on it." He paused, chuckling. It was the first glimmer of humour. "It's always good to better the Sassenach."

Hravn laughed out loud, "Aye, and as one who is part Norse, part Cumbric, I couldn't agree more."

The king hesitated, then patted Hravn affectionately on his back. "Norse-Cumbric! I was forgetting. You could almost be Scots. Come, my apartments and the hall are on the top floor. I have a room for you below. My steward will show your staff whilst we discuss my cousin's message." His tone changed, "Ealdgith, I suggest you change before meeting Queen Margaret. She has strong views about how her ladies dress."

*****

Hravn and Ealdgith climbed the wooden stairs to the great hall. Ole and Ada had already been sent to join those who would be serving the tables at the King's feast. Ole greedily anticipated easy access to food. Ada was intrigued but wary. Orme followed them, knowing that he would be seated separately, somewhat lower down the table. They could hear that the hall was already packed, the sound of boisterous, mainly male, voices echoed above them

King Malcolm met the couple as they entered. For once Ealdgith was pleased that she wore the best of the gowns that Aethelreda had given her. Green silk with wide gold-embroidered cuffs, a red woollen over gown and her hair platted under a close fitting green silk head dress, complemented the King's ermine-trimmed red cloak worn over fashionable tight green leggings. Ealdgith quipped as he complimented her on her dress, "And to think that Hravn and I spent most of

34

last year living in just the clothes in which we escaped from Ghellinghes-scir."

Canmore led Ealdgith to an armchair to the right of his, at the centre of a long table mounted on a low dais. Queen Margaret took Hravn by the arm and led him to sit to her left. He held her chair attentively as she seated herself next to her husband. Hravn was struck both by her beauty and how different she was to Ealdgith. Where Ealdgith was tall, with an athletic body tanned by a life outdoors, Queen Margaret was petite and pale. Hravn had heard that she was as pious privately as she was in public, and that she spent much of her time in prayer, devotional reading, and ecclesiastical embroidery. In their first day at the palace he had seen already that she had a considerable effect on the more uncouth Malcolm who, like himself, was illiterate. It was said that he so admired her piety that he had her books decorated in gold and silver. Her dress too was simple: a pale cream silk gown, pale blue over-gown and a white wimple held in place by a small gold circlet over her plaited blonde hair.

Hravn knew her to be of the English royal line and the House of Wessex but was unprepared for her heavy accent with hard, indistinct vowels. She sensed his surprise and placed her fingers delicately upon his. "I was raised in the Hungarian court where my father was exiled as a child when Canute deprived him of the English throne. Mine is the English of that court. Some find it hard to understand. Hungarian and English are enough for any one woman to speak." She laughed, "It is the reason I insist that English alone is spoken at court here. I could not cope with the Gaelic of my husband's Pictish lords."

Hravn's laugh broke any ice between them. "I understand your plight, My Lady. I was raised to speak English, Norse and Cumbric. It can be a challenge at times, although Pictish-Gaelic is from the same source as Cumbric, and indeed Breton. It was a God-send to be able to talk to the Norman's Breton knights at Richemund."

"Tell me of England and the plight of our people. I have heard little since my brother and Earl Gospatric led the rebellion that brought so much suffering down upon them all." Hravn could see sorrow and regret in her eyes. He knew that Queen Margaret's brother was the young prince, The Atheling Edgar, whom the English thegns had chosen as their King instead of William. "I have not seen my brother since he fled to Flanders. I fear he will never live to gain his rightful throne." She hesitated, "Though I have found a people and a love I never thought to see..." Hravn saw her instinctively reach her right hand out to touch that of her husband.

As she turned to smile at Canmore, Hravn glanced about the room. The King's guests were seated around a horseshoe of tables. Two other, as yet unintroduced, nobles sat to his left. Trestle tables ran at right-angles to the King's raised table and he could see Orme talking animatedly to two knights' attendants at the foot of the table in front of him. He was surprised that the tables were covered with brightly coloured red and green cloths that added to the richly coloured gaiety of the scene, but would surely soon be spoiled by gravy and grease. He fingered the silver platter, cup, knife and spoon in front of him. Never before had he dined at such a table. It surpassed even Earl Gospatric's and was a far cry indeed from past feasts in Ealdgith's father's hall.

Oil lamps were set on sconces between the many tapestries that hung on the walls: bright scenes of the hunt, craggy mountains and sea battles off a rocky coast. A brazier on thick stone flags, burned at the far end of the hall, and he could feel the warmth from another behind him. Above the feast, blue-grey wood smoke curled into the rafters and out through louvered openings in the wooden roof. A great iron chandelier, with close on a score of large white candles, hung from the ceiling above the centre of the horseshoe. Hravn chuckled to himself; any wax would doubtless drip onto those serving them. He knew Ole would find this amusing.

The man to Hravn's left leant over and growled in his ear in broad Gaelic that he could just understand. "Y'er Cumbric, I ken. Dinna listen to the pious bitch. She's too English for her own good."

Hravn sat back, surprised. The man had fair, almost white, hair and the eyes of Canmore. "I'm Domnall mac Donnchada, Canmore's brother." He nodded towards the King. "He's more Sassenach than me, brought up in their court whereas I was taken to the Isles when Macbeth slew our father and took the throne." Hravn nodded, intrigued. "It was a Cumbric earl, Siward was his name, who helped put my brother back on the throne. If y'er Cumbric, y'll do for me. What about your lass?"

Hravn laughed, rather captivated by the Scot's bluff openness. "Edie's English, but no Sassenach. She's an Angle, but now holds lands in Westmoringaland in her own right. We both do, or will when we can reclaim them." He winked confidentially, "She'll be Cumbric yet. I'll see to that." They both looked up, their attention suddenly upon the serving staff as they entered the back of the hall carrying jugs. As Domnall banged the table, Hravn gestured to Ole to serve them.

Ole beamed as he poured a heavy red wine for Hravn and Domnall before placing the jug in front of them. Hravn noticed that he kept glancing across to Ada as she served Ealdgith and the stout balding man to her right. Hravn was relieved to see that Ealdgith had the good sense to immediately add water to the wine. He sipped slowly at his, unwilling to lose face in front of Domnall, but wary of the strength of the sweet heady liquid. Domnall had no such reservations. He downed the cupful in one long swig then poured another in contrast to Queen Margaret who took the jug from her personal servant, then served her King before pouring a small measure for herself. Hravn could see why there was tension between the pious, dutiful and very English queen and her bluff, assertive Scot's brother-in-law.

As Ole and Ada left the hall to collect further jugs of ale with which to serve the lower tables, other staff entered with platters of hot food and placed them in front of the King and Queen and then progressively along the tables in front of the, by now, boisterous and demanding household. As the Queen again served her King, Domnall nudged Hravn, as he stabbed a herring and spooned shellfish onto his platter. "Dig in, lad, y'll no be served y'sel." Hravn copied, tearing a wedge from a loaf to complement the fish. Meat followed, with a whole piglet carved in front of the King.

The noise abated as they ate and Hravn divided his attention between Domnall and the Queen, as he held two very different conversations. He couldn't help but contrast the extravagance of the royal table to the past two years during which Ealdgith and he had nearly starved, a condition in which the Northern peasantry and dispossessed nobility still existed. He could see sorrow and concern in Margaret's eyes as she listened and encouraged him to say more. She spoke at last and gestured to the food around them. "I understand. Whilst my husband's generosity helps bind his lords to him I do ensure that we always cook more than we need and afterwards, whilst the food is still wholesome, it will be given to the poor hereabouts."

The queen paused and Hravn was momentarily aware of the quiet strumming of a harp behind them. The royal bard was starting to play, slowly gaining their attention before beginning to sing.

Queen Margaret placed her hand upon Hravn's. "Thank you for the warning that you brought us. I appreciate the risks that you took." She paused to glance to her right, "though I cannot understand how Ealdgith can live as she does. Surely it is too much for a woman to risk?"

Hravn nodded, smiling. "Perhaps so, My Lady, but she has always been a risk taker, even when we hunted as children. How we live has been forced upon us and has become the way in which we can best serve our people...and take revenge for the slaughter of Edie's family." He paused, his eyes suddenly hazy, as if looking inward at a different time and place. "Mayhap, once we can reclaim our lands in Westmoringaland, Edie will be able to focus more on her people. Our lands will be secure so long as the Normans keep to their side of the border. The Vale of Eden is a place of plenty and I hope we can use our energies to better effect there." His eyes refocused on the present, "Anyway, I believe she has Queen Aethelflaed's blood in her veins. Edie's mail and sword were mayhap once the Queen's, so who knows her future."

Margaret's eyes widened in surprise and she sat back silent, thinking. Those in the great hall took her lead and listened as the bard began to sing.

Later, after platters of sweetmeats had been served to the tables, Hravn sensed a sudden tension of anticipation within the hall. He started with surprise at a sudden harsh squeal. Queen Margaret jumped too. Domnall scoffed, "Sassenachs! Tis but the pipes. They'll lead a man to war, y'ken."

Queen Margaret leant across to speak into Hravn's ear. "We have them in Hungary too; crude, noisy things." She paused, with a pointed stare at Domnall, then turned and tapped her husband on the shoulder and whispered. He in turn stood up and invited Ealdgith to swap places with his wife. Hravn suspected that the act was more to do with the Queen's lack of patience with Domnall's coarseness than out of a hostess's concern for her guests.

39

Two pipers entered the hall and bowed to the King just as Ealdgith took her seat. They wore simple clothes: drab plaid thigh-length tunics, knee length braies and tightly bound leggings. Domnall led most of the men in the room in banging on the tables and beating a rhythm in time with the skirl of the pipes. The music enveloped the hall, as it echoed from the stone walls and deafened all within.

Domnall pushed back his seat, pulled his boots off, then stood and mouthed a question to his brother, who nodded. Turning, he clicked his fingers towards a man standing in the shadowed corner behind them. The man stepped forward, bowed and handed Domnall two large swords. Both had plain cross pieces and the longest blades Hravn had seen. Hefting the sword blades uppermost, Domnall strode round to the centre of the horse-shoe space. bowed to his brother and placed them on the ground so that their blades crossed at right-angles.

The fist-drumming and piping stopped. Domnall stood and faced the King, with his toes touching the point of a sword. As he breathed in, he turned slowly and stared at the audience, demanding and holding their attention. He raised himself onto his toes, then straight-backed and square-shouldered, placed his hands on his hips, arms akimbo, and nodded to the pipers. As the rhythmic music skirled across the hall he danced around and across the swords, flicking his toes between the crossed blades, turning, smiling proudly, careful not to touch blade or hilt. No one spoke. All watched, enthralled.

Ealdgith stared, mouth agape, until Canmore spoke into her ear. "He does me a great honour. When you were but a babe, I reclaimed my throne from the usurper Macbeth, slew him on the field of battle at Lamphanan, then danced over his sword and mine. Domnall does this in memory of that day, and what it means to our family and our people. He must do it without touching the swords; to do so would bring disgrace upon us all."

Ealdgith leant and whispered back into the King's ear, "Doubtless a great honour, but surely a great risk too?"

Canmore nodded. "Domnall is no fool. He knows the risk. That makes the honour all the greater. These men," he glanced at the nobles within his household, "will follow him anywhere and Domnall will serve me in anything." The King leant forward to draw Hravn into their conversation.

"Domnall will lead my men against King William as and when he crosses into Lothian. Thank my cousin for his warning and tell him that I will bide my time to hear what that Norman King has to say before I react. Much is at stake." Both nodded, watching Canmore intently as he continued. "As to Cumbraland, the Earl holds it for me, but Elftred is his man there and in Westmoringaland too. I'll be honest, my control there is less than I would like. Kingship has long been debatable and since the Normans seized the English crown it is something of a no-man's land. If you can keep the southern border peaceable you will be of service to me and I will endorse the Earl's grant of lands to you."

They were both effusive in their thanks, diplomatically giving Canmore credit for generosity that was perhaps not his to confer.

"Now, Hravn, I'd like to know you better before you return to Bebbanburge. Join me tomorrow on the hunt; my household needs more venison for Yuletide, and Edie..." She smiled, anticipating an invitation to hunt, "...Queen Margaret will be pleased to show you our new stone-built chapel and statues of the saints."

"I'd be delighted." Ealdgith's heart sank behind the façade of her smile.

Chapter 4

Ealdgith turned and waved to Ada to join her on a vacant sea chest in the bow of the snekkja. She drew Ada to her side, unclasped her cloak and wrapped it around them both to keep out the swift breeze resulting from the snekkja's brisk ebb-tide passage down the River Earn. The girl looked at her, quizzically.

"You know that I would like you to assist Frida as my maid and then take over from her when she has her baby?" Ada nodded. "Well, I'd like you to do more than that. When Hravn and I ride out to raid Norman lands I will be the only woman. I would like you to be my companion and my servant, just as Ole will be Hravn's servant. Could you do that?"

Ada looked at Ealdgith expressionless, her brown eyes wide with surprise. Ealdgith felt a pang of guilt. Ada was young. Was she still affected by the trauma of her abuse by the Norman knight who had slain her father? "I'm sorry, Ada, perhaps I am asking too much of..."

"No, My Lady..." Ada interrupted quickly, nervously. "...I mean, yes, My Lady. If Ole is with me, and Hravn and Ulf, then yes." As Ealdgith squeezed her shoulder reassuringly, Ada continued, "Will you teach me to fight like you taught Ole?

Ealdgith drew Ada to her and kissed her forehead. "Off course, Ada. I'll teach you how to use the short seax and the bow but, more importantly, I'll teach you how to throw a man twice your size, how to read what he is thinking and where to hurt him. A very special man taught me how, and it has saved my life many times. It'll be hard and you'll get a lot of bruises." She watched as Ada's thin smile turned into a distant stare.

It was moments before Ada brightened and spoke again. "Thank you, My Lady. I won't let anyone hurt me again, not like that. I want to be like you. To ride, to raid, to kill Normans."

Ada's earnest intensity chilled Ealdgith, but she knew that the girl had every right to feel as she did. Her desire for revenge was good motivation for her to learn. Ealdgith was sure that she could temper aggression with caution.

"Upon our return, I'll have clothes like mine made for you, a padded leather jerkin and helmet too. You can choose a horse from my uncle's stables; there's a young chestnut mare I'll introduce you to." She paused and held Ada's hands. "Now, listen. Call me Edie, not My Lady. My household is my family. We've all lost our own families and the household is our new family. We are bound to each other now."

Ada leant forward to kiss Ealdgith and was hugged as a sister in return. Ole, making his way towards the bow, paused and watched then returned to join Hravn and Orme by the helmsman. He knew something had changed and it could only be for the better.

*****

The snekkja sliced through the grey foam-flecked waves, borne along by a cold northerly wind that brought flurries of snow. Ole didn't know that such speed was possible. He stood in the bow with Ada, his feet feeling the vibration of their passage through the water, laughing as the high prow, carved in the shape of Our Lady Mary, Star of the Sea riding upon a sea serpent, rose and dipped, spraying them with icy salt water. A month ago, he had never heard of the sea, let alone seen it. Now, he loved it: its smell, its taste, its constant movement and changing moods. Meanwhile, the crew slept, chewed air-dried fish or gazed at the rock-bound sandy bays fringing the Northumberland coast.

"Why's it called a snekkja?" Ada asked, carried along by Ole's enthusiasm.

Ole chuckled, "Because it's long and thin like a snake and is the fastest of ships. Hravn told me." He turned, braced himself against the stempost and looked back along the length of the longship. "Isn't she beautiful, and so cleverly built? See how she cuts through the water like a knife, yet she flexes to withstand the strength of the waves."

"Yes," Ada took up his line of thought, "and every man has a chest to keep his clothes and weapons dry and they are pinned to the deck and sat upon to row. Even the oars fit through holes that can be closed to keep the sea out, as they are now."

"It's a different life." Ole sounded almost wistful.

"But not one for a girl." Ada gave him a sideways glance. "I'd rather ride and fight, serving Hravn and Edie. Wouldn't you?"

Ole's slight nod and the gentle squeeze of his arm around her waist was all the reassurance she wanted.

"Come," she said, "let's go aft and cuddle the hounds to get warm."

*****

The helmsman's cry roused the dozing crew and passengers. "Bebbanburge! Man the oars, you lazy fish heads! You've slept enough this voyage."

It was as if the crew had never slept. They woke as one and within moments had dropped the sail and pushed the oars out through the open ports in the upper strake. As the snekkja's speed fell away the helmsman heaved on the long steer-board, using the longship's momentum to swing it shoreward, cutting across the northerly wind.

Hravn waved a raised thumb at Osgar in a sign of appreciation and made his way forward to the bow, his feet braced against the roll of the snekkja in the cross-sea. Ealdgith followed. "I'm glad you've got your sea-legs at last. You've not turned green once on this trip," she teased.

"Look!" Hravn pointed to a cluster of dots on the broad Bebbanburge beach. "Ulf has the men training. I think we should join them. Can you go aft and ask Osgar to run the boat up onto the beach behind them?"

All on board lurched forward as the snekkja's forward hull scraped against the fine sand of Bebbanburge bay. The vessel was still moving as Hravn leapt from the bow into the thigh-high water, Ealdgith and the others close behind, wincing as the cold water numbed their legs. They had barely cleared the bow when Osgar ordered the oarsmen to back paddle to keep the snekkja afloat on the ebbing tide.

Hravn led a sprint through the shallow water, reaching Ulf a furlong beyond the tideline. The big housecarl turned, a teasing glint in his eye. "Was your stomach that bad that you had to abandon a perfectly serviceable ship, eh?"

"Good to see you too, Ulf." Hravn clasped Ulf on his mail-clad shoulder, then nodded towards the group of men-at-arms that seemed to be tumbling through the high dunes that bordered the Bebbanburge cliffs. "That's good to see. How're they enjoying it?"

Ulf gave a dry laugh, "As much as we did when you had us doing it up the fellside at Mersche. They're to have one last go...if you care to join in?" He added, teasing.

Hravn grinned, glanced at Ealdgith, raised a challenging eyebrow, then nudged Orme in his ribs with his elbow. "Come on, Orme, over onto my shoulders. Ulf, set them off after me, and Ole, look after the hounds." Crouching down whilst Orme bent forward across Hravn's right shoulder, Hravn took a deep breath, then strode forward in a long gait, adjusting his grip on Orme's legs as he went.

Ealdgith groaned, raised her eyes in mock despair then turned to Ada. "If you're to train to fight you might as well start now. Ready? Lean forward over my right shoulder, place your left arm in the small of my back, your right across my chest and hold my left shoulder. I've got your legs."

The girl gasped as Ealdgith stood up and started forward, chasing Hravn. Ada's startled expression caused Ole to poke his tongue at his friend, forcing her to smile as she bounced, half upside down, against Ealdgith's back.

"I'm glad...you're so light...Ada." Panted breaths interrupted Ealdgith's speech. "When Oswin started training Hravn and me...I was carrying him up the hill!" She heard Ulf yelling at the men at arms to swap over and start another race up the dunes. Their laboured breathing behind her drove her on.

Ealdgith knew she had the edge. Orme was every bit as heavy as Hravn whereas Ada was much lighter than her. The advantage began to tell as they reached the steep sandy slope and, no longer running, began the lung-bursting climb, her thighs forcing her upward faster than Hravn. She moved, slowly, into the lead.

After two false summits, Ealdgith knew that the third was the last. She could just see Hravn from the corner of her eye, maybe ten feet behind. A cacophony of grunting, gasping, cursing and spitting told her that the pack of men was close. Ada, too, was winded by the constant pressure of her stomach on Ealdgith's shoulder; she could hear her gasping. There was no point in trying to ask her just how close the men were.

As Ealdgith crested the dune for the final run to the finish at the base of the cliff she stumbled and almost tripped, as her left shoulder was jostled roughly.

One of the men at arms, taller even than Hravn, edged past her; the soldier across his shoulders urging him on. Sweat poured from his brow, splashing onto her bare arms as he forced himself forward, his longer stride taking him ahead of her.

The soldier stopped at the cliff foot, bent forward to lower his comrade to the ground and then stood upright, head back, gulping air. Ealdgith, moments behind him, lowered Ada to the ground then lay back against the cold rock, breathing in through her nose and out through her mouth, relishing the pure air infused with the scent of the sea and wild thyme. Eyes closed, she heard, rather than saw, the next of the panting, sweating men reach the cliff.

Ealdgith opened her eyes as her pounding head cleared and turned to the tall soldier next to her. "Godric, isn't it?" He nodded, still catching his breath. "Well done! I knew I'd beat Hravn, Ada is so much lighter than Orme, but you beat us both, coming from behind. That's impressive."

Godric pulled himself upright then, looking down at Ealdgith, said, "I had to My Lady. Beating Sir Hravn was a bonus, but I had to beat you."

Ealdgith frowned, puzzled. "Why? I admire your achievement, but surely there was no reason to beat me?"

"Forgive me, My Lady," Godric spoke softly, respectfully, still short of breath, "but there are those amongst us who cannot be bettered by a woman..." He hesitated, "no matter how noble her birth right."

The young woman nodded slowly. "I see. Did Eadwulf demand this?"

"No, My Lady. Rather, some of the men-at-arms expect it. They respect you for winning your contest against Eadwulf but they need to believe in themselves as men."

Ealdgith continued to nod, thinking as she listened. "And what of you, Godric? What do you feel?"

The man hesitated and relaxed his pose slightly as he looked directly into Ealdgith's eyes. "I will follow whomsoever commands me, so long as they inspire me, understand their men and know how to fight...man or woman alike."

A thin smile on her lips, Ealdgith held Godric's gaze. "Thank you. I respect your honesty and would expect nothing else. I know you to be one of Eadwulf's section leaders. I want you to accompany me when Hravn and I raid into my homeland in Aefter Yule. Mayhap, afterwards, you will be able to reassure all the men that they should have faith in me, just as I have faith in them."

"Yes, My Lady."

They both turned as Hravn cleared his throat. "I agree, Edie." He stepped forward, offering his hand to Godric. "Well done. That run inspired us all. Now, Edie speaks for me, as do I for her and we lead as one, I hope by our own example. Have the men understand that. Now they, and you, need to get a well-deserved meal. I'll speak to everyone later, after we've reported to the Earl."

Ealdgith turned to look for Ada and saw that her new maid and companion had already run back down the dunes to join Ole and the hounds.

*****

"Thank you, Hravn. From what you say, I can't put my trust in Canmore to fight William when he goes north. He always was wily. I'm pleased, though, that he's admitted that his hold on Strathclyde and Cumbraland is not as strong as he would like. I think you should meet Elftred sooner rather than later. He needs to know that you both now have lands in the Vale of Eden and are going to secure them for me."

48

"We thought that too, Uncle," Ealdgith interrupted, "perhaps we should go there next, before we raid into Count Alan's lands."

The Earl nodded assent and flicked his eyes to Hravn, inviting the young knight's advice.

"Lord, we must secure our base at the fort called Chesterholm first. I want to leave before the Yuletide festivities are over and strike when least expected. Edie and I will then continue to Carleol to meet Elftred and go on to Morlund. Gunnar, can help prepare for the move against the Pendragons too. I trust him totally."

Ealdgith interrupted again, keen for her uncle to understand that it was their joint plan. "We'll take our own men with us, leaving Eadwulf to build the base whilst Orme arranges to supply it." She hesitated, aware that they would start to drain her uncle's winter food reserves. "Are you happy with that?"

"Why wouldn't I be, Edie? But rather than cart everything from here I will have instructions drawn up for those who hold my lands along the North Tinan to supply you."

A slow smile spread over Hravn's face, "Thank you, my Lord, we'll leave on the fourth day of Yule. That will allow the men to celebrate without getting too drunk."

Gospatric raised his hand as they turned to leave, his expression suddenly serious. "A word of caution. Many of the lands of south Westmoringaland and Furness are held by a Norman, Ivo de Taillebois. He is said to be hard and arrogant and quick to take revenge. Elftred will know more, but that is why I want that border made secure...and peaceful. He's said to be with William, subduing Hereward and the rebels on his other lands in the Fens. We must be prepared for him to come north sometime after that." Both nodded their understanding as he added, "And be wary of those who may play on what they perceive to be your youth and lack of experience. You grew up overnight after the

49

harrowing. I know that and respect your counsel, but others may not...Elftred for one."

*****

"Ulf! You old dog! Where did you get that?"

Ulf looked up from the table in one of the rooms he shared with Cyneburg but carried on oiling the long oak haft in front of him. "The armoury of course. Where else would a huscarle find a Danish Axe?"

"It's a thing of beauty." Hravn complimented Ulf on the traditional symbol of a housecarl's status. "That haft must be at least five feet long and the blade a good foot wide. It would surely cleave a man in two."

"Come closer. Just look at the blade."

Hravn whistled as his fingers traced the line of the brass patterns inlaid into the blackened steel of the broad, triangular axe head. "Have you ever used one in battle?"

Ulf shook his head, "No, but I was trained after Fulford, when Edie's father chose me for his house guard. Cenhelm has a saddle holster for it, though it's for fighting on foot, used two handed, not on horseback. I've seen one, used properly, take down a horse and slay the rider in two swings. Mayhap I'll take it when we ride south."

"So you must, Ulf, so you must. But we have other business first. I've agreed with the Earl that we'll secure the old fort before the end of Yuletide, then you'll ride with us to Carleol and Cumbraland, leaving Orme and Eadwulf to build up our base there. We'll take Edric and our own men with us." Hravn's enthusiasm buoyed Ulf, though he put the axe down and quickly went to Cyneburg as she entered the room holding a babe in her arms. Hravn was always impressed by Cyneburg's unusual prettiness. Her mousy hair, high cheekbones, wide-spaced blue-grey eyes and snub nose gave her an exotic, almost sultry appeal and he could see why Ulf had fallen for her at first sight, albeit when she was heavily pregnant.

"Adelind! Let me, my dear." He said, as he gently took his six month old daughter in his arms, then, with a wink at Hravn, jiggled her up and down to make her giggle, taking care to support her head with his giant hand.

Cyneburg smiled, shook her head resignedly and whispered to Hravn, "Don't tell Ulf that I've just fed her."

Aefter Yule 1072

Chapter 5

Ole blew onto his icy fingers whilst Ada held hers to her chestnut mare's mouth, inviting them to be licked warm by her rough tongue. A smoking oil lamp cast long flickering shadows around the stable as they strove to ready the five horses for the day's ride to the old fort by the stone wall. They turned as the stable door opened and let in a draft of icy air from the pre-dawn night. Ulf ducked under the wooden lintel and and briefly stamped his feet and patted his arms to body to restore his circulation. Frost glistened on his leather boots.

"Well done you two, that's what I like to see. Up, working and sober, unlike a couple of Eadwulf's lads. They're in for a hard ride this morning."

Ulf placed a brotherly arm around the two youngsters, pulling them close. "Ada, I told Edie that I thought you were too young to ride with us, but I understand why she wants you with her. Cyneburg is going to miss you though. Now, both of you, stick together and, when the dung gets kicked in the air, stay close to me and I will look after you. Understand, eh?"

They both nodded and smiled up at him. Neither thought of doing otherwise.

"Don't let the men distract you. Your job is to cook and look after the horses for the five of us. We'll take care of our own weapons, even Edie. The others will look after themselves. Remember, we're the family within the household. We might lose some of the men in a fight, but I'll be damned before we lose anyone in our family."

Ulf squeezed Ada's shoulder gently, "Your chestnut looks well groomed and Edie's bay too. She will be pleased." He turned to Ole, "How's my stallion? His temper can be as black as his colour sometimes."

Ole stepped sideways sharply, anticipating getting his ear tweaked. "Really, Ulf? It must be his rider. He's like a placid foal with me."

Ada giggled, then said, "Ulf, we're about ready here. When will we form up to ride out?"

"Once the dawn starts to break. You've a little time yet. Go to the kitchen and get your fill of warm soup and bread. When we ride, we won't stop 'til late in the forenoon."

*****

A clear sky, in which a few bright starts were visible already, prolonged the daylight and heralded another cold night. Hravn held up his hand to halt the column of riders. They had ridden hard and fast to, make the most of the short day. Heading southwest from Bebbanburge, they had joined the old stone road at Alnewich and followed it south until they hit the line of the old Roman wall where they turned to follow it westward along another, narrower, stone road just to its south.

"Hold! There's Godric returning." As the column slowed, it split into three. Hravn and Ealdgith stayed on the road with their two servants and Ulf and Eadwulf, whilst the sections under Eadwulf's command moved to secure the ground to their flanks, leaving Edric and his men to guard their rear and control their remounts and pack ponies.

Hravn glanced across to Ulf and the two men shared a nod of approval. The benefit of their weeks of training was evident in the way in which the score of men dominated the ground around them. Their mottled green cloaks blended with the winter grassland, and the low sun glinting on their spear tips offered the only reflections. Hravn had insisted that they dull the shine on their burnished steel helmets by rubbing them with soot from a smoky flame. The last two years had taught him and Ealdgith the benefit of camouflage and concealment; it was an art that their men must also learn.

Godric reined to a halt alongside Hravn, almost as breathless as his horse, and tapped his right temple with his fingertips in a salute of respect.

"Nieweburc is but two leagues off My Lord, just south of the wall. I've spoken to the headman there and we will have shelter, stabling and food." Godric laughed, "He was a little reluctant 'til I said you had the Earl's word that he could forgo some of his dues later in the year, though I suspect we will finish off his Yuletide reserve."

"Good work Godric. I trust you didn't explain our purpose here?" There was a hint of a tease behind Hravn's serious question.

Godric pulled a face, "Lord! A good soldier never gives away the element of surprise."

Eadwulf almost growled, not happy with his deputy's informality and Hravn's encouragement of it, "Aye, but you can be sure that someone there will inform on us."

Hravn nodded, "Mayhap, Eadwulf, but if we strike tonight they won't have the opportunity."

Ealdgith sensed the tension and interrupted quickly. "Dudda and Cola know the fort and adjacent vill, having crawled through them when we were last there. It's barely two leagues yon side of Nieweburc. If they return tonight to confirm where the guards are, we can raid at first light."

"I agree. We need to get the men fed and rested as soon as we can, sleep 'til midnight then move against the fort." Ulf spoke on the assumption that the plan was agreed. "I'll warn Dudda and Cola now."

"That's settled," Hravn quickly summed up his outline plan. "The fort has four entrances and the ruined vill abuts its western edge. Once we know exactly where the outlaws are I will take Edric and his men through the gate nearest to them. From what we saw last Blót-month, they live within the fort, not the vill. Eadwulf, split your men into three groups and on my signal, block the other three gates to prevent any escape, then move in quickly to join me. We'll keep the ponies and remounts stabled at Nieweburc."

Ulf glanced at Hravn and raised an eyebrow. He always asked the same question. "Prisoners?"

"Those whom we seize will be returned to the Earl to face his justice. The dead will be strung from the highest tower to deter others. Any who are badly wounded will be sent to their maker before they join those on the tower. Eadwulf, you will see to that."

"Aye, Lord. It will be done." Hravn sensed that the order met with Eadwulf's satisfaction."

*****

Dudda levered himself up onto the stone sill, swung his legs across and slowly lowered himself down. "It's their stable," he whispered to Cola. "Follow me in."

The smell of horses had drawn the two men to the stable. It formed one side of a square of long single storey stone buildings near the centre of the old fort. They were aware that a low fire burned in the building opposite; wood smoke hung in the crisp night air and a dull glow lit the inside of the shutterless window frames.

A warm, fetid, horse-smell dominated the room that was now the stable. Grunts, moans and the occasional wet fart masked the sound of Cola's entry. Squat and swarthy, he lacked Dudda's agility; a horse

55

whinnied at the sudden noise as he slipped on unseen rubble on the floor.

Dudda tapped Cola on the shoulder to draw his attention then, waving a forefinger towards the doorless gap in the far wall, he led the way to an entrance that opened onto an enclosed paved yard. As he crouching in the shadows, Cola pointed across the yard. A man lay slouched against the open doorway, his head on his chest, snoring. Beyond, lit by the low flickering flames of a fire in the middle of the room, a dozen or so men lay wrapped in cloaks. All slept. Dudda smiled and moonlight glinted on his eyes and teeth as he nodded his head back towards the window in the far wall. Cola turned and they retraced the route.

"Here they come." Ealdgith's whisper sounded louder then she intended as it cut through the still cold air. Hravn nodded, but he did not avert his gaze from the edge of the wood outside the fort. His eyes tracked two figures as they emerged from the shadow of the archway in the northern tower and ran towards them. Light from the waning moon threw faint shadows and Hravn noticed that the men's ash and soot streaked faces didn't reflect the moonlight and were almost invisible. It was another of the arts of camouflage that he had discovered.

The success of their mission was evident from Dudda's wide grin. "It's as you thought, Lord. They're using the old headquarters block by the cross roads in the centre of the fort..."

Cola interrupted, impatient for his share of the glory, "It's to the left of the road in from the western gate, the one from the vill. There's only one entrance. They're sleeping in the block on the left, the one on the right is stabling."

"Hravn nodded. "Good, I remember it. Well done." He gestured to Ealdgith to come closer with Ulf and Eadwulf.

"Eadwulf, take Cola with you as a guide. Have your section leaders take the northern and southern gates, you take the eastern. I'll enter through the vill and take the western one." He glanced at Ealdgith, "When you hear a fox bark, followed by an owl hoot, each group is to move in towards the crossroads. I should be in your line of sight by then, so watch for my signals. Follow me in when I enter the yard and have your other two groups secure the outside of the buildings. Is that clear?"

"Aye, Lord. We'll have the little skitas yet." Eadwulf's approval was all Hravn needed. He turned to Ole.

"Stay here with Ada and guard the horses. Be ready to lead them in as soon as you hear my horn. String them together on long reins, one string for each group and take two groups each. That way we can regroup and mount quickly. We'll use their own mounts for any prisoners we take."

The false dawn's dull yellow glow silhouetted the outline of the hill that dominated the east side of the fort. As Hravn approached through the ruined vill to the west, the glow threw the old buildings into dark shadow. The others followed at five-pace intervals.

Pausing under the arch of the western tower Hravn gestured for Ealdgith to join him. "Edie, it's time for the fox to startle the owl, Eadwulf should be in place by now."

Ealdgith nodded, tipped her head back, took a deep breath and cupped her hands around her mouth. It wasn't the first time that they had used her skill in mimicking animal and bird sounds.

Sköll and Hati's ears twitched as the calls echoed through the icy night. Hravn moved onward briskly, hugging the shadows, then paused by the edge of a building twenty paces short of the old headquarters block. He waved Ulf forward and pointed to where Eadwulf had already taken up a position just beyond the crossroads. "You, with me. Then Edric and his men. Edie will follow with the hounds. They should deter anyone who is putting up a fight."

Hravn hesitated as he entered the yard. The guard was no longer sleeping in the doorway. He crouched below window height and moved to the door post. As Ulf joined him, he stepped inside.

A man, presumably the guard, was stoking the fire. He turned as Hravn's foot scuffed the edge of the doorpost and, with a roar more of panic than rage, flung a burning log towards the doorway. Hravn sidestepped and slashed forward and down with his sword. *Nadr*, with the adder-like speed of its namesake, sliced through the man's wrist. He fell, screaming, as he rammed the blood-spurting stump under his armpit.

Shouts echoed around the room as sleep befuddled men grabbed weapons and lurched to their feet. Two who grabbed their swords were felled instantly, the others froze, quelled by the shock of the attack and the snarling fangs of the two wolfhounds that herded them into a corner.

"In there!" Hravn yelled at Eadwulf as he led his men into the room, "Check any rooms beyond."

The aged oak door burst apart at Eadwulf's leather-booted kick. "Stop! Godric, seize him!" Eadwulf yelled to his men outside the building as he saw a man's naked buttocks and legs disappear through a window in the outer wall. He froze as a woman screamed, then sobbed hysterically.

"I'll see to her. Have your men clear the rooms then leave." Ealdgith stepped through the door.

A black-haired young woman, perhaps in her late teens, crouched naked and shivering in the corner. "Here." Ealdgith flung her a blanket that lay on a filthy straw-stuffed mattress and then crouched, her hand on Hati's collar. "Are there other women?"

The woman stared, not comprehending. Ealdgith tried again, in halting Cumbric instead of English.

The woman shook her head. Ealdgith persisted, "You're safe. No one will touch you. Now, who are you and why are you here?"

Ealdgith watched the woman's eyes flit to and fro, from her face to Hati. Ealdgith realised that her own dress was probably intimidating. She spoke again to reassure her. "I'm Lady Ealdgith, we're here at Earl Gospatric's bidding, to clear his land of outlaws." She raised a questioning eyebrow, waiting. The woman spoke at last.

"Aerona, Lady. I'm from Twisla. They took me from there and made me cook for them, and..." Aerona hesitated, "...look after other needs."

Ealdgith held Aerona's gaze and nodded her understanding. "Show me those who took you by force and my husband will ensure they hang for it. We will return you to Twisla, too, if that is what you want, or else you could mayhap stay in a vill hereabouts if you fear your family will think you too disgraced. Now, where are your clothes? Find them and I will take you to Ada, my servant. She doesn't speak Cumbric, but she will look after you."

Ealdgith left the room to inform Hravn and find Ada. Eight men, their hands bound behind them were being led out of the building. Three bodies, including the guard, were piled in the yard. She watched as two of Godric's men slung a naked corpse on top.

"Eadwulf!" Hravn's shout caused all in the yard to stop and turn. "Have the prisoners lined up. The woman you found was badly abused by some of them. Anyone she identifies will join those corpses on the tower."

Eadwulf chuckled, "Fewer mouths to feed then, Lord."

*****

Hravn glanced across at Ealdgith, pushed his trencher to one side and rapped his knife hilt on the table as he turned to the men sitting around them in the hall at Nieweburc. It was early in the forenoon, but felt much later.

"That fight was easier than I expected. Be assured that our dealings with the Normans will be harder. Tell the men that they did well today. They behaved as I was sure they would, in particular those who brought my justice to the two who violated Aerona. It was rough justice and perhaps not what the Earl would expect, but it is important that they understand I will not countenance the violation of women." He paused as he recalled the fate of his half-sisters in the harrying two winters ago.

"Eadwulf, before you take the remaining six prisoners back to the Earl, I want you to visit the vills of Hēg Denu, Simundeburn and Beltingham." Hravn passed a heavy ring across to Eadwulf. "This is the Earl's token. Use it to prove you speak on his behalf, then return it to me when we next meet. Have them gather the grain, meat and fodder we will need. They must expect to sustain us whenever we are here, from now until Lencten at least. When you return here with Orme, bring Aelfric with you. His skills will be invaluable in roofing and weatherproofing buildings for us to use. I'll let you choose which ones. I think it will be at least a fortnight before we are back from the Vale of Eden. That should give you time to finish establishing a base. We'll then go back to Bebbanburge together, before returning to raid into Ghellinghes from here."

"Aye, Lord." It was becoming obvious to Hravn that Eadwulf spoke little. He also sensed that he was beginning to gain the master-at-arms' confidence, though no doubt, Eadwulf would enjoy his independence during the next two weeks.

"Ulf, Edric, we'll ride to Carleol tomorrow and return Aerona to her people as we pass Twisla. Ulf please have Ole and Ada lead two remounts and the pack ponies when we depart and, Edric, I want two scouts riding a league ahead all the time. We've more vills and crumbling forts to pass through yet."

Chapter 6

Carleol stank. The red sandstone walls of the old town and fort and the clusters of thatched wattle and daub, or turf-walled, houses clustered outside, were reflected in the still water of the River Eden. The flowing tide was almost at its height and the town's fresh sewage hung, floating in the river, penned against the Solway's rising salt water. That, and the tannery down river from the town, combined to create the stench borne towards the eleven riders by the westerly breeze. The late afternoon sun shone dimly through the river's miasma.

Hravn called the riders to a halt and pointed down from the crest of a low hill to a sprawling jumble of fallen walls. "See how the Stanegate follows the wall down to the old barracks and then on to a bridge? That's our route. The Earl said Elftred lives in the fort behind the walls beyond the Eden."

When they had passed through Carleol three months earlier Hravn had been worried that Ada might be abducted by Dyflin slavers, and they had found shelter in a damp, dilapidated inn. This visit was different. The body of armed men, wearing dull green cloaks and with eye-catching black and red shields slung over their shoulders, drew stares of respect and caution. The gate in the town walls was unguarded and they rode through close together, to thread their way through the jostling crowd of townspeople and merchants. A small flock of sheep being driven from the market to the shambles blocked their way momentarily and the smell of the slaughterhouse distracting the hounds until Ealdgith called them sharply to heel.

The fort was at the northern edge of the town, on a peninsular between the rivers Eden and Caldew.

Hravn halted the troop fifty paces short of the fort's open gate and rode forward with Ealdgith. Ulf followed. As she rode, Ealdgith removed her leather helmet and shook her long hair free, keen not to be mistaken for a young squire again. "Sir Hravn and Lady Ealdgith to see Lord Elftred on Earl Gospatric's business." Hravn spoke in Cumbric.

The guard looked past Hravn and gave the mounted men a questioning look. Hravn understood his concern. They were an unusual sight in peaceful Cumbraland. "We will need rooms for our household and our men. Perhaps you can take us to the Constable whilst they wait here?" His firm but friendly tone reassured the guard who, barely hesitating, shouted back over his shoulder in a heavy dialect that Hravn struggled to understand.

"Berwyn, take his lordship and his lady to the Constable and get Ceri to take his men to the stables." Pausing, he addressed Hravn, "Lord, welcome," then, glancing at Hati and Sköll, added, "best keep those hounds close. Lord Elftred's own hounds have their free run around here."

Ealdgith felt suddenly self-conscious, aware that several of the men-at-arms were eyeing her strangely, staring at her shimmering mail hauberk. Whilst Hravn talked, she glanced around, stern-faced. The fort was similar to the Roman one they had just commandeered for their own use, though in a much better state of repair. Although some buildings had fallen into disrepair and their stones removed to create space, the majority of the tiled roofs had been replaced with thatch or turf. At the central crossroads, the headquarters building had been demolished and replaced with a large Norse-style wooden hall. It looked strangely out of place.

As he dismounted, Hravn turned to Ulf. "Take our horses. We'll join you in the stables once we've made our introductions."

Berwyn led them to a large stone building with a small yard and rapped loudly on the door. As he entered he bid Hravn to wait on the threshold, but returned momentarily to lead them through a torch-lit passage to a high-ceilinged anteroom. "The Constable will be with you shortly."

The room was Spartan, the walls a mix of old flaking plaster and new dun-grey patches. It was unfurnished, save for two stools by a low fire burning in a central brazier from which the smoke escaped through a capped hole in the ceiling.

"Mmm, homely," Ealdgith muttered, as the two hounds stretched out in front of the brazier.

Hravn pursed his lips and nodded, "Think how old it is. It's a miracle it's still used..." he broke off as a squat, middle-aged man with receding black hair walked in and held out his hand to greet them.

"I'm Maldred, the Constable. Welcome. I hear you have news from the Earl for Lord Elftred. He, unfortunately, is away in Allerdale 'til late..." He paused, looking quizzically at Ealdgith.

Hravn grasped the outstretched hand firmly. As he introduced them both he debated whether to keep his counsel or take Maldred into his confidence about their plans to destroy the Pendragons' stronghold in Westmoringaland.

"We've had a long ride, Maldred, and cleared a nest of reaving outlaws on our way past Twisla. A room for our men and stabling for our horses would be appreciated, as would a good rest before we pass on the Earl's instructions," he hesitated slightly, coming to a decision, "My wife, Lady Ealdgith, has news from her uncle that we must discuss with Elftred personally. Mayhap you can arrange an early audience tomorrow?"

Maldred's shoulders stiffened and his tone became more formal, "Lady, I did not know that you were the Earl's niece." He cleared his throat, "Your...dress puzzles me though, why ..."

"...Am I dressed to fight?" Ealdgith interrupted Maldred with a captivating smile. "That, I will explain to Elftred tomorrow, save to tell you now that Hravn and I spent the last year fighting the Normans that took my family's land in Gellinghes-scir, and that we now serve my uncle in a similar way."

"Indeed?" Hravn enjoyed the constable's look of bewildered surprise.

"Maldred, once we have seen our men and servants settled, perhaps we could join you with our huscarle and tell you a little of our story over a meal?"

*****

Maldred called for them early the next morning. "Lord Elftred is breaking his fast; he would like you to join him to eat and talk."

They walked across to the longhouse, taking Ulf with them and leaving the hounds with Ole and Ada. Hravn wasn't sure how the Cumbric lord would welcome others interfering with his control over the lands he held for the Earl, and he felt that the housecarl's presence would add status and gravitas to their meeting with Elftred.

A tall man, thinning on top with a full, fleshy face and thick beard rose to greet them. He wore heavy woollen breeches and tunic under a wolf-skin cape. Ealdgith was surprised at how reserved his clothes were; Hravn was more surprised that Elftred was obviously English, not Cumbric. "Hah! Hravn, and Ealdgith too. May I call you Edie? The Earl has spoken of you more than once and Maldred has told me more of your work just now. Come, sit and eat with me, your huscarle too."

Hravn and Ealdgith were taken aback by the warm familiarity of their welcome. As they joined Elftred at a table by the blazing hearth in the centre of the longhouse, he clicked his fingers and summoned a

65

man with beakers of small beer. "No one drinks the water hereabouts," he warned dismissively, "now tell me what the Earl wants of me?"

Ealdgith took a vellum scroll from within the lining of her cloak. It was secured with the Earl's seal. "My Lord Elftred, my uncle sent this for you. It may come as a surprise to you, for I understand that it explains his plans for us here and why he has granted us both lands on his southern borders."

Elftred's expression froze, joviality replaced by a questioning frown. "I will read it shortly, just tell me what it says."

Hravn took over the conversation. "Our Lord wants that viper's nest of Pendragons cleared for good. We have a troop of his men in addition to our own and plan to move against them this sumor, once we have completed a mission for the Earl yon side of the Pennines. You may not know, but the lands that the Pendragons control were once my family's. Uther and his father took them from my great ealdfader. He has granted them to me on condition that we are successful."

Elftred nodded, "I see, and what lands has the Earl granted you, Ealdgith?"

Ealdgith let Hravn speak for her. "The Earl and King Malcolm, from whom we have just come, want the southern border to be kept quiet. Both fear that lawlessness could entice the Normans to interfere."

"King Malcolm, you say?" Elftred leant forward, his eyes fixed on Hravn.

"Yes, Lord. There is a bigger picture to this. As you have heard, I was for a while a spy in Count Alan's camp in Richemund. We know that King William will come north and move against the Scots later this year. Count Alan, Bishop Walcher and Earl Walthoef are to provide support in Dunholm and Ghellinges-scir, 'though not Earl Gospatric; he's been excluded from all correspondence. That is a concern. We took this news to Forteviot just before Yuletide."

"Go on."

"The Earl's personal plans will depend on how King Malcolm reacts. He wants us to make it difficult for Walcher and Count Alan to feed the King's army as it passes through, then he wants the Pendragons dealt with. We know their lands and how they work better than anyone. Once those lands are secure we are to keep the border from Stanmoir to Ulueswater peaceful. The lands of Hep and Ulueswater have been granted to Edie in recompense for the loss of her family land in Gellinghes-scir. We will, of course, need your support with food and fodder until we are established in our own lands."

Elftred sat back, rubbing his chin with his fingers. "Ah...your uncle is a clever man, Edie. Mayhap he didn't tell you that, whilst the lands he has gifted to you are his to do so, they have been under my control, whereas yours, Hravn have been lost to that nest of vipers, as you rightly call them. My lands, however, lie both sides of what you call the border. I have interests in Amounderness and north of Loncastre that I still take revenue from and have an...understanding...with our Norman friends there."

Ealdgith gasped.

Hravn caught Ulf's questioning eye. He nodded, slowly, then smiled conspiratorially at Elftred, "Now, that is interesting. I can see why the Earl would want to keep that sort of relationship quiet...I assume he does know?"

"He is aware of it, of course." Elftred's smile belied the cold look in his eyes, "It is not something that either of us want widely known."

A silence hung in the air. Elftred spoke at last. "Very well, this may serve us all. I need a peaceful border and, perchance that matters do not go well with the King, the Earl may be forced to flee to his lands

67

here." He hesitated, "Did the Earl talk about the value of Ulueswater?"

"Do you mean the lead?" Ealdgith spoke before Hravn, "We intend to exploit it to fund the cost of maintaining enough men to keep the border peaceful."

Elftred smiled slowly, his joviality returning. "I thought as much. You're sharp, Edie, and as shrewd as your uncle. He is aware that I have yet to start mining so it is not as if he is depriving me of it. It will be a while yet before you can mine, but if you export it through Carleol when you do, I will see that we are all well served. Mayhap I can help find you miners too. Now, let us eat. We can talk more later."

*****

As they rode south along the stone road from Carleol the fells, grand and forbidding, filled their horizon, and Ealdgith let her mind wander. She imagined the days of the long-dead Cumbric kingdom of Rheged that had once flourished there. It really was a mountain fastness. To her left, snow capped the tops along the length of the Pennines, where the north-easterly wind whipped shredded rags of cloud past the summit of Fiends Fell, or Cross Fell as Gunnar said it was now called. On her right, the blue-grey blocks of the fells began to close around them, etched in white, with snow-lined ridges and snow-filled gullies. She wondered whereabouts the lake of Ulueswater lay within the maze of ridges and valleys. This was to be her new home.

"Well, what did you make of Elftred?" Hravn asked, interrupting Ealdgith's thoughts.

"Canny." Ulf's understated reply made Hravn smile.

Ealdgith was more critical, "He's certainly a survivor, but should we trust him? He obviously has dealings with the Normans."

68

"You're right, Edie, you're both right." Hravn paused, "It was only when we were talking over breakfast that I realised that he plays the same game as your uncle; they're very alike."

Ulf laughed at Ealdgith's expression of surprise and indignation. "What is it that the Earl says? 'Keep your friends close, but your enemies closer still.' Is that not what they both do?"

"And Elftred is Gospatric's man," Hravn added, agreeing.

"You mean that he's right to deal with the Normans?" Ealdgith's bewilderment cleared slowly. "Yes, I suppose you may be right. What better way to look after your interests than pretend to befriend those who threaten them?"

"Hah! There you have it, Edie." Hravn's chuckle made them all smile. "That's just what the Earl does. He bought back his lands from the King whilst conspiring against him. He befriended Count Alan whilst he had us resisting him. He had us visit Canmore to sound out the Scots' King's intentions without committing to him. It's the politics of survival and a game we too must learn to play."

"But there's more, isn't there?" The tone of Ulf's question implied that he knew there was. "Edie and I saw you in deep conversation with Maldred just before we rode; you were talking with him whilst we attended to the men."

"Aye, Ulf, there is, and I'm not sure what to make of it. I mentioned Elftred's Amounderness and Loncastre lands to Maldred. I tried to sound casual, as if they were of no concern. Maldred obviously feels otherwise."

"Go on." Ealdgith and Ulf spoke as one.

"Elftred's son, Ketel, is married to Ivo de Taillebois's daughter, Christiana."

"What! You recall what my uncle said about him?" Ealdgith's exclamation startled her horse and

69

she tugged urgently on her reins as it skittered sideways.

"I'm not sure how much the Earl knows. Maldred inferred that there is little affection between father and daughter. Mayhap that is why she was tempted by Ketel; she has a son and another child on the way, apparently. He also said that de Taillebois is every bit as unpleasant as the Earl implied."

Ulf's deep laugh surprised them. "Now that's what I mean by keeping your enemies close. If Elftred can stand up to Ivo de Taillebois then I'm sure we need to keep on the right side of him."

"You're right again, Ulf, for sure. Come, let's get to Morlund!" Hravn spurred his horse to a canter, challenging them to catch up.

*****

"Edie! It's Edie! Fader, Edie's here. Hravn too, and lots of men. Come on Tyr." A nine-year-old girl, long blonde hair flailing behind her, ran down the track from a Norse longhouse that dominated the low ridge above the vill of Morlund. She almost tripped, before lifting her skirt to her knees to run faster. A brindled collie, just out of puppy-hood ran behind her, barking excitedly. "Edie, you've come back...what...?"

The girl slowed and stopped. She stared, open mouthed, as Ealdgith swung herself down from her saddle, the gap in her green and tan cloak exposed the mail hauberk beneath. Bronze, silver and copper rings glinted in the setting sun. As Ealdgith laughed, the girl ran forward again and flung herself into the young woman's embrace. "Aebbe, did I not promise you that we would return?"

Tyr followed at a more measured pace and Hravn spurred his horse onward to meet him. As he swung his leg over the saddle and jumped down in a swift easy motion, he clamped his hands on the boy's

70

shoulders. "You've grown, Tyr, and you're filling out. You'll be as broad as your fader soon, let me guess; you've turned twelve already?" He hesitated, catching Tyr's anxious glance towards the men behind him. "But don't look so serious. Come, meet Ulf. He's a true warrior as well as my deputy and closest friend. Meet Ole too, my servant and a lad it takes both Ulf and me to keep out of mischief. Now, mayhap you can show Ole to the stables whilst I introduce Ulf to your fader."

Ulf swung down and, passing the reins to Ole, joined Hravn on the path to the longhouse. "You're on home turf here, Hravn," he joked, as he glanced towards the large dragons' heads carved into each end of the massive oak roof beam. "Just look at those handsome fellows. You Cumbric-Norse certainly know how to build a house to impress a man." Then he chuckled, flattered, as Ealdgith quipped from behind him.

"They're almost as fearsome as you, Ulf."

Aebbe just looked in awe at the threesome as she walked alongside Ealdgith, holding her hand.

"Hey, Gunnar! I've come to empty your larder." Hravn shouted to a blond, stocky man standing, thumbs tucked into his belt, in the gabled entrance to the longhouse. Hravn could tell by the broad grin in the whiskered, ruddy face that his jest was well received.

"Hah! The cockiness of youth. Hravn, I see that old sword I gave you has served you well and..." Gunnar paused, grinning even more, as Ealdgith swung the left half of her cloak over her shoulder to expose Queen Aethelflaed's hauberk and sword, "Edie, you departed as a young lady determined to be Hravn's Valkyrie and have returned as the goddess Freyja herself. Come here, My Lady." He stepped forward and swept Ealdgith up in a warm bear hug.

Releasing Ealdgith, he turned to Hravn, "Now. We'll get your horses stabled and then have all your men join us here. I'll have Aleifr and Mildgyd roast a sheep for us all." Gunnar referred to the two house staff that Hravn remembered from their visit fourteen months earlier. "I can tell that you have news and I am sure that this is more than just a casual call."

The air in the longhouse was heavy and blue with smoke from the fire in the large central hearth. Mutton fat spat, dripped and sizzled from the roasting sheep as Ada helped Mildgyd serve horn cups of ale to the men clustered around the long trestle table. Aebbe refused to leave Ealdgith's side as she sat opposite Gunnar, with Hravn and Ulf either side of him. Ealdgith remembered how the young girl had come to her early one morning desperate for a mother's hug; a hug she had craved ever since her mother had died giving birth to her younger brother, Magni, months earlier. Ealdgith felt honoured by the special place she held in the young girl's heart.

Hravn's men watched quietly, awed by the Norse lord of the manor of Morlund and intrigued by his jewellery. Each of his bare upper arms was bound by a mass of engraved gold and silver rings. Some were undoubtedly old and very traditionally Norse and contrasted markedly with the silver cross that hung from the lowest ring on his left bicep, making a very obvious mix of old and new religions.

Gunnar clicked his fingers to attract Mildgyd's attention, then with a wink across the table, said, "Find the mead, Mildgyd. I recall that our Edie has a liking for it." He banged his cup on the table again. "Let me get this right. You both led a resistance, slew countless bastard Normans, conned your way into Count Alan's headquarters, led a hundred of Edie's people to freedom in the upper dale and are now Lord of Ravenstandale and Lady of Hep and Ulueswater?"

Hravn sat back and smiled. The alcohol was going to his head and he was more relaxed than he had been for many weeks. He laughed, "There you have it,

Gunnar, well almost. All we need is your help to clear the Pendragon curse once and for all."

Gunnar stabbed at a hunk of mutton on his platter, then chewed on it thinking, before he washed it down with a swig of ale. "The Pendragons have started raiding again, using men that have fled the Normans. I don't know how many they have, but it is more than ever before. I can provide maybe a dozen men and sound out neighbours to gain their support. For sure they will want to squash this menace before it bites us all."

Ealdgith spoke before Hravn. "We can ask for nothing more, but we must take care not to give the Pendragons warning. I know Uther has his spies and pays well; that is how he has survived for so long. Do not be too trusting of your neighbours."

Ulf interrupted and echoed Ealdgith's concern. "My Lady is right, Lord Gunnar. Mayhap we should work with the men we have, yours and Lord Hravn's. Ours are well trained and I am sure that, when we are ready, we can train your men too. Others would be untested and could hinder more than help our fight."

Gunnar glanced at Hravn, his question unspoken. Hravn stood to gain attention and impose his authority so that all could hear. "That's sound advice. I agree with Edie's caution and Ulf's ability to train men to fight is second to none. Thank you, Gunnar, I cannot ask for more. Yours is the offer of a true friend. We will return in May and train our men to work together. In the meantime, find out what you can about the Pendragons' strength and where they base themselves, but don't give them cause to think they are threatened. Mayhap we can use their overconfidence against them."

As Hravn sat down Gunnar clasped his shoulder, "Your men have ridden hard to get here. Don't rush back. Stay two days more, rest them whilst we plan our move. Besides, I want to hear more about Edie's lands and your thoughts for mining lead."

Chapter 7

"This rain's the curse of the gods!" Hravn pulled his lanolin-oiled cloak close, ran from the makeshift armoury to his impromptu headquarters in the old fort and cursed as the wind whipped the newly hung door from his hand, slamming it shut behind him.

Godric chuckled, took a glowing poker from the hearth, dipped the tip into a horn of ale and passed the steaming brew to Hravn. "Here, Lord. At least it will warm you."

"Thanks." Hravn raised the horn as if toasting Godric, then drank the warm weak ale quickly, before wiping his lips with the back of his hand. "Are Edie and Ulf back yet? I thought I heard horses come in."

"Aye Lord, they're inside," Godric nodded towards the inner sanctum of the time-scarred Roman building, "they're warming by the hearth."

A gruff bark from within the smoky room was echoed by Sköll and the hound bounded ahead to great his friend.

"Hravn!" Ealdgith ran to meet Hravn in the doorway and reached up to kiss him as he pulled her to him in a close hug. "Come, Ulf's here, let's swap news."

"Welcome back Ulf," Hravn clasped him warmly on the shoulder, "how were the family?"

Ulf laughed, "Good, but Adelind's teething and bawling like a good 'un, so I'm glad to be back...what?!" He flinched, then rubbed his upper arm as Ealdgith punched his bicep.

"Don't lie Ulf, I saw the tear in your eye as you handed her across to Cyneburg before we rode. You're the softest huscarle I've ever known."

Hravn laughed at Ulf's sheepish grin. "And how was Frida?"

"She's got a good two months before she's due, but cursing the number of steps at Bebbanburge. I think she's bigger than Cyneburg at the same stage, don't you Ulf?"

Ulf nodded, then changed the subject, keen to move the conversation on to the matter of their forthcoming raid into Ghellinges-scir. "I've brought the extra crossbow bolts and arrows you wanted. The Earl tactfully reminded me that his spies will be ready to lead us into Dunholm in Hrēðmonath, which means that we've barely two weeks left in Solmonath to hit Edie's uncle's manors, return and sort ourselves out."

"I know," Hravn responded, starring into the glow of the hearth's embers, "it took longer than I thought it would to get this place ready. Thank Thor for Aelf's skills, and Gamel the blacksmith. I trust you returned them safely?" he added, remembering the reason for Ulf and Ealdgith's trip back to Northumberland.

"Aye, we did and it looks like this storm is testing their work. All seems weathertight?" Ulf glanced around the room.

"I hope you reassured your uncle, Edie? He's no need for concern. Grab your cloaks and I'll show you the armoury and the stocks in the buttery. The lads have worked well and we are ready to go in the morning."

Ealdgith glanced at Ulf, who nodded, then turned to Hravn. "I saw my uncle with fresh eyes when we returned; I fear that he has aged. There are streaks of grey in his beard and yellow in his eyes. I think worry about the King's campaign into the north is getting to him."

Hravn took hold of Ealdgith's hand with a gentle squeeze, "I'm not surprised Edie. That's why he wants us clear of Bebbanburge by sumor and is looking to send Aethelreda and the children to Flanders."

As they returned to the outer room Hravn turned to Godric. "Find Eadwulf, Edric and Osric. I'll brief everyone here in an hour."

*****

"Thank you Eadwulf, good point. Now, to summarise." Hravn stood at the edge of the model that he had made on the floor and held the attention of those clustered around it, deliberately encouraging his master-at-arms' participation in the planning. "Edric, you will remain here to demonstrate a strong presence along the line of the Tinan and reassure our Norman neighbours that this is not the seat of any outlawry they may experience. The route into Ghellinghes-scir is about thirty-five leagues and should take us three days. We'll rest up for one day before raiding at night and crossing back north of the Tees. Edric, have the pots bubbling with stew for our return in a week."

Hravn turned to Eadwulf, "I want you with my household party. Your section leaders, Godric and Osric and two of their men will take turns to scout our route. We'll follow Dere Street, the old stone road from Corbricg, here," he tapped the model with his spear point, "to Saint Æbbe's monastery where there is a ruined fort. That's where we will shelter on the first night." He paused and glanced at their eyes to confirm understanding, then added, "We'll each stand guard in turn, except Ada, though she may want to keep Ole company... just to keep him awake, of course." His wink reassured the lad before his mouth dropped too much.

"Next morning, we'll cross a ford and should then see Dunholm on a hill three leagues off to the east, here." Another tap. "I want us to keep moving quickly; this is where we will be most vulnerable. Then, as we keep going south, we should see the River Uuire to the east. We'll cross it at a loop in the channel. From the Earl's map, it looks as if there is a smaller river to cross within another league or so and then we will reach a further ruined fort at Bincastre. This is all church land so I'm not sure quite what we'll find, but we'll stop there for our second night. On our third day, it will be three leagues until we reach the Tees. It's the boundary with Count Alan's lands and the bridge at Persebricg is likely to be guarded. I want us to cross by the ford at Gegenforda, a league and a half upriver, here."

"I know it." Ulf interrupted, "We can use Earl Edwin's Pommel as a reference point after that."

"What?" Eadwulf's rare gruff laugh set them all chuckling.

Ealdgith smiled across at him. "It's the highpoint on the ridge west of Ghellinges. There is a clump of trees that dominates the forest all around. It looks just like the knob of a pommel, and of course Ghellinges was Earl Edwin's seat...why, what did you think it was?" She quipped, drawing an embarrassed twitch of the lips from Eadwulf.

"And Richemund lies just beyond, over the ridge." Hravn's voice was sober. "Take a moment or two to remember the route then come across to the model of the ground for the raid." Hravn had used the same technique when making the second model, placing differing size stones to represent the vills and granaries, reeds for the rivers, lines of soil for the tracks and moss for woodland.

"I'm impressed, I've never seen the like." Eadwulf muttered, half to himself.

"I'm pleased, because this is really for your benefit. It's home ground for Edie and Ulf." Hravn continued with his briefing. "Once we cross the Tees we will make for Cattun. We know it's waste with only a couple of families scratching a living there. We've nothing to fear from them and will lay up for the next day, move into our positions at dusk, then raid after sunset. We'll work in two groups." He paused.

"Eadwulf, you're with me along with Osric and his man...what's his name?"

"Alfric, Lord."

Hravn nodded his thanks, "And Ole too, of course. We'll go south, staying east of the Swale and raid Mortun before coming back to hit the granary and mill. We raided both last year and I know that Elreton's granary has been rebuilt in the same place. I assume Mortun's has too. The roofs will be newly thatched and should catch and burn quickly; we need to take that into account. Understood?" Hravn continued without waiting for an answer.

"Edie will lead the second group with Ulf and Godric. Ada, keep close to Edie throughout. Raid Corburne first, cross the Swale by the ford at Esebi before returning to burn the granary at Esebi. Then, go straight to Elreton and block the road from Richemund until we join you after we've fired the mill. Once together, it's straight to Persebricg and across the bridge. We will take it at the charge if needs be. I want to avoid the ford in the dark. We will rest briefly at the old fort and then return north at first light. Now, Edie, I know you've some thoughts about coordination."

"Not just coordination. We don't know what state the granary at Corburne is in, though we do know that the thatch on Esebi's is very mossy and will be difficult to ignite. I'm concerned also that Corburne is at least ten minutes from the ford and the ford is barely a league from the castle at Richemund. Once the garrison reacts, as it will, we are at risk of getting cut off."

"I agree, My Lady." Ulf spoke for the first time, addressing Ealdgith formally in recognition of the seriousness of the situation. "Remember how quickly the granary at Elreton exploded last year. I think we need to get into the granary, where it will be dry and dusty and set light to the grain inside, closing the doors as we leave to keep air out. Hopefully it will burn more

79

slowly and give us time to cross back over the Swale, without forewarning the castle or Esebi."

"You're right, Ulf." Hravn and Ealdgith spoke as one, Hravn adding, "Take Cenric with you for the task. Edie and Godric should hold the crossing at the ford. Do you agree, Edie?"

"Yes. Now, about Esebi. We're forgetting the impact that this is going to have on all the vills and we owe Father Oda at Esebi a great debt. He is my uncle's man after all, and he worked closely with us last year."

Hravn nodded slowly, sucking his lip whilst he thought. "The impact won't be that great. We know that all these granaries hold only wheat, and that the Normans reserve wheat for themselves because they think it below their status to eat bread made from barley or rye; so, the people won't go without wheat because they will never have it anyway." He paused again, before coming to a decision. "Edie, we'll see Father Oda as soon as we're secure in Cattun. Just you and me. He needs to know what we are doing and we can give him a couple of hours to get the villagers organised, empty the granary, and stash the grain. They can take it for themselves in the sure knowledge that we will be blamed for their granary's destruction. It'll be an extra bonus for them and should secure their silence."

"Hah! Yes! That's just what was on my mind." Ealdgith clasped Hravn's hand in thanks. "Don't you agree, Ulf?" The big housecarl's broad grin was all the answer she needed. "We'll fire the inside of that granary too," he said, "it will give us time to get to Elreton before we awake the wasps' nest. Once we are clear from Esebi they won't know where to go next, hopefully it will be to Corburne, particularly if it's burning by then."

"Agreed." Hravn tapped his spear butt on the stone flags as if to emphasise the point. "But, Edie, I think there is more yet?"

"Oh, how you know me," she laughed. "When you fire Mortun it will be seen from the castle at Richemund. That alone could be enough to provoke a reaction and if it is before we are clear of Corburne we could still be trapped the other side of the river. We need a signal that will coordinate our moves."

"Moonrise, Lord." Eadwulf broke into the discussion. "Today it will rise a couple of hours before dusk. Four days from now it will rise just after sunset. From what I know of My Lady's homelands, both of our groups will see it rise over the moors in the east. So, as long as the clouds are thin and we are already in position, we will have a clear signal as soon as the moon cuts the horizon."

"Of course, that's the answer, Eadwulf," Hravn's praise was very obvious, "and what's more, it'll be a waning three quarters moon, so good enough to see by but not too bright. Ideal for raiding, I'd say, but we must make full use of the shadows. Right, if there are no more questions we'll prepare weapons and food, ready the horses, then ride at first light tomorrow."

As they left the room Eadwulf pulled Ulf to one side. "Does our lord always go into such detail and involve his men in his orders with such informality? I've never seen the like."

"He's a rare leader Eadwulf. You should know that by now. He's always planning ahead and he cares for his men like few others do. We've a lot to learn from him." Ulf clapped Eadwulf on his shoulder. "But don't forget Lady Edie. Her influence is considerable. They always get their heads together first; that double act just now was really for our benefit, to get our input. Don't be fooled by their youth either, they're as mature as you or me, maybe more so in some ways."

"Hah! I'm beginning to think I underestimated them both, Lady Edie in particular." Eadwulf cleared his throat, "Now, where can I find a woodcutter's axe? That Danish beast of yours would fell any door in the land. I can see that I'll need to smash my way into the Mortun granary and set that alight from the inside to give us time to get to Elreton."

*****

Sleet, swept by an icy north wind, whipped across their backs and plastered their cloaks. Ealdgith silently thanked the gods that the wind was from behind, pushing them southward; its bitter blast would have made a northerly journey unbearable. It also, she thought, helped to shield their progress from any prying eyes. She glanced back at Ada, then across to Ulf; both were stern-faced, hunched forward in the saddle, concentrating on guiding their quick-moving mounts between the potholes and ruts on the old, slippery, Roman road. Swapping her reins between hands she sucked the numbed fingers on her free hand then tucked them under her cloak; sensation returned slowly. It had been a long, cold two days enlivened only by the hounds catching a deer early that morning. It now hung over the back of their one pack-horse. At least they would eat better than expected.

Hravn held up his hand to halt the party when he saw Cenric galloping towards them, closing the gap quickly. He halted slowly, careful to avoid his horse's hooves slipping on the half-frozen stones.

"Godric is at the fort, Lord, across the river just over the next crest. It's deserted though there's a vill clustered onto its south side. Several of the towers are still standing and some of the barracks are roofed and dry inside, but the rest are tumbling or roofless." Cenric spoke quickly, breathless as he wheeled his horse alongside Hravn.

"Good, well done Cenric. Lead us in." Hravn urged his horse forward, then called to Eadwulf, "Have the men dry and shelter the horses first on arrival, Ole and Ada will tend to ours."

Hravn left his deputies to secure the fort, prepare their camp and gather firewood whilst he explored the double towers of the eastern gate, three floors of which were still intact. Taking time to gather his bearings in the fading light he was relieved to see that the vill did not intrude within the fort's walls and that they should be able to keep themselves secure. He had no doubt that a party of armed strangers would be noticed. He mused to himself: why not make the most of that and buy fodder from them for the horses? That might help buy the villagers' loyalty and silence. The only other sign of habitation was a thin wisp of wind-whipped smoke almost a league to the east.

What pleased him more than the prospect of buying fodder was a second stone road. Leading from the eastern gate, it turned north and ran as straight as an arrow. Narrow, overgrown with moss and little more than a man's height in width, it must be an old military road, built for fast movement rather than trade. Hravn wondered: could it be the backdoor for their attack into the shire's heartland? He could just see the night fires of Dunhelm off to its right, four or five leagues away.

"Edie, find Ulf and Eadwulf and come up here...keep to the walls, the rafters look weak. There is something you need to see." Hravn leaned over the parapet and shouted down urgently.

"You could be right." Ulf's eyes narrowed as he scrutinised the old road in the hastening dusk. Eadwulf simply nodded in silent appreciation.

"I'll talk to the Earl's spies first. Mayhap we can strike from here rather than across the Tinan, raid manors on the west bank of the Uuire and use the road to move quickly north." Hravn talked to himself as much as the others. He turned, "Now! To the task in hand."

The following morning dawned cold, but clear, with a weak sun that brought at least an illusion of warmth to exposed skin.

After crossing the Tees at Gegenforda, Ulf closed up alongside Eadwulf and Godric and bade them to stop. "Look yonder," he pointed with his spear shaft, "that clump of tall oaks atop the hill on the skyline, that's Earl Edwin's Pommel."

They nodded, it was a very obvious landmark.

He shielded his eyes with his hand, "Now, to the right. See how the forest is blackened by fire. That was Hravn's parting gift to the Count last sumor."

"What?!" Their heads turned in surprise.

Ulf grinned briefly, then his expression hardened, "The forest settlements that I told you about were further along the ridge, to the west. We were betrayed for a sack of grain, and a hothead Norman knight raided us with a dozen of his men-at-arms. They murdered Hravn's father, who was the headman, and were torturing the people when we caught them unawares and slew the lot, Edie took two with her bow, and her hound killed another." He spat. "Miserable bastards! Well, we knew we couldn't remain, so Hravn set a line of fire right across the tops from the Swale northwards. We led the people from the settlements up into the upper dale, leaving the Normans to stop the fire before the west wind swept it across Richemund. As it happened, a storm broke, but we were all already clear." He paused and smiled wistfully, "I'm glad the clump survived."

Chapter 8

Hravn slid from the saddle, left his horse and moved through the low scrub, where he crouched at the edge, his hand on Sköll's collar. Godric, fifty paces behind, raised his hand to halt the others a furlong away along the ridge, before the track dipped across neglected fields to the wasted vill of Cattun. The setting sun cast a red sheen over the cluster of thatched houses in an apocalyptic echo of the slaughter and rape there just two winters earlier. He waved Godric forward.

"Those who survived the harrying and haven't been starved into servitude live in the buildings on the far side of the vill. We'll shelter in those on this side and stockade the horses there. Call the others forward. I'll take Edie and Ulf to make our introductions whilst Eadwulf gets everyone into shelter and secures a perimeter. Can you brief him?" It was an order, not a question, but Godric appreciated Hravn's manner. He already had great faith in his young lord's leadership.

"Will this do, little lady?" Godric pushed the wood-framed house door open with his foot. As the evening light flooded in Ada heard the scuffle of vermin across the floor. "We'll take the house opposite. This'll be fine once you get a fire going, I'm sure even Ole can find something to burn." He liked to tease the pair, and he sensed that Ada's reservation towards men, and him in particular, was diminishing. Ulf had told him in confidence about Ada's background and asked him to look out for her.

"Come on, Ole. Sort out the hearth whilst I open the shutters and get some light and air in." Ada glanced back with a smile over her shoulder. "Thank you, Godric."

Ole struck a spark against some tinder and lit a rush-candle that he kept in his saddle bag. There was one large room with a central hearth under a hole in the thatched roof, a sleeping platform under the rafters at one end and an assortment of tools and clothes strewn across the floor. "I think those who remained in the vill have ransacked this place for food and clothing. We'd best tidy before Hravn and Edie get back." He spoke to Ada as he picked up a broken stool. "We can get a fire going with this and I'll see what's in the other houses."

Ealdgith and Ulf rode alongside Hravn across open grassland that separated the two halves of the vill, past the stark skeletal remains of the two buildings that had once been at the heart of village life. Blackened timbers were all that remained of the granary and barn that had been destroyed along with the grain and animals inside by Normans sweeping through Cattun on that fateful winter's day. Ealdgith bit her lip as she remembered the screams of the people of Dune, caged in the vill's barn and then burnt alive and shuddered at the thought of that happening here. She glanced at Hravn and could tell by his frozen expressionless face that he was haunted by the same memory. The hounds broke their trance.

Sköll growled and ran forward as two men moved in the shadow of a house. Hati followed until Hravn called them to heel. "We mean you no harm," he called out as he slid from his saddle and passed his reins to Ulf. Ealdgith did likewise. "This is my wife, the Lady Ealdgith. Her father was Thor, Lord of Hindrelag. I am Sir Hravn and this is Ulf, our huscarle. Who is the headman here?"

The men remained concealed in the shadow, one spoke. "You are not Norman?"

Ealdgith replied. These were once her people and she hoped they would respond to her. "Please, step from the shadow so that we may speak openly. I assure you, we are not Normans and have no love for them. I know that this vill was once under the charge of Ulf, who held it from Earl Edwin. What became of him?"

86

The men hesitated, then stepped forward. The same one spoke. "He fled, Lady, the day after the Normans came, taking his family and others with him. For sure they perished in the snows that came after."

Ealdgith nodded, her eyes holding those of the spokesman. "I understand, we fled too." She glanced at Hravn. "Though, as you see, we survived. But what of the other villagers? I can see that the land is mainly fallow now."

The man glanced up the hill towards the skeleton of the barn. "Those few of us who are left were in the fields. The Normans sought out Ulf, held him with his family whilst they cleared the houses, raped those that took their fancy, then pushed men, women and children into the barn. What you see now is all that is left of them."

Ealdgith felt a tear on her cheek. "Whose is this land now?"

"The Count's, Lady, though he concentrates on other manors and has left us alone, for now. We have nothing that he can tax."

Ealdgith hesitated, then decided to risk speaking openly. "We are here to settle a score with my uncle and will be gone two nights hence. I command that you do not speak of our presence here before then, it will be better for all our sakes. I assure you that you will know when our business is finished and, if you think you may gain a reward by speaking out, please do so. I regret that there is little we can do for you as food and seed corn will be what you need, and coin will doubtless draw attention if you spend it."

"Mayhap this will help?" Hravn opened his saddle bag and took out a fist-sized pouch. "Hack-silver will raise fewer eyebrows in the marketplace," he paused, "and if you are asked for a name, mention just Lady Ealdgith."

Ealdgith interjected, "No, please do not risk your head by speaking to any of the turncoat English lords or the Normans. Instead, spread the word openly that I will take retribution for the murder of Lord Thor and his household, and that any treacherous lord needs to consider his loyalty. If any ask whence we came, tell them it was from the direction of the moors. As I say, you will know when to speak, just wait 'til then. Can you do that?"

The man took the pouch, then nodded to Ealdgith with a thin smile, "Thank you My Lady, I will. I appreciate your confiding in me. Your father was not my lord, but I remember him as a just man. I am sure that we are best left in ignorance." He stood watching as they remounted, turned, and cantered back, leaving the survivors of the wasted vill of Cattun in peace.

Ulf paused in the doorway and gave a loud laugh as he entered the house, "You'll make Ole a good wife one day, Ada. A pot of broth bubbling already and meat roasting too. Eadwulf and his lads will be after it..." He stopped mid-sentence and shook his head in embarrassed amusement.

"Aye, we will that, Ulf." A chorus of laughter echoed from the shadows and, as his eyes grew accustomed to the gloom, he saw the rest of their men sprawled on the floor.

"Don't think we've taken advantage of Ada's good nature, Ulf. We've done all the other chores, watered and tethered the horses. Eadwulf's just setting the guard now." Godric spoke quickly, very aware of Ulf's concern for Ada and Ole.

Ada's quick smile reassured Ulf, he was pleased her confidence was finally building. "Aye, happen. You're still a bunch of rogues though. I hope you've a couple of stools for our lord and lady. I know they want to talk us through the plan for tomorrow whilst we eat, and shift your butt Alfric, unless you want to be mistaken for a hunk of venison."

*****

Hravn told the guard to rouse him when the false dawn backlit the eastern moors. He woke Ealdgith and they rode quietly out of the vill, keen to reach Esebi and find Father Oda before local people awoke. It was a good three leagues ride to where the priest lived near the Swale. As the couple crested the hill north of the church and descended to tether their horses alongside Father Oda's small cottage, smoke was rising from domestic fires in a couple of cottages to their left. Their attention, though, was to their right; as they rode they both stared at the stone tower of the castle of Richemund that grew ever larger on the Hindrelag bluff, barely a league up the valley.

The hounds sensed that the priest was within and ran forward to scratch at the door. It opened a crack and the questioning face of a dark-featured man in early middle-age peered out. His surprise turned to delight, then concern. "Hravn, Lady Edie, come in, quickly!" He closed the door with a cautious glance around the vill and ushered them to sit down by the hearth, where the recently stoked fire threw out light and warmth. "It's good to see you for I feared we would never meet again, but I sense that you may herald trouble. What is it that my master, the Earl, has in mind now?"

Father Oda was one of Earl Gospatric's network of spies within the church and, following Hravn's recent flight from Count Alan's coterie, the only one able now to report on matters in Gellinghes-scir. They could see that the constant strain of sudden discovery and risk of torture was telling on him.

Ealdgith spoke first. "The Earl is under no illusion that his future is uncertain and he wants to hinder the King's progress into the north as best he can. We are to burn granaries and mills in Dunhelm in the coming weeks. Once we do so the road south will doubtless be closed to us and we are here now to pay

89

my father's brother a final visit. I cannot call that man 'my uncle' anymore."

Hravn saw consternation on Oda's face. "We are repeating our raids of last year and will hit Mortun, Elreton, and Corburne tonight. We know those manors are producing wheat solely to feed the Normans. The destruction of their stores will not harm our people, for they grow what little barley and oats they can on their own meagre lands, but we could hinder the Count's ability to feed the King's army when it comes north." He hesitated, "Esebi too. If you think you can trust your people, we suggest you get them to break the granary open before dusk and take what they want for themselves and hide it well. We will burn the granary tonight on our way from Corburne to Elreton. The blame will be ours."

Father Oda paused before responding. "It should work, but have you thought of the risk? There will be a dozen mounted men-at-arms here within twenty minutes of the first sign of fire." He glanced towards the shuttered window. "That's not all. Since you burned the forest they are building another wooden castle at Gellinghes to secure the tops behind Richemund, so don't be tempted to escape that way. It's on the site of Earl Edwin's burned hall."

Hravn gave a low laugh. "I'm not surprised. Worry not, Father. We know how quickly the Normans can move, but we know what we are about and will act before they can think and react. We will be north of the Tees whilst they are still searching in the vale of the Swale. We have arranged for word to spread that we rode from the moors, so do not gainsay any rumours you may hear."

"You should know, Father, that the Earl has great faith in Hravn's ability to plan and lead these raids. We have a troop of his men under our command and..." Ealdgith placed her hand on Hravn's arm, "he has knighted him and granted both of us lands in

Westmoringaland. We are to hold the Earl's southern border there once we are finished in Dunhelm."

"Ah! God be praised! That is well deserved." Father Oda's face broke into a broad smile and he held out his hands to touch them both. "You have my blessing and, yes, I will arrange for my people to look to their needs. None here has any respect for the Normans and you can be sure that the granary will be empty when you burn it. I will have kindling stacked within to assist your work. Now, you must leave before the presence of two armed horsemen draws any attention. After all, we are within sight of the castle."

*****

Godric guided his horse slowly across the ford. The river, as it lapped against the rocks at the edge, sounded unusually loud in the still air. Sound carried clearly on such a night and he took care to speak softly when he halted in the shadow of the large oak tree by which Ealdgith and Ada sat on their horses. "They're on their way back, I heard them coming down the track through the woods."

"Good, go and make a start on firing the granary, I want us away from the shadow of that castle. I'll send Cenric to you and then take Ulf to the top of the hill. Meet us there when you're done, I want five minutes to get clear if you can do it."

Godric left as Ulf and Cenric splashed through the ford with far less caution than Godric. As they halted, Ealdgith sent Cenric onward and called Ulf to her side. The grin on his soot-blackened face told her that he had good news.

"We found two granaries, my guess is they've been stockpiling for the King's army. I think the new one will go first, I think we've only minutes more."

"Godric's setting this one to go within a matter of minutes. He'll meet us at the top of the hill. Come, I want us all out of sight of the castle before its roof burns." Ealdgith turned and cantered the three furlongs back to the vill, then up the hill past the church and through the cluster of houses. She was sure that many eyes watched from behind shuttered windows. Ulf waited, then followed behind Ada as she led the pack horse. He turned as Godric galloped up behind.

"Quickly! The priest stuffed the place with so much brushwood and dead bracken that it will explode any time now. The Normans will never guess it was empty." Godric carried on past to warn Ealdgith.

Ealdgith led them swiftly, out of the valley and up over a hill bounded by a large loop of the river, across Schirebi Beck in a jump, then over the stone road that led down to the old Roman fort of Catrice. It was land she had explored and hunted over with Hravn for most of her childhood; a fast ride on a moonlit night was a challenge she relished. The others followed with a blind faith. A distant red glow off to their right signalled that Hravn's raid at Mortun had been successful.

The climax of Ealdgith's raids came suddenly. Esebi's granary exploded with a loud crack and shower of sparks and leaping flames as the massive roof beam broke.   Seconds later the first Corburne granary followed, prompting a long trumpet blast to rouse the Richemund garrison. She halted where the track entered a copse on the crest of a low rise and signalled to Ulf and Godric to close in.

"We've a good view back for almost half a league from here. We'll wait to see if we are followed, then join Hravn at the mill."

They saw Corburne's second granary explode in a shower of sparks, as flames reached skyward. The slow-burning fire had smouldered through the grain and eaten into the thick thatch, before finally opening a way for air to rush into the oxygen starved space below the roof. Dry dust had then fuelled an explosion that threw back the roof in a loud crack that reached them across the still valley. Godric gasped and Ada flinched at the sudden burst of light.

"Look! Riders on the track. See the glint of their spears." Ulf pointed urgently, "The light is reflecting off their mail. Four, no, five of them. They'll be here in a couple of minutes."

Ealdgith's decision was immediate. "Back into the trees, stay mounted. We'll take them with crossbows. Ulf take the first, then Godric, and Cenric the third. I'll take the fifth and set Hati on the fourth. If you're confident aim for the man, if not take his horse. We'll slay them once they're down. Ada, get behind us with the pack horse."

They reacted quickly, wheeling their horses into the shadow of the trees. Ulf moved fifty paces down the track, positioning the men at intervals so that they each had space to cover their appointed targets. Ealdgith remained by the entrance. She intended to take the last rider in his flank and then act as cut-off to prevent any escape. She placed an arrow between her lips and notched another onto her bow string. Ada, watching from behind, tethered the pack pony to a branch and did likewise. Hati, trained and practiced in ambushes, lay by his mistress's horse, panting in anticipation.

The Normans had been moving at a quick canter, but slowed as they reached the wood. It seemed to Ealdgith that rather than sensing danger they simply couldn't see clearly in the shadow of the trees.

Ulf, astride his black stallion, raised his crossbow into the aim and slowed his breathing whilst he tracked a point just in front of the lead rider, estimating the time it would take the bolt to strike the rider's chest. Godric and Cenric did likewise. The sound of Ulf's shot was their signal.

The impact of the ambush was dramatic. The first two riders were flung backwards out of their saddles by the shock of short heavy bolts smashing into their ribs. The third rider struggled to stay mounted as his horse squealed in pain and reared up before collapsing forward, a bolt embedded deep into its chest, where it had ruptured a lung. As its rider fell to the ground, Cenric leapt from his horse, grabbed his spear and strode forward to thrust it through the horseman's back. Cenric moved so quickly that he was onto the track before Hati. The fourth rider's horse swerved as Cenric leapt in front. Its rider wheeled sharply in an attempt to escape the killing ground and the hooves skittered on the frozen earth, kicking at Hati. It swerved past the fifth horse just as Ealdgith's arrowed pierced that rider's midriff. The fifth horse ploughed on, tripping and stumbling over bodies as its rider slipped from the saddle to be dragged with his head bouncing along the ground.

Ealdgith whipped the second arrow from her teeth, notched it and drew her bow as the fleeing Norman galloped past. She flinched and ducked instinctively at the twang of a bow behind her back and the thrum of an arrow past her right ear. Ada's arrow caught the Norman in the side of his neck. He pitched sideways and, as he hit the ground, Ealdgith's arrow tore into his back. She turned with a smile of surprise and admiration and shouted "Stay there!" As she dismounted, she called Hati to heel and went to check the bodies. She felt nauseous and breathed deeply through her nose to calm herself. Killing always unsettled her and she recalled Brother Oswin's warning that it becomes easier with practice. She doubted that it would for her; it was evil, but necessary. She, they, had no choice if they were to survive in this new Norman world.

"Godric, Cenric, cut that horse's throat, then take your horses and drag it off the track. I'll kill any Normans still alive, then we need to drag them out of sight too. We'll let the other horses run loose." Ulf's voice resonated through the trees.

Ealdgith ran up to him. "I'm sure they weren't looking for us, they only seemed concerned about the track. I think they were heading for Mortun. Thank the gods we got to them before they found Hravn's group."

Ulf's reply was gruff, as he heaved a corpse into the trees. "Aye, we need to get across to him now. I reckon we've bought a bit of time."

*****

"By Thor, Edie, that's cutting it fine!" Hravn exclaimed out loud as he saw the sudden pyres at Esebi and Corburne. He was with Eadwulf, running back from the Elreton granary where a slow fire was burning through the grain within. He was sure the new fires would rouse the vill and he wanted to set the mill alight before they attracted attention. "Osric, Alfric. Be quick, force the mill door and set fire to the upper floor. Get it going quickly. We'll block the track from the vill. Eadwulf, let's get remounted."

Osric shattered the cross bar securing the mill's door by a single blow from the woodcutter's axe. He shouldered the door open and Alfric followed as he clambered up the ladder to the mezzanine floor in the loft. They ripped open sacks and, striking flint and steel, set light to the dry hemp. Satisfied with the fire, Osric swung down from the loft and dashed to the door.

Alfric tripped as he turned to follow and lunged forward pushing a stack of grain sacks. He pulled himself upright and he watched in horror as the sacks fell from the mezzanine onto the stone flags below. "No!" He screamed. Clouds of dust and dry grain from the bursting sacks billowed back into the loft. Myriad fine particles were ignited by the naked flames that already licked through the loft. Rapid combustion in the confined space exploded in a fire ball that thrust Osric out of the mill door and consumed Alfric in flames.

Osric rolled forward, staggered to his feet and ran back into the mill. A wall of searing hot smoke hit him and burned the exposed hair on his face. He gasped at the hot pain in his lungs. Crouching down below the layer of smoke and taking a deep breath, he pulled his lanolin-proofed cloak over his head to shield his hands as he started to climb the ladder. His eyes stung from the heat and smoke, his head throbbed as his steel helm radiated heat into his skull. His breath gave out as he clutched at the top rung. It came away in his hand, burning at either end, and he fell back as Hravn and Eadwulf grasped his legs and took his body weight. The three men staggered backwards out of the mill, blindly gasping lungfuls of fresh air.

"Ole! Water!" Hravn croaked, "Here, pour it over Osric's face and hands. There's another water skin on my saddle, get it."

Ole felt strangely calm, although dazed by the speed of disaster he had grown used to violent change and he obeyed Hravn instinctively.

Hravn checked Osric quickly. His face was red and his beard and eye lashes badly singed, but his helmet and cloak had saved him from further burns. He had some nasty blisters on his hands, but thankfully they didn't appear to be charred.

Eadwulf shook Hravn's shoulder. "We have to go. Nigh on a dozen men are coming. Alfric is gone, we can do nothing more here."

"I know. Osric, we'll help you mount, then follow behind me. We'll stop further up the track and wait for the others. Ole, lead Alfric's horse."

They galloped away from the inferno, but slowed and then stopped as the shadows claimed them, their eyes still blinded by the light and unable to cope with the dark. "We'll wait here. Osric, are you able to hold your reins and ride?"

He nodded slowly, grim faced, silent for a moment until he spoke with a soft croak. "Ole, have you more water?"

Hravn jumped with surprise as Ealdgith's group of riders burst upon them suddenly. He realised that he must still be deafened by the blast and noise of the explosion. As Ealdgith reined to a halt beside him her expression changed from glee to consternation when she saw the empty saddle and grim faces of the four men. "Alfric?" She asked urgently.

She took Hravn's hand in hers as he reached across to her. "The mill exploded. Alfric was trapped inside. Osric was burned trying to get to him." He spoke without emotion and Ealdgith realised that there was a risk of shock setting in.

"Come, what would you have us do now, for we have to get clear before the Normans gather their senses. We've already slain five that were on their way here." Ealdgith held Hravn's eyes with hers and stared intensely, urging him to act.

Hravn shook his head as if to clear his thoughts. "Five! Where?"

"This side of the stone road to the old fort. I think they were heading to Mortun. Others will be at Esebi by now and this latest blaze will no doubt attract more here. Can you not hear the castle bell tolling?"

"Bell? No. I fear the blast deafened me. All I can hear is a dull roar in my ears." Hravn released her hand with a quick squeeze. "Lead us to Persebricg Edie, you and Ulf. Take charge until my eyes and ears recover. Godric and Cenric, bring up the rear. Eadwulf stay with Osric, I fear he's in a worst state than either of us."

"Ole and Ada, lead the spare horses and follow Eadwulf. Hravn, stay close to me until your eyes recover, we'll ride fast." Ealdgith wheeled her horse, nodded to Ulf and urged her horse forward.

They moved swiftly. Ealdgith took a route that looped north towards Middeltun, until they found the stone road and followed it towards the Tees; the moon, at its zenith, lit their way.

Ealdgith halted the column on the ridge above Persebricg and sent Ulf forward to observe the bridge. He returned moments later.

"There're two guards Edie, at this side of the river. Yon side is clear. We'll be in view for the last furlong once we go around the next corner, but we can cover that at the charge quicker than they can react."

She turned in her saddle and spoke clearly. "Ulf is correct, we'll take them in a charge, with spears. Ride three abreast with Hravn between Ulf and me. Godric, go with Eadwulf and Osric. Ada, ride between Cenric and Ole. With hounds in front, I think the guards will scatter before we hit them. Don't stop until I do. We'll walk the horses silently down to the bend, then follow my signal."

Ealdgith walked her horse around the final bend in the stone road. Two guards lounged against the bridge parapet, talking. She assumed that others were sleeping in an adjacent hut. She glanced over her shoulder to check all were ready, raised, then lowered her spear point and dug her spurs in, urging her black mare into a gallop. The guards reacted as anticipated, scattering as the wall of horses and mail-clad bodies rolled towards them and crossed the bridge. Ealdgith kept the pace going for five minutes before they slowed on the crest of a hill. The road behind was quiet.

"I want to get to the fort at Bincastre, then rest and have a look at Osric's burns. How are you now?" Ealdgith conferred with Hravn. His smile told her all she needed to know.

"Better, Edie. My head has cleared and I can see and hear again. I agree with you. Lead on with Ulf, I'll follow with Osric and Eadwulf."

A clear, frosty dawn broke and cast a pink glow over the old fort as they crested the last of many rolling ridges. Hravn took Ulf to the top of the gatehouse tower to check for any sign of pursuit whilst Eadwulf, with Cenric and Ole, tended to the horses, rubbed them down with hay, watered them and used the last of the oats, carried by the pack horse, to supplement the village fodder.

Ealdgith led Osric into the old headquarters block where they were encamped and, whilst Godric rekindled the fire in the hearth, she lit a torch, sat him down and turned to Ada. "Go to my saddlebag, fetch my herb roll and spare undershift, then bring a bowl and pitcher of fresh spring water. Oh, and ask Ole to go and fetch me dock leaves for Osric's hands as soon as there is light to see by."

"I'm going to have a careful look at your burns, Osric, and see what I can do for you." Ealdgith bent down, her head close to Osric's, then, seeing his frown, added with her most reassuring smile, "Hravn's ealdmoder was a herbalist, she taught me well and gave me the secrets of her potions. There's no magic, just the lore of our people." She knew the Church frowned upon the practice of healing, particularly by women, "Are you happy for me to touch you?"

"Yes, of course, My Lady. I'm sure you will help me more than Eadwulf's home-spun wizardry will...I just didn't expect you to tend to me."

"Oh, Osric! There's a lot more to me than Eadwulf seems to think," she teased. "Though I sense he may be changing his view."

"Oy aye, My Lady. He is that." Osric smiled at last. He relaxed and sat still whilst Ealdgith unbuckled his helmet and eased it gently from his head.

"It's best I do this, Osric, I can see that your fingers are too raw to manage." Ealdgith turned to Ada, "Use your seax and cut my undershift into strips."

Osric gasped, "No, My Lady. You cannot do that." He sounded genuinely shocked.

Ealdgith laughed. "And why not, Osric? It is but a piece of linen, nothing more, and your need is greatest." She peered closely at his face. "You were lucky, your face is badly singed but the skin is only reddened and your hair burnt away. Your eyes may irritate until your lashes grow back, but there's no lasting damage that I can see. I will make a salve to help keep your skin moist. Now, Ada, moisten a strip of linen and pass it to me. I'll gently clean your face, Osric."

Ealdgith work carefully, dabbing the burns and wiping away soot and sweat. The cool moisture soothed Osric's pain and he felt the heat in his skin diminish."

He flicked his eyes up to look at Ealdgith's. "How is it that your touch is so gentle, My Lady?" Ealdgith felt her face blush, but she knew by his tone that Osric wasn't being flirtatious. "I heard that you killed two men with your bow, just last night, and you weald a sword that would stop any man but, forgive me for being outspoken, your touch is that of an angel."

Ealdgith stopped her wiping and stepped back, a slight smile on her lips. "That is a great compliment, Osric, thank you. I think you now know just who I am."

Osric carried on looking at her face, waiting for her to tell him more.

"My family and my people are everything to me. I do all that I can to care for them and, in these times, that means fighting for them and healing them. One day, I hope, it will also mean providing shelter and food; peace and security too, when we take our lands in Westmoringaland. I am just so fortunate that a remarkable man taught me to fight," Ealdgith glanced at Ada, "for unless a woman can defend herself she will always be ruled by men and at risk of abuse.

"Hravn taught you?" Osric was surprised.

"No, though he tried. Hravn and I were taught by a soldier turned hermit monk. He learned his skills serving the emperor in the east, though he taught us a lot more besides. Now, let me bathe your hands, I am afraid that they are more badly burned. Once I have applied a salve I will wrap them in dock leaves and bind them with linen. I will also give you an infusion of herbs and poppy to drink. It will help with the pain, but may make you drowsy. When we ride on I want you to have Ole sit in front of you and take the reins. You must hold onto him."

Ealdgith continued quickly, when she saw that Osric was about to demur, "I want you with us on the next raid, Osric, so you must rest your hands until then...and that is a command, not a request."

Osric smiled shyly.

Lencten

Chapter 9

Hravn was true to his promise. With five days left before the start of Hrēðmonath they paused and looked in wonder at the beauty of Bebbanburge, side-lit in an ethereal glow by the setting sun. Having forced the pace to Chesterholm, the raiding party had rested for two days before returning to Bebbanburge with a more leisurely ride. Ealdgith had insisted that Osric's burns must have time to heal and that she needed to dress them twice daily. Edric and his small section remained in the fort, patrolling the Dunholm border, pending their lord's return.

With more than a week to plan and prepare for the Dunholm raids, Ealdgith gave her time to her friends; seeking out Bebbanburge's birthing woman, introducing her to Frida and sitting with Cyneburg when she sang with Lady Aethelreda's music group. She realised also that the risk of injury would be their constant shadow in the months ahead and that the men would look to her to tend them. Her care for Osric had earned their respect but had also placed a heavy burden upon her. Resolving to improve the quality and scope of her medicinal herbs, salves and dressings, she went in search of the Earl's physiker. Hravn sought out the Earl.

"Come in." Earl Gospatric embraced Hravn warmly and gestured for him to sit at the table in his private quarters. "Ulf, Eadwulf too. Welcome. I want to hear of your success before I introduce you to my men from Dunholm."

Hravn summarised quickly, reporting his impression of Dunholm and Gellinghes-scir as well as details of their route and raids. Gospatric was especially interested to hear news of Father Oda and the new castle at Gellinghes. "The Count's grip on the north is firmer than ever, I'm sure he will start to bolster Walcher in Dunholm. Your raids will pose a challenge that will annoy and stretch him too." He paused. "I'm sorry about the loss of your man, Alfric. He was a good man-at-arms, as I recall. I will replace him in time for the next raid. Eadwulf, choose someone you can trust and who will need little training. I've been thinking, too, about your return to Cumbraland. You will need to keep your line of supply secure whilst you deal with the Pendragons. Hravn, work with Eadwulf and choose a further six men."

"Thank you, my Lord, I was reluctant to ask, but it was on my mind to do so. I will have Orme work with them whilst we are away. As my steward, he will be responsible for resupplying us. I'm minded to use Edric and his men for that task and keep all Eadwulf's men under me," he paused, "though on reflection, Edric might need reinforcing if he is to oversee the stone road as far as Carleol."

Gospatric laughed, "I'm sure you would have asked. Believe me, you'll need them. By the way, thank Edie for taking care of your wounded. I expected nothing less from her."

"Ahem!" Hravn cleared his throat nervously, "There is something else, though I fear it will be another drain on your coffers."

As Gospatric nodded assent, encouraging him to speak, Hravn saw tiredness in the Earl's eyes and a wan complexion only partially masked by his weather-beaten skin. Ealdgith was right to be concerned. "We'll need fell ponies as well as horses if we are to fight the Pendragons on equal terms on the fells. Horses will never cope with the rough ground and the Pendragons use only ponies."

"My coffers be damned! I'll spend a lot more yet ere this business is finished. What's spent in Cumbraland and Westmoringaland can't be claimed by that bastard William when he comes north. Be assured that I'll fund what you need, we'll talk later. Now, wait whilst I summon your guides."

From the corner of his eye Hravn glimpsed Eadwulf's mouth drop and Ulf wince as the Earl ushered four men into the room. Their undyed woollen tunics and clean-shaven tonsured heads drew Hravn's attention. He grinned but held his tongue.

The Earl wasn't smiling, "Brothers Ealhmund, Bilfrith, Cedd and Sicgred. Don't let their appearance deceive you. They work for Ligulf and have authority to move at will across Dunholm. No-one knows the shire's byways better than they."

Hravn stepped forward, hand outstretched. "Welcome brothers, come, meet Ulf and Eadwulf, my masters-at-arms." He turned to the Earl's map, unscrolled on the table. "Show me the granaries and mills of Dunholm. Ulf, Eadwulf, please join us."

The candles had burned down and been replaced before Hravn finally stood upright, stepped back from the map and clapped his hands in appreciation. "Well, gentlemen, I think we have a plan. Eadwulf, take the brothers to eat whilst I brief the Earl. We'll join you shortly. Ulf, can you find Edie, she will want to be in on this."

*****

Hravn drew Ealdgith to his side and embraced her slim waist, the warmth of her skin through the thin linen of her under dress enticing his fingers to caress her gently. "They're just as we were," he said, nodding towards Ole and Ada as they raced, galloping across the firm beach below the Bebbanburge crags. Wet sand thrown from their horses' hooves glistening in the early morning sun.

Ealdgith rested her head against his shoulder. "Yes, it feels as if it was a different life, though it was but a blink ago.

"Maybe." Hravn gently kissed Ealdgith's hair, his heart still racing after their early morning love making. "I'm glad you dismissed them from our chamber. We need time together, just as they do."

"Hah!" Ealdgith smiled up at Hravn. "But not in the same way. Their only interest is to prove they can hold their own on horseback and with bow and sword. It will be a long while yet 'ere Ada has the feelings that we do. Ole too, I think."

Hravn laughed loudly. "I hope you're right, Edie. Now, I told Ulf I would speak to all the men at midday. You'll need to change into your mail first, otherwise they'll think you've gone soft if you turn up in a gown and mantle."

*****

"Eadwulf, form the men into their sections, then join Edie and Ulf. I want everyone to be able to see the model." Hravn stood in the centre of a sand model. His men-at-arms, split into their four sections, gathered around three sides of the model, whilst Eadwulf joined Ealdgith, Ulf and the four monks on a broad flat rock overlooking the fourth side. He waited, resting on the butt of his spear, studying his men intently whilst they chattered, bemused by the intricate carved lines, groups of pebbles and patches of seaweed and earth. Then, glancing at Ulf, he nodded.

The housecarl's bellow resonated across the beach, "Listen in, pay attention, and woe betide anyone who can't answer our lord's questions when he's finished."

"Thank you, Ulf. Now, you've all been warned."
He grinned at the men clustered around him. "This,
lads, is a model of the land of Dunholm, south of the
Tinan. We'll be livening things up for the Normans
there within a few days. I'll point out the key features.
Remember them, remember what you are required to
do and understand what those in the sections alongside
you are to do. We're going to make our way into
Dunholm as a troop and return, reaving and burning,
in four independent sections. We'll move hard and
fast." Hravn hesitated as a gasp of surprise rippled
through the ranks around him.

"Have no fear, by the time we ride you'll will be
more than ready for the task ahead. Once I've finished
explaining my plan, each section will practice the drills
for burning and destroying a dozen or more mills and
granaries. You'll raid by night but you won't be
travelling blind." He pointed his spear towards the
monks on the flat rock. "The brothers, here, are the
Earl's men in Dunholm. They will guide you. Trust
them, they may be men of God but they are at the heart
of our resistance against the Normans. With their help,
I have planned four routes that will avoid many of the
Norman castles. We are in their hands, just as their
safety is in ours. Guard them well." He paused, to check
for understanding, reassured by a dozen pairs of
attentive eyes gazing at him.

"Where I'm standing is the old fort at Bincastre.
Some of you know it already. This is our start point and
we will go there from our forward base in the fort at
Chesterholm, following the stone road of Dere Street.
The line of seaweed below Ulf and Eadwulf marks the
river Tinan. That is the northern edge of the shire of
Dunholm. Follow the line of seaweed around to where
the river joins the sea, there the weed marks the
coastline. Below the Tinan is another river. That is the
Uuire. See how it winds its way to Dunholm, then to
where I am standing. The lines of pebbles are the stone

roads that we will use. The clusters of stones are the manors that we will raid. Other rivers that you need to be aware of are shown by the broken reeds. You can see how these run between the areas of high ground and woods that I have marked with moss. Finally, our routes are the deep grooves in the sand. These follow tracks that the brothers know well. Take note of how they zig-zag between the manors and avoid the rivers. Where they do cross the rivers, there are fords which the brothers assure me, are crossable at low tide." He paused again and glanced around. The men's attention was focussed on the model. No one spoke.

Hravn turned to the section on his left. "Section one. Godric and Osric, I couldn't ask for two more able lieutenants to take care of Lady Edie. You too of course, Cenric. You are on our left flank, raiding north along Dere Street." Hravn indicated the route with his spear tip.

"Start at Bishop Walcher's manor at Efenwuda, then go four leagues north west to another of his manors at Wlsingham. West again to Gaitte near Stanhopa, then north up a valley and east, back onto the stone road. Follow it north for a few leagues before cutting west again along the River Defena to Muclingwic." He paused to glance at Ealdgith, then tapped the line of the stone road with his spear tip. "Take care along here. Having well and truly poked the wasps' nest further south it is possible that you will meet a swarm of them heading south to give help. They won't expect you, but you should expect them. Finally, continue further west along the Defena to Hunstanwortha. I am sure it will be dawn by then. Make your way north on tracks to cross the river at Corbricg, then hold the bridge until Ulf returns; unless he has beaten you to it."

Hravn's tone changed and he lent forward to emphasise his next point. "Be under no illusion, we are all expendable, except Lady Ealdgith. A woman can expect little mercy if taken by the Normans and, as niece to Earl Gospatric, she will be of considerable value to them. Ensure that doesn't happen."

Godric glanced at Osric, "I speak for the three of us. We have given our Lady our oaths. Where she leads, we will follow gladly."

Hravn nodded and his face relaxed. "I know, thank you." He turned to the next section, "Ari, you have section two, with Paega and Tófi. You will be with Ulf, raiding along the west of the Uuire until you meet up with Lady Edie. Take the narrow stone road north from Bincastre, then east to Beaurepayre, just north west of Dunholm itself. I'm told that Beaurepayre is the French for beautiful retreat and I'm assured its being built by monks for the benefit of Walcher's knights, with a small mill on the river to supply a granary and barn. It is likely to be one of the biggest wasps' nests we poke. Strike quickly, then be gone...and avoid shedding monks' blood."

Hravn stopped and caught the attention of the men around him. "A general point. I have chosen those manors that support Bishop Walcher and, through him, the bastard Norman king. They are our target, not men of God or the people suffering under their yoke."

Turning his focus back to Ari, Hravn continued. "Cross a tributary of the Uuire, then move north on the road to Langelye. It's a new Norman manor, just south of Langecestr by an old Roman fort. Burn granaries and mills at both, then finish with a long ride north west, cross country, to meet the stone road and then away north to Corbricg. If Lady Edie isn't there, wait for her, as she will for you.

Hravn stopped, stepped back slightly and pointed his spear towards a tall broad youth with long plaited blond hair and a short beard. He laughed to break the tension. "Tófi, you're new, replacing Alfric I think. Welcome, though I fear you will need to train hard to catch up with these others. Eadwulf told me you were big, but he didn't say just how big." He glanced up at Ulf, joking, "Tófi's as big as you Ulf. Your section will need double rations by the look of it. Feed him well and work him hard, for I think only you are big enough to handle him."

Tófi grinned, "Worry not, my Lord. I have a warrior's blood in my veins and..." He paused before adding with a low laugh, "...I am a Dane, after all."

Hravn rolled his shoulders and raised an eyebrow. "That I can tell, Tófi, for only a Dane would dare interrupt my orders, but now you have our attention tell us whose blood is in your veins."

Tófi hesitated, only momentarily chastened, "Earl Siward tumbled my ealdmoder, or so my family claims.

Hravn's laugh was echoed by several of his men. Even Eadwulf chuckled. "That's good to hear Tófi, though given what I've heard about the Earl's ways I'm sure you will have many cousins hereabouts who may make the same claim. You've set yourself a high mark to live up to, that's for sure. Prove yourself to Ulf, that's all I ask for now."

"See me after, Tófi." Ulf's voice cut through the air. He could see that the young Dane showed promise, but his cockiness could do with tempering.

Hravn continued. "Dunstan, with Ealhstan and Snorri, you are section three with Eadwulf, raiding east of the Uuire." He pointed with his spear. "Your route is long and you will need to cross the Uuire at Lamburne and then the Tinan at Neuburna. Speed will be important as you need to be across both rivers by dawn, before the tide floods. I will meet you at the Neuburna ford with Section four. When you leave Bincastre, cross the river and stay south and east of it. Your first target is Crokesteil. It is between two rivers and you will be shielded from interference from Dunholm by the river Uuire on your left. Then go four leagues north east to Shaldeford where there is a shallow ford by a mill and granary. Thereafter you have a good five or more leagues to cover in order to cross the Uuire by the ford at Lamburne. Your targets there are the mill, granary and sheep folds north of the river. Break the gates on the folds and release the sheep, they may cause enough chaos to help cover your retreat. It is then a straight route over higher ground to cross the Tinan by the ford at Neuburna. The tide should still be hanging between the ebb and the flood. Wait for me there. I will join you from the east. Is that understood?"

Hravn waited whilst Ari paused and nodded, "Yes Lord."

He continued, "Hrodulf, that means that you will be with me, along with Hrodgar and Ragnarr. We have the longest route and, unlike the others, we will move from the fort at Bincastre the morning before the raid and get into a position nearer the coast at Iodene. From there we will raid up the coast as far as Helton, on the north bank of the Uuire, before cutting across to Neuburna. Iodene is on old moated manor with a mill on the north side of the moat. From there it is two leagues north east to Horedene. The vill has a mill and is at the top of a valley leading to the sea. Then we go three more leagues north to Saeham followed by four more to Helton. The manor at Helton is on the north slope of the hill overlooking the ford. We, too, need to cross before first light in order to get across the high ground and cover the five leagues to Neuburna." Hravn turned and shouted up to Eadwulf. "Hold that crossing for me Eadwulf, I fear that we will be there well after you."

Hravn paused again, to give the men a moment to look at the model and understand the lie of the land. "Before I introduce you to your guides and have them go through the detail of which manors you will raid I want you all to remember two things. The night of the raid is a full moon. That will give us the very low water of a spring tide as well as light to see by, but it will make us more visible. Make sure you darken your mail and weapons, blacken your faces and wear your green cloaks. Also, speed and surprise are our best weapons. Our attacks are not expected and, good as they are, the Normans will not be able to react quickly enough to catch us. But as our raids develop and fires are seen across the land we must expect chance encounters with armed groups on our route, particularly when those with Eadwulf and me cross the high ground between the Uuire and the Tinan just as dawn breaks. 'Swift and Bold' will be our watchword. Remember it."

As Hravn clambered onto the rock to join Ealdgith, Ole's questioning expression caught his eyes. He laughed. "Yes, Ole, of course you're coming with me. Just as Ada is going with Edie. Now, both of you, go and join the sections that you will ride with and listen to what the monks advise.

Chapter 10

"Eadwulf, take your section to buy fodder from the vill. Ulf, set the guard and get the men and horses under cover, it looks set to be a cold night and we could all do with getting out of this wind." Hravn took charge, the troop having arrived at Bincastre just as the sun set behind the Pennines to the west. Rooks croaked and fussed in nearby trees as they settled for the night and the lookout rubbed a sleeve across his damp beard and stifled a sneeze. It felt raw in the open and little encouragement was needed to complete tasks and get under cover.

"We'll share a common hearth tonight," Ealdgith called across to Hravn, adding, "Ole and Ada, give the lads a hand with the meal, the sooner we eat the sooner we can rest."

Hravn called his section leaders to him after their meal of venison stew and bread. "At first light, before we breakfast, join me on top of the main tower. I want to show you the land hereabouts and the routes to your first targets. Hrodulf, have your men ready to move after we've eaten. I want us undercover near Iodene as soon as possible. We can rest briefly once we've scouted out the best routes into the manor. The rest of you can move out in your own time, but give yourselves time to get into position and decide upon your routes. Remember, we attack together just as the sun drops below the horizon. The moon will have risen by then, so we will have sufficient light to move by."

*****

Brother Sicgred raised his hand and slowed his horse to a halt. Hravn gave a secret sigh of relief. It had taken longer than he had planned to cover the ten leagues from Bincastre and the sun was already sinking in the sky behind them. As Hravn closed up alongside, Sicgred dismounted and signalled for Hravn to follow. He passed his reins to Ole and swung down easily from his saddle to move with Sicgred into the dense leafless copse on their left. Sköll stayed close to his master as Hrodulf motioned to his men to walk their horses carefully under cover of the trees.

Sicgred led Hravn quickly down into a narrow valley. They cut through the trees, across a wide shallow stream, and up to the edge of the wood and the cover of a broad oak tree. A man-high earth bank was barely fifty paces to their front, beyond which Hravn could see the roof-line of several thatched buildings.

"That's the manor and vill of Iodene. We're on its east side," Sicgred whispered. "The beck behind us is tapped off higher up the valley and feeds into a moat on the other side of that bank. The moat surrounds the vill which is maybe a furlong wide and the same across."

Hravn gave a low whistle. The moated vill dominated a small plateau between a low hill to the south west and a steep wooded valley along its northern edge. "You said the only entrance is on the south side and that the mill is outside the moat on the edge of yon deep valley."

Sicgred nodded. "Aye, but the granary and barn are inside the moat, opposite the mill. Come, we'll make our way there." They dropped back down into the shallow valley and ran a couple of hundred paces to their right. Sicgred stopped Hravn with a tap on the arm. "Look yonder. There's the mill, just where the stream drops down into the steeper valley. If we cut up here we can crawl to the edge of the moat. You can tell from the scrub along the top that the banks haven't been patrolled for a while, at least not since the harrying."

Hravn's heart sank. He lay on his stomach alongside a clump of briars on top of the outer earth bank. The scummy brown moat-water stank. It was a good ten paces to the far side and Hravn thought he could see sewage floating on it. "How deep is it?"

Sicgred shrugged. "The bank's as high as a man. Mayhap it's not that deep, but there will be a bed of filth in it."

Hravn sucked his lip, thinking, "That puts paid to wading through it. I feared it might. We'll have to use Cenhelm's fire-arrows. Which are the roofs for the barn and granary?"

"Directly ahead, Lord. Side by side. The granary is the one that looks like it was re-thatched a year or two ago. The barn is mossy roofed."

Hravn peered at the granary, "Forty paces, no more. That's amply close enough." Then he flinched as a loud grinding screech echoed across the valley. He looked backwards over his shoulder. "That's the millstone grinding. Hel's teeth, it's close." He cursed, then grinned sheepishly at Sicgred, "Sorry Brother."

Sicgred gave a low laugh, shaking his head. "I've heard worse curses. It's close, half a furlong away, maybe more. But we're screened by the trees and that sound may help to cover any noise we make."

"Thanks, Sicgred. I've seen enough. Can we drop down into the valley and see what tracks are there? That'll be our way in and out tonight. I want to hold the horses in the valley bottom and give them and the men a couple of hours rest. I'll use the fire arrows against the granary and hope it sets the barn alight. They won't set light to that mossy roof. Hrodulf can secure the outside of the mill to guard against the miller raising the alarm. We'll torch the mill roof as we leave, that should give those inside enough time to escape."

The men lay on the ground, backs propped against trees, their thick green cloaks keeping the damp out and body warmth in; but even so, it was cold in the gloom of the valley bottom. Ole took the horses down to the river to water them, then fed them oats from his saddlebag before letting them browse on whatever limited foliage they could find. Hrodulf chewed on a hunk of dry venison whilst Hravn checked the flights on the five fire arrows which he hoped would be enough to ignite the granary roof.

"Its time," he said at last. "Ole, stay here with Brother Sicgred and ready the horses for a quick departure. Ragnarr, you're with me. Hrodgar, go with Hrodulf. Let's go!"

The first raid was simpler than Hravn had anticipated. Once they were committed to action, events took charge of time itself.

Hravn showed Hrodulf the mill, "Don't light your torch until you see my first arrow, but don't fire the roof until we return." Continuing up the valley side, he crawled the last few feet to the top of the earth bank. The setting sun was just touching the horizon. "Light the kindling, Ragnarr. We're right on time."

His first arrow sliced through the air on a fast, flat trajectory, straight into the granary's steep thatched roof. There was no sign of smoke. "Damn!" he cursed under his breath as he dipped the tip of the second arrow, bound with wool and well coated in oil, into a small flame that Ragnarr shielded from the breeze. This followed a slightly higher, slower, trajectory than the first arrow to fall in the centre of the thatch. Ragnarr grinned as he watched a thin wisp of smoke rise. Hravn's third arrow landed in thatch on the far end of the roof. He smiled to himself, then at Ragnarr. The thatch had caught. Flames tore upward from the centre of the roof and smoke was rising from the far end. He shot his next two arrows in quick succession, aiming for the windward side of the roof. As they turned to run, shouts sounded from beyond the moat.

Hrodulf didn't see the fire arrows, but a thin column of smoke above the trees told him it was time for action. Striking flint and steel he lit the torch whilst Hrodgar stood, sword in hand, by the mill door. On hearing Hravn and Ragnarr slide back down the valley side he quickly held the torch up to the low eves of the roof and walked briskly around the mill. The scream from inside coincided with Hravn's arrival. As the four men ran down the slope the mill door burst open and a man and two women staggered out.

"Don't look back!" Hravn shouted a warning as he heard a loud crack and sudden explosion, "That's the granary, protect your night sight if you can." An eerie glow lit the forest as they mounted and galloped up the track leading out of the valley and east towards Horedene. A second explosion told them that the mill was destroyed. Their night-long race had begun.

*****

Ulf was also watching the sun sink towards the grey line of the Pennine fells, but he wasn't waiting for it to set. He was judging how long it would take them to compete their task and to then withdraw as rapidly as possible up the steep hillside as the sun disappeared behind the ridge. With luck, it would shield their presence from anyone on the opposite hill.

He had left Bincastre shortly after Hravn to lead Ari's section along the west bank of the Uuire and then it's tributary, the Browney. They had ridden in the open, green cloaks thrown back over their shoulders to expose their mail, hoping to be mistaken for a Norman patrol. Before midday they had crested a hill and looked down upon the new Norman fortified manor of Beaurepayre, which sprawled across a broad plateau on the side of the hill opposite. A mill stood by a small bridge over the river between the hills and a granary stood amidst a cluster of hayricks on the far bank. He hadn't needed Brother Ealhmund to explain the lie of the land. It was obvious that their every move would be observed and that the first naked flame would be seen at night by the guard. He needed a new plan.

Ulf moved carefully from the cover of a tree from which he had been observing the mill and granary. It seemed as if the mill was closed for the day and that the miller and his family were working in their own fields behind the mill house, a couple of furlongs away along the river bank. Within a few moments he re-joined his men, who were lying concealed in a fold in the ground, whilst their horses grazed on the hillside.

"Come on big lad," he tapped Tófi's leg with his foot. "It's time we did some acting. Follow us down, Ari, and stay under the trees by the bridge."

Ulf and Tófi rode nonchalantly down the track, left the cover of the wood and crossed the bridge at a trot. They rode abreast as they swung left and followed the perimeter of the fields by the river, ignoring the granary fifty paces to their right. Both felt that the eyes of Beaurepayre were upon them.

Ulf stopped suddenly, swung down from his saddle and ran his hands up and down the front legs of his horse. He glanced at Tófi and then led his mount slowly towards the granary and a side of the building that shielded them from the manor on the hill and the miller in the fields across the river. Tófi followed, hoping they looked like two men-at-arms seeking to tether their mounts whilst they attended to an injured fetlock.

Tófi grinned, impressed, as Ulf drew the huge Danish axe from its saddle holster and swung it with a single blow that shattered two of the boards that clad the side of the granary; but turned in haste as the crash startled a flock of pigeons. They burst from the trees and circled overhead in confusion. Any pretence at leisurely examining a lame horse gave way to an adrenaline-fuelled urgency.

"Quick, Tófi! Pull the boards back whilst I light a torch," hissed Ulf wishing that they had already done so. As Tófi heaved on the boards Ulf squeezed past. The granary was stacked with hessian sacks. Ulf slashed at the hessian, spilling grain and tearing the sackcloth into long strips. "That's it." He touched the torch to the shredded sacks and stepped back. "Come on, stay on my left and help shield this torch from view. Mayhap we'll get back to the mill before the alarm is raised."

As the two riders cantered across the field towards the bridge, Tófi glanced back. A thin column of smoke rose from the far side of the granary. He chuckled to himself. When the granary ignited, the fire should spread to the hayricks.

Ulf rode with the burning torch held at arm's length, low down to one side. It was still too light for the flame to be seen at any distance. On crossing the bridge, he halted and passed the flaming brand to Ari, who promptly lit Paega's torch. The two men ran to the mill to set light to the thatch on opposite sides of the building. Once they were sure that the roof was ablaze they flung the torches onto the roof, for good measure, and re-joined Ulf, breathless as they mounted. As the five men galloped back up the hillside track a horn sounded the alarm behind them. Ulf whooped with exhilaration. "Come on lads, Langelye is only a league away on yon side of this hill. I want to get a quick look at it before the light goes."

*****

Ealdgith rode at a brisk trot following the stone road through broken woodland. She forced a quick pace and reckoned that their third target, the small manor of Gaitte, was already a couple of leagues behind. All had gone well, mainly thanks to Brother Cedd's invaluable advice and knowledge of the land and the manors. On each attack, they had split into two groups, Ealdgith taking Osric and Ada, whilst Godric led Cenric and Cedd. They had simply lit their torches, galloped up to their targets, fired the thatch and disappeared into the dark. Her mind wandered as she rode and she mused about how the mottled links of her mail tunic shimmered in the patches of moonlight. It was as if her body was coated with a mysterious glowing liquid.

Cedd closed up alongside Ealdgith and motioned for her to slow to a halt. "Over the next hill, My Lady, we'll drop down into the valley of the Defena and take a track off to the left to Muclingwic."

Ealdgith nodded her understanding, then froze, raising her hand for silence. The sound of galloping hooves, many hooves, carried on the still air. She glanced at Godric, they had to set an ambush, they couldn't risk letting the Normans see them and then loose the advantage of surprise. "Quick, Godric, we'll ambush them as at Catrice. Get the men back under the trees. Stay mounted and use crossbows first. Godric, you're first in line, then Cenric, Osric and you too, Ada, use your bow. Brother Cedd, stay back. I'll force them to slow, then we'll take them in the flank."

The moon broke from behind a cloud, throwing patches of light through the trees and casting dark shadows. Ealdgith dismounted quickly as an idea came to her, "Cedd, take my mount. Hati, heel!"

As the section took up positions and loaded their cross bows, Ealdgith ran fifty paces back up the track to where a large tree cast a dark shadow. She drew her sword and waited, her hand on Hati's collar.

The Norman men-at-arms arrived at a rush in single file, concentrating on the track ahead. Four? Six? Ealdgith struggled to count them as they loomed ever closer, the drum-beat of their horse's hooves resounded through the wood. She felt suddenly very lonely and exposed, with no sight of her men or Ada. Estimating twenty-five paces, she fixed her eyes on that point on the track. As the first horse reached the mark she stepped suddenly sideways into a patch of bright moonlight, her sword raised.

Ada gasped. Ealdgith's movement startled her and she stopped tracking a rider with her arrow. A faceless wraith-like form danced, floating in the moonlight, liquid copper flowed over it, glistening but not dripping, it's head was a skull with black sunken eyes. Ealdgith's multi-coloured mail and tanned-leather helmet with eye and cheek guards transformed her appearance when caught in a shaft of bright moonlight.

Ealdgith held her breath as she swayed, making the moonlight shimmer on her mail, poised on the balls of her feet, ready to jump to avoid the onward rush of the horses galloping at her. Blood pounded in her ears. Time froze, then suddenly the leading horse reared, neighing with fright. As it rose in the air, hooves poised above Ealdgith, Ada loosed her arrow. She had aimed at the rider but, as he was thrown up and backwards, the barbed head struck the horse in the soft flesh of its unprotected belly. It grunted, sank to its knees, then recovered to stagger, screaming, into the night.

"Go, Hati!" Ealdgith urged her hound to attack and it leapt at the legs of the second rider as his horse skittered sideways. Hati gripped the man-at-arm's leg in his jaws and pulled him down just as the horse fell, and rolled onto the man's legs. Hati, sensing that his prey wasn't going to move, snapped at the man's face then leapt over the thrashing horse to pin the first fallen rider to the ground.

Ealdgith paused briefly, feeling strangely detached from what was happening as she watched the effect of the ambush. Two men-at-arms were already down. Crossbow bolts took down three more as they slammed through mail and bone. The only man-at-arms still mounted was the third in line. His horse had reared when halted, deterred by the carnage in front.

Without hesitation, he urged his mount forward at Ealdgith, his sword raised to slash down at her.

The blow never fell. Osric's spear cut through the air, pierced the man's mail hauberk and penetrated deep into his exposed armpit. He collapsed and slid down the side of his horse. His head bounced on the ground as he was dragged past Ealdgith. She froze, momentarily stunned by the impact of their merciless attack. Hravn's phrase, 'shock action', had become a stark reality.

"My Lady?" Osric snapped Ealdgith out of her trance. As she looked across at him in the moonlight his concerned expression turned into a reassuring grin. "That was bravely done, My Lady." He laughed as a surge of relief swept through him, "You surely are a Valkyrie sent to lead us all."

Ealdgith smiled sheepishly, relieved but still shaken; surprised but grateful for Osric's praise. "Thank you, but it is I who should praise you. I've never seen a spear thrown with such haste and accuracy."

Godric ran up to them. "Osric, give Cenric a hand to roll the horse off that man. He's alive but I don't know the state of his legs, they'll be knackered anyway. There're two more that live, My Lady. One with a bolt in his guts and another that was thrown. I'd guess that he's just stunned and bruised, but no one's going near him whilst your hound has his nose to his throat."

Ealdgith glanced across the track, "Hati! Heel! Now!" Hati slunk backwards with a low growl, head down, hackles raised. Ealdgith praised him as he returned to her, relieved that he hadn't savaged the man and gained a taste for human blood.

The soldier with trapped legs screamed in pain as his horse was dragged clear. "Cenric, put a bolt into the beast's head and put it out of its misery." Godric then gestured to the wounded men. "I'll despatch them all if you wish, My Lady."

Ealdgith was about to say 'yes' but hesitated, her promise to Brother Oswin had been in her mind during the brief, vicious, engagement: *'teach me how to fight, Brother, and I will only use that skill to save life and protect others'*.

"No, Godric, enough are dead already. We can't take prisoners with us, but we can take the risk of leaving them here 'til daylight. I'll give the one that is dying with the stomach wound something to chew to help with his pain. Ada, bring me my roll of medicines please." Ealdgith turned and looked for the monk. "Brother Cedd, do you speak French? Can you talk to these men?"

"Some, My Lady, and Latin too. I can get by well enough." Cedd joined Ealdgith and together they crouched down by the man with the injured legs. He watched warily, unsure of their intentions and confused by the presence of a woman and a monk. He flinched, more in fear than pain, as Ealdgith lifted the bottom of his mail hauberk clear of his legs.

"Tell him that I will do what I can for him. It looks as if one leg is badly bruised, but the other is broken below the knee. See how it is bent though the bone hasn't punctured the skin. I'm going to pull it straight and bind it to a splint. There's nothing else I can do. It will hurt, a lot. Make sure he understands." Ealdgith looked up at Godric, striving to sound calmer than she felt. "Bring the other prisoner here. He can help hold this one. Does one of them have a spear I can use as a splint? Break it into a three-foot length."

Godric ushered the soldier at sword point and forced him to kneel beside Ealdgith and Cedd. "Cedd, tell him that I am The Lady of The Greenwood and that my argument is with the King and the Bishop, not his soldiers. When we ride on I will leave them here to fend for themselves and find help in daylight. I want their word they will cooperate." Cedd translated and both nodded, with questioning glances at Ealdgith.

Ealdgith steeled herself for her next task. "Osric, find something for him to bite on whilst I straighten his leg. Cedd, have his friend hold his shoulders, then help me pull his leg straight. Godric hold his good leg firm. He'll have good reason to kick out." She took a deep breath to control her racing heart and the nervous knot in her stomach, felt gently for the point of the break and then pulled quickly. The soldier bit down hard upon the cloth wad in his mouth and trembled as sweat beaded on his face, but relaxed slightly when Ealdgith took a linen pad from Ada and wiped his brow.

Osric placed his hand gently on Ealdgith's shoulder. "Well done, My Lady. Leave me to splint his leg whilst you tend to the stomach wound."

Ealdgith was about to move, but glanced up at Ada as she shook her head. "He's dead, Edie."

"Thank you, Osric, I appreciate that. Bind him carefully. Cedd, perhaps you could see to the other one's passing." Ealdgith stood. "Come, Godric, let us get clear of here. We've still two manors to raid and mayhap ten more leagues to ride." She stepped back and turned to look each of her men in the eye, suddenly weary. "Thank you. That was a nasty fight. I'm proud of you all and proud to call you my 'green men'. We've still got a hard night ahead, let's finish it."

Later, as they crested the ridge above the south bank of the Tinan, Cedd rode abreast of Ealdgith. "I can't return to Dunholm, My Lady. I'm compromised now that the Normans have seen my face and know that I am a monk."

"I know, Cedd. I realised that as soon as I asked you to speak to the prisoners. I am sorry for that but I'm sure the Earl will want to keep you in his employ." Ealdgith paused, looked across at Cedd then added, "I would like you to stay with me, I'm sure my uncle will permit it. My husband is still open to the influence of the old Norse gods, as are others amongst us, but many will welcome your attention and administration, as will I. If you can keep an open mind, a guiding hand upon all our consciences will doubtless be good for us all.

"It would be an honour, My Lady. Men-at-arms always welcome a priest nearby when there's fighting to be done, whatever their bravado, and I've had my fill of living the life of a spy. As to the old gods and an open mind, I always find that Wyrd and God's Will are closer than we all think."

*****

Eadwulf slowed his horse on a crest overlooking the south side of the Tinan. As he dawdled, waiting for his small group to close up, he marvelled at the panorama that had opened up behind them. The dawn picked out the river and lifted their spirits. It had been a long night.

He started and his relaxed posture stiffened as he raised his gloved hand to shield his eyes from the bright low sun just breaking above the horizon. "Dunstan, look back the way we've just ridden and tell me what you see."

Dunstan turned his horse and stood up in his stirrups. "Riders, the sun's glinting on their mail." He held his arm out and used the width of his fingers to help judge the distance. "Mayhap a league away, maybe five or six of them...and...a second larger group, a half league behind them, but closing. He turned back to Eadwulf with a questioning shrug.

"My silver is on Hravn having poked a wasp's nest." He turned to the monk, Bilfrith, how far to the ford?"

"Nought but five minutes, the track leads down through the forest."

Eadwulf formed his plan instinctively. "We'll ambush the second group at the ford. Bilfrith, lead the

124

way as quick as you can. We've time, just," he shouted, wheeled his horse and spurred it to a gallop.

Their route down the hill opened onto a small clearing crossed by three tracks all of which led down to the ford. As the five horses slithered to a halt on the muddy approach to the water, Eadwulf turned and shouted his orders. "Bilfrith, cross the ford and wait on the far edge. Pretend to gallop off as soon as the riders see you, I want them to give chase. Dunstan and Ealhstan, get into the trees on the left, Snorri, you're with me on the right. Stay mounted. Hravn will join us then we'll take them with a crossbow volley before charging with the spear."

Although short of time and options, Eadwulf had chosen well. In their rush to give pursuit across the ford the Normans would have their backs to the men on the top of the slope behind them. The thrum of approaching hooves resounded through the trees and spurred them to action.

Eadwulf urged his horse down to the track and held up his hand in a gesture of greeting and a command to halt just as Hravn burst around the corner. "Lord, I know what's behind you. We're ready for them." He shouted at the men as their horses slid to a halt behind Hravn. "Sicgred, cross the ford, now. Bilfrith is waiting for you and has his orders. Lord, take Hrodulf and Ole and join Dunstan up there on the left, Hrodgar and Ragnar you're with me on the right. We'll take them in the back with a volley of bolts when they start to cross the ford, then ride them down from behind."

Hravn flashed a relieved grin at Eadwulf, then raised his voice so that all the men could hear. "You're a life-saver, Eadwulf. Now, all of you, listen in. We must hit them hard and fast. Mark the man nearest to you and aim for the man, not the horse. Sköll will deal with the horses. Do not hit Sköll. My arrow shot will be the signal. Drop your crossbow once you've loosed your bolt, then charge in with the spear. Get ready!"

The men were barely in position, their crossbows cocked and half-raised in the aim, when the Norman men-at-arms hurtled across the junction, their horses lathered and foaming at the mouth. Seeing Sicgred remount at the far edge of the ford the leading Norman spurred his horse into the river, intending to risk a mounted crossing. It was the last thing he did. Shot at close range, Hravn's arrow punched through his mail hauberk, pierced the padded jerkin beneath, and penetrated his spine. He jerked upright then slid slowly out of the saddle into the river: paralysed, conscious, drowning.

As the leading Normans turned to face the threat, those behind them collapsed and fell from their saddles as short, heavy, cross-bow bolts ripped into them with terrifying lethality. They strove to turn their mounts as they were forced onto the mud at the water's edge by the press of rider-less horses, panicked by Sköll snapping at their legs.

Hunters became prey. The four remaining men-at-arms realising their plight and, with a collective effort born of training and experience, they succeeded in forming a line. They drew swords and moved forward. But their heroic effort was swept aside by a phalanx of spears borne by Hravn's armoured riders who tore into man and horse alike. Two died instantly, one fell, dragged into the water by his dying horse and the fourth staggered towards the deeper water before Eadwulf's sword blow half-severed his head. The call of Hravn's horn echoed across the valley. His men paused and looked towards him.

"Well done, all of you. Now, that is what I call an ambush. Only moments ago, we were pursued and in fear of our own lives, yet now we are the victors. We have suffered barely a scratch whilst our foes lie dead around us. That's due to your skill, your nerve, your discipline and," he paused, pointing his sword towards Eadwulf, "the training that Eadwulf and Ulf have given you. Today you've proven yourselves. I'm proud to lead you and glad that you serve me."

Hravn smiled as he watched his master-at-arms blush, then the normally gruff man laughed.

"Aye Lord, they're not bad for a scabby bunch. Don't praise them too highly though. Right, lads, let's strip these bodies of their mail and weapons. I'm sure our Lord could do with some more for his armoury. Hrodulf, round up what horses you can and, Dunstan, take your men and throw the stripped bodies into the centre of the river. The longer it is until they are discovered the better it will be for all of us."

"Yes, Master." Dunstan shouted back as he bent over a body by the water's edge, "but one of us has more than a scratch. Snorri has had his arm sliced. Our Lady must see to him soon."

*****

"Ole, hold that torch a little closer, I want to see Snorri's wound more clearly." Ealdgith bent down to cut the blood-hardened remnants of Snorri's shirt way from the deep wound in his upper arm. Her eyes were gritty with tiredness and the dull ache of fatigue hammered her forehead. She concentrated, as she sought to block out the raucous sound of matey storey swapping. Hravn, Ulf, Eadwulf and their section leaders were still on the high that follows every battle. She half wanted to join in, but could hear that Godric and Cenric were giving her more praise than she would have claimed for herself. Snorri was her priority now.

She sensed Edric behind her. "Edric, bring me the strongest mead we have. The more I can dull Snorri's senses the better, and the stronger it is the better. It will help cleanse this cut."

"The salt water is ready, Edie." Ada said, testing the temperature of the boiled water with the tip of her little finger. "It's cool enough now."

Ealdgith pushed her hair behind her ears and turned to Snorri. "You were lucky, that sword tip sliced your arm without driving much material or dirt into the cut. I've cleared away everything I can. Now, I'm going to bathe it with mead. Hravn's ealdmoder was sure that alcohol helps stop infection. Then I'm going to wash it with salty water to promote healing. It will sting, mind you. But it's a good pain, not a bad one." She looked into Snorri's eyes. He nodded, understanding.

"Once I'm happy with the wound, I will stitch the edges together." Ealdgith paused, a slight smile on her lips. "My mother always cursed my needlework, I could never pay attention, but I'm sure you wouldn't fancy lacework decorating your arm."

"Snorri forced a weak smile. "No, My Lady, anything that holds it together will do for me."

"Finally, I will add a salve of honey and egg white to help soothe and heal, then I'll bind it with linen. First, though, you're going to drink this." Ealdgith took a horn from Ada. "It's strong mead. It won't stop the pain, but it will dull the sharpness. Mayhap you'll be less likely to lash out."

Snorri shook his head. "Never fear, My Lady. I've more control than to do that." He drank the mead in one quick long swallow then lay back on the table top and gripped the edge with his hand. "I'm ready."

Ealdgith took a linen strip from Ada and began to clean the cut with the remains of the mead. Snorri bit his lip, but held his nerve.

"No," Ealdgith joked, anticipating Snorri's unspoken question. "It isn't my undershift. I can see that Osric has been talking. Lady Aethelreda's seamstress had raw linen to spare. More than enough for any dressings I'll need." She passed the swab to Ada, who threw it into the fire.

Ealdgith caught Ulf's eye and gestured for him to come to her. "Can you hold Snorri's shoulders whilst I stitch the flesh together. It will help me, and him, if his arm doesn't twitch. Ealdgith took a thin steel needle and length of catgut from her leather medicinal roll, threaded the catgut through the needle's eye and pulled it straight. She glanced at those helping her. Raising her voice, she spoke a little more curtly than she had intended. "Ready?"

The room fell silent as all eyes turned to watch. Ealdgith bit down hard on her lower lip, blocked distractions from her mind and started to stitch the soft, warm, fleshy edges together. The tension in her fingers relaxed as Ulf's hand gently touched her shoulder.

Chapter 11

Hravn paused before he placed his foot in the stirrup and turned to Edric. "I'm sorry to leave you here again, Edric, but I need you to keep the fort secure. Within a month, I should have more men to send so that you can also patrol the stone road down towards Carleol. I'll want a secure line of supply when we move into Westmoringaland."

Edric chuckled through the mass of red beard that hid half of his face. "The truth be known, I'm happier holding the fort than raiding Norman lands. Last summer was different, we had to fight for our survival, but what we do now is best left to Eadwulf and his men. I know a couple of my lads feel likewise, though others would rather be with you."

Thank you Edric, I'm glad, though we'll all face challenges enough when we hunt down the Pendragons. What's the news from the ford?"

"All quiet, Lord. The lads have watched it for the last two days, since you returned, but no one's been near."

Hravn nodded, satisfied. "Good, call them back and concentrate on the lands around here until I reinforce you. Now, Edie needs to attend to Frida's confinement and I have some monks to return to their monastery...all but the one that Edie seems determined to retain as a household priest." Hravn raised his eyes heavenward.

Edric laughed out loud. "Hah! Lord. Mayhap it's for the best. Many of us have more respect for the One God than you do, and care little for the old gods. Sometimes it helps to have someone to confess your fears to without worry of judgement. Our Lady has a wise head, for certain."

Hravn clasped Edric's hand firmly. "Thanks." He turned and swung into the saddle.

*****

The snow came late that year. The wind swung to the east and its bitter blast caught them three leagues away from Bebbanburge. As yellow snow-laden clouds loomed ahead they urged their horses forward, gasping as the cold air bit at their throats, numbing all exposed flesh. The wall of driven snow hit them just as they reached the fortress's wooden ramparts.

"Thank the gods you're here! The guard sent a runner for me as soon as he recognised you approaching." Orme caught up with Hravn just as he dismounted inside the upper ward, his face was ashen. "Where's Edie?" Orme looked around, searching.

Hravn caught hold of Orme's shoulder. "What? Is it the Earl?"

Orme stared back blankly, momentarily uncomprehending. "N...No," he stuttered, "it's Frida. She's started with child."

Hravn relaxed and called to Ole who was still mounted. "Fetch Edie, she was at the back, keeping an eye on Snorri in case the ride caused his stitches to split." Turning back to Orme he placed his arm around his friend's shoulder, "Come, take me to Frida. Edie will catch up with us. Surely Lady Aethelreda's birthing woman is with her?" As Orme nodded, he continued, "Then there's nothing you can do. We are all in Wyrd's hands now and Frida has the best of care."

Edie ran to their small hall in the upper ward. Ada followed, leaving Ole to take their weapons to the armoury. Ulf clasped the lad warmly on the shoulder. "Don't fret for your sister, it's as natural as popping peas." He lied deliberately. His stomach's tense knot of worry during Cyneburg's labour a year ago was still a

131

painful memory. "Come, we've work to do oiling these blades."

Ada helped Ealdgith unbuckle the leather straps on her mail tunic then, as Ealdgith pulled on a simple cotton shift and wool cloak, she quickly pulled off her leather jerkin and breaches, cursing as she fumbled. Ealdgith touched Ada on the arm and teased her softly, "There's no rush, others are with Frida already. If we arrive breathless and flushed we will only unsettle Frida. No matter what you feel inside, you must appear calm and in control. Now, take a deep breath and let me help you."

Ada took another deep breath as she entered the birthing chamber. Cyneburg glanced across to her, smiled and stood up, "Here, take Adelind from me and keep her calm. I'll help Frida just as Edie helped me last year." Ada relaxed, the warmth of the baby in her arms distracted her from the sight of Frida, kneeling naked on a bed of ferns that covered the floor. Cyneburg knelt in front of Frida, took her hands in hers, looked into Frida's eyes and encouraged her to take slow deep breaths in time with the birthing woman's instructions.

Ealdgith realised that the moment of the birth was very close. She glanced about the room to check that Sunngifu, the birthing woman or midwife, had everything ready: boiled water, a small sharp seax and burning oil lamp with which to sterilise the blade before cutting the umbilical cord, clean lint, feverfew and fennel to ease pain and cramp, flax oil for cleansing. She smiled to herself, reassured, content that Sunngifu had all the essentials to hand as well as complying with the folklore customs that guaranteed a safe birth. All midwives kept their secrets close; secrets that, as a herbalist, Ealdgith had been permitted to share. Folklore served to reassure mothers to be and the men and women around them: the untying of knots, unbraiding hair and opening of all locks in the house to ensure that the birth canal was clear and unblocked, small charms, chanting verses to Freyja and the old gods or prayers to Our Lady and Saint Dorothy. They all helped reassure those that didn't know the secrets of childbirth.

Sunngifu started to massage Frida's back and encouraged her to breathe deeply. "Now! Push!... and relax." Beads of sweat bubbled on Frida's forehead, her eyes stared at an unknown world, fixed within herself. She groaned, then strained, pushing with a strength that seemed about to tear her insides, then suddenly it eased and she felt a rush as her baby moved within her, from her. She felt hands about her then, as Sunngifu eased her slowly onto her side, Ealdgith said softly, "Frida, you have a boy. A beautiful, perfect boy."

Frida lost track of time as Ealdgith and Cyneburg eased her gently onto a straw-stuffed pallet and, wrapping a gown around her, placed her son upon her breast. She lay back and looked up at her friends. "This is Agnaar." They nodded, understanding. There could be no other name for him than that of Frida's father, slain by the Normans for defending his family.

Cyneburg settled herself next to Frida and, as the young woman lay back exhausted, she sang softly to her friend:

Sleep, wee bairn, on her breast,
Warm and soft it will be;
Around thee thy moder's arms are folding,
In her heart a moder's love;
There, no harm will come to thee,
Naught will ere break thy rest;
Sleep, wee bairn, warm thee will be,
Safe on moder's gentle breast.

*****

Hravn walked across the cobbled yard towards a large barn-like building. His boots slid on the icy surface though, thankfully, the snow had been swept aside into great piles. He grasped Orme by the hand and then pulled him close in an embrace. "Well done, Fader. You certainly beat me to that."

Orme grinned and blushed. "Planning was never my greatest strength."

"Hah!" Hravn chuckled, "I would say it is your self-control that isn't. You fell for Frida the day you first saw her, remember?"

"Aye, and now we have Agnaar, and wouldn't be without him. It's only two days, but it feels," he hesitated, "as if he's been ours forever."

Hravn laughed loudly, "Well, Orme, it's time we got down to work before you lose your mind completely to the bairn's spell. Come on, introduce me to the men you've been training." He steered his friend into the hall that doubled as a barracks and training area.

Orme lacked Hravn's height and natural authority, but his open-faced good humour always endeared the stocky young man to the soldiers that he led. Most recognised him as one of their own, but with the wit and confidence to lead rather than be led. The men were gathered around a fire blazing in the hearth at the side of the hall. "Bondi, Saxi, Gyrth, Carl, Cerdic and Wulf. They're quite a bunch and volunteered altogether to join us. I daresay they might have some history, but Ulf and Eadwulf will soon sort that out, I'm sure."

They turned as Hravn strode towards them, a couple casting uncertain glances at Sköll. He held out his hand and greeted each man in turn before taking a step back and looking each in the eye, well aware of the impression that his weather-stained and battle-marked mail hauberk would have upon them.

"Welcome, I'm sure that our Lord, the Earl, will be as sorry to see you leave his service as I am glad to have you join mine. Orme will have explained something of what I expect, but I want you now to work with my masters-at-arms. They set and expect a high standard and I want you ready to march with me by the end of the month. If you fail, I fail...so don't let me down. Is that understood?"

As they nodded assent and understanding, Hravn gave a wry smile and added, "You may have seen my wife, Lady Ealdgith. Her word is mine. She will lead you and fight alongside you. Does that pose anyone a problem? Speak now if it does."

Wulf glanced at the men alongside him. "No, Lord. We have seen Lady Ealdgith. It was her reputation, as well as yours, that brought us to you and it was me who suggested it. We welcome adventure and the chance to ride with your men."

Hravn's face broke into a wide grin. He felt an instinctive liking for the tall wiry man with a lopsided smile. "Hah! Thank you, Wulf. Adventure is something I can certainly guarantee. I hope that you are all just as enthusiastic after a week of Ulf's training." He turned as he noticed their eyes glance beyond him "Now, speak of the devil."

*****

Earl Gospatric stood with Hravn and Ealdgith on the rock alongside which Hravn had, many weeks before, made a sand model and briefed his men about the Dunholm raids. Hravn looked down upon his men with pride. They looked tired. He was too. It had been a long, hard, five days. He was pleased, too, at the close interest the Earl took in the men and his warm praise for the testing training they had been put through. He listened to the Earl's closing words.

"You've done well, all of you, not just the winning section. Serve Sir Hravn and Lady Ealdgith well, just as you have served me. Mayhap one day I will see you in Westmoringaland. I hope I do, it would be an honour. Now, as to the winner, Ari, take your men to my armoury. Each is to choose a sword for their themselves. Choose well and think nothing of the cost. Chose a sword that will serve you, and in so doing you will continue to serve me. Thank you."

As Ulf dismissed the men the Earl turned to Hravn. "Tell me more about this latest training? From what I gather it was novel and challenging."

Hravn laughed. "It was certainly challenging to run it. As you saw I've split the men into four sections of four, taking Godric and Osric into my headquarters. They're good, very good, and future masters-at arms I'm sure. They've both sworn to serve Edie and would fight to their death to protect her. We put each section through a series of tests on successive days: sword skills such as man against man, in pairs, forming a shield wall; use of the cross bow at different ranges against moving and static targets, and on horseback too, though reloading is still a challenge; use of sword and spear whilst mounted; concealment, movement and scouting; then finally how to survive in the field, including applying the medical skills that Edie has taught them: staunching bleeding, keeping wounds clean, using herbs to control pain and bleeding, and the like."

The Earl's eyes widened in surprise. "How in the name of God did you keep track of all that?"

Hravn nudged Ealdgith. "It was Edie really. She's the only one of us who can make sense of words and numbers on paper. She thought it would be a good test for Orme too. He's been sticking to his studies and will do well as my steward. Edie thought it would test his record keeping and stock taking."

The Earl stifled a laugh and turned to check that Orme wasn't in earshot. "I hope his adding up was correct, else Ari's men might be handing their swords back."

Ealdgith was quick to defend Orme. "Fear not, Uncle. I checked his sums as he went along. As Hravn says, he's doing well. I always knew that he was undervalued as my father's groom."

Gospatric glanced up at the sky. "The weather's turned at last. That snow was winter's last roll of the dice. Let's enjoy this sun and walk along the beach; the wind is still too cold for standing still. The couple fell in alongside him."

"Now that you're ready to go I want to confirm exactly which lands I'm granting you. I'll have this written on parchment with my seal in case Elftred objects, and my steward will prepare a map too." He stopped and turned to Hravn.

"You'll have charge of my southern border in Westmoringaland. It's long and much of it, as you know, is just rough fell-land, good for sheep but not much else. Though there is timber to harvest too. It's land that nobody really wants, which is why it's been neglected and why the Pendragons have been able to thrive there. By joining it to the land I am granting Edie, at Ulueswater, you should be able to exploit the lead there and pay for the keep of the men you'll need to employ to hold the border."

Hravn nodded as Gospatric continued. "You'll be able to reclaim your old family lands of Mallerstang and Ravenstandale. They are fertile and mayhap there's lead to be found in Mallerstang. You'll be responsible for the Haugr-Gils too, the headwaters of the river Lauen and the southern watershed of the Eden. That way you'll control the passes to the Norman lands in Loncastre and the south. North of Ravenstandale you'll have the small manors along the foot of the escarpment, that's Crosebi Raveneswart, Sulebi and as far east as the Eden and Nateby, but not Kircabi Stephan. That remains with Håkon."

Gospatric turned to Ealdgith. "Edie, I want you to hold Ulueswater. The mines at the head of the lake are the key to your future. If, God forbid, anything happens to Hravn, I want you to be secure and for no one to have cause to challenge your authority to hold them. By giving you the lands of Hep, Askum and Ulueswater, and the watershed of the Eamont as far west as Stantone, you will hold all the lands adjoining Hravn's. The two of you will then control the border of the upper Eden vale from west of the Eden by Kircabi Stephan, embracing the lands of your good friend Gunnar of Morlund, to those Cumbric passes west of Penrith. Håkon will hold the border to the east as far as the stone road over Stanmoir."

There was little new in what Gospatric gave them. It was as he had promised when he had knighted Hravn, but it reassured them both to hear it confirmed. Hravn was about to thank Gospatric, when Ealdgith grasped Gospatric's hand and raised it to her mouth to kiss.

"Thank you, Uncle. I think, too, that by holding land in my own right men will grant me respect that would otherwise not be given. But, what of Elftred's dealings with Ivo de Taillebois and access to his own lands in Amounderness?"

Hravn laughed, interrupting before the Earl could respond. "Hah! I think I should make it quite clear to them both that they can have free movement on their personal business along the stone road south of Hep but that all other passes will be closed on my authority, and yours, my Lord." He deferred to Gospatric.

"And that is what I shall say in my letter to Elftred," the Earl smiled broadly, "just as I will also say that Edie has the right to export lead, and silver if you find it, through whichever Cumbric ports she chooses." He paused and looked at them with a sudden sternness. "I trust Elftred. He is kin and is sworn to me, but his son's marriage to Christiana de Taillebois does complicate things and he is playing a two-handed game to control his Loncastre lands. Keep him close, but always keep your counsel."

Relaxing again, Gospatric turned, clasped them each on the shoulder as he walked between them. "Let's head back. Now, Hravn, there's a fell above Kircabi Stephan called Standards Rigg. Have you heard of it?" As Hravn shook his head, Gospatric continued. "Good, it's where several boundaries come together, yours included. Great men have placed their cairns there for many generations. You must too. One thing I know for sure is that you will be leaving more than one mark on those lands."

Chapter 12

Hravn leant forward and braced his arms against the top of the small wooden balcony outside their chamber. He looked down onto the sea below and inhaled deeply, the ozone borne on the warm late-spring breeze invigorated him. He would miss the sea and not just for the beauty of its wild ceaseless motion. The ocean-road was a lifeline to places far away. Places and people. He waved at Osgar who was tightening the lines that secured the snekkja, where it bobbed gently in the small harbour below the fortress. He thought of the message that Osgar had brought the evening before. He stretched and ran down the stairs to the hall.

The men around the long table stood as Hravn entered, sitting again as he pulled back a chair alongside Ealdgith. He had summoned his headquarters, section leaders and those of prominence in his household.

"I've called you here so that I can go through the detail of my plan for our move to Westmoringaland, but first I must tell you of the message that the Earl received last night." He glanced at the faces around him. Ealdgith knew, as did Ulf, but no-one else. He read the tension in their eyes. He knew they anticipated bad news.

"The Earl, as you know, has his spies in the King's court. He has had warning that the King will move against the Scots in early Weodmonath, maybe even as soon as late Æfteraliða. He wants to hit the Scots whilst they are still at haerfest, and he's going to strike quickly, moving by sea with a smaller force coming overland. Mayhap our raids in Dunhelm forced his hand, but we can be sure that his ships will be on this beach in a little over two months from now."

He watched faces drop, eyes widen. They had all known that the Norman army would come, one day. The immediacy of a date made the threat tangible. Hravn was saddened, but pleased. It would spur them all onward in his quest to scourge his lands of the Pendragons. "The bastards!" Eadwulf's outburst spoke for them all.

Hravn maintained the sombre mood. "You're right, Eadwulf, but we'll all be long gone by then. The Earl has yet to decide what to do with his family, but he will send them either to Flanders or Carleol. Orme, you were to stay back here and keep us supplied. Instead, this means that you will now have to be clear of here well before then, women and children too. I want you to work with Hrodulf's section now and start to build up the base at Chesterholm. Get word to Edric and have him assist. It will be a long slow business moving everything by ox cart, but you will have the carts' drivers to assist you. Aelf and Esma, I want you to move there now too. Have a household ready for Cyneburg and Frida when they bring the children. The Earl is as yet undecided what to do with Cenhelm and Gamel, but I anticipated he may move the better part of his armoury to Carleol, leaving only that with which he will equip the men he retains here. Are there any questions so far?"

Hravn watched their heads shake and then continued. "Ulf, Eadwulf, I want the rest of us ready to ride four days from now, on the first day of Thrimilce. We will take all the ponies and remounts to use as pack horses. Edric has enough fodder for them at Chesterholm, so concentrate on taking our own food and weapons. We will go via Carleol. I want to ensure that Lord Elftred fully understands his role in all this. Then we will go to Gunnar at Morlund. He is already expecting us for mid Thrimilce."

The masters-at-arms nodded seriously. Hravn grinned to lighten the mood. "Now, as to the Pendragons, we'll finalise our plans when we sit down with Gunnar and find out how many of his men we need to train. Suffice to say, I don't intend marching all over the Haugr-Gils to find them. Their greed will be their downfall and I will draw them out and into a series of ambushes on our terms, to whittle their numbers down."

"We'd best clean out Cenhelm's stock of cross bow bolts, then." Hravn chuckled as he heard Eadwulf's gruff aside to Ulf.

"Right, you two, let's do a stock check. Mayhap I'll speak to Cenhelm before you plunder his armoury."

*****

"Hel's teeth! This place still stinks!" Hravn grimaced and tried to hold his breath as he led the way over the bridge into Carleol. He glanced back over his shoulder, impressed by the identically dressed warriors, Ole, Ada and himself included. Each wore a mottled green cloak over their mail, a black and red shield over their shoulders, armed with lance and sword and leading a laden remount. It was a sight of power and intent. The bustling crowds fell away as the twenty warriors, forty horses and two wolfhounds pushed their way along the narrow street from the town gate to the fort.

Hravn was aware that their arrival had been anticipated, it being impossible to move a large body of armed men without attracting attention. The fortress gates opened at their approach and, as they entered the courtyard, he recognised Maldred's squat frame at the top of the steps, waiting for them. He lent across to his housecarl. "Ulf, tell the section leaders to go to the stables with all the mounts. I want you, and all the

142

headquarters with me. The eight of us will see Elftred whether he wills it or not."

Hravn swung down from his saddle and strode across to the steps, just as Maldred walked down. "Maldred," he held his hand out in an effusive warm welcome. "We're passing through on our way to Morlund, but I must first speak to Lord Elftred. I hope he is at hand?"

Maldred smiled, slowly. "I am impressed, I see your plans are coming to fruition." He nodded appreciatively. "I will have my men assist yours with tending to your mounts though I am surprised that the Earl can spare so many?" He gave Hravn a sceptical look

Ignoring the jibe, Hravn continued with a cold urgency. "Those and more Maldred, which is why I must see our Lord. Is he here?"

The Constable nodded, "I'll take you and Lady Ealdgith now."

"Nay, Maldred. My huscarles and servants will attend too." He turned and shouted across the noise in the courtyard. "Godric, Osric! Bring the chest for Lord Elftred."

Elftred stood by the hearth in the main hall as Maldred ushered the party in. "My son, Ketel." Elftred introduced his son dismissively with a wave of his hand. Ealdgith was surprised that despite the warmth of the day Elftred wore the same wolf skin cloak as he had on their last visit. She sensed he wore it to signify status rather than for comfort. If Elftred was phased by the sudden presence of Hravn's housecarls he didn't show it. Hravn retained the initiative. He wanted to impress his will upon Elftred and then move on quickly.

"My Lord, thank you for your hospitality, though we will not tarry. I want to reach Morlund by last light. The Earl sends his regards and bids me update you on his affairs."

143

Elftred stepped back, momentarily surprised, then ushered Hravn to a seat by the long table. "Come, Lady Ealdgith too. Settle your men at the end. Maldred, bring ale if you will and mead for Lady Ealdgith and her maid," he cast a glance of surprise and distaste towards Ada's boiled-leather jerkin and soft leather breaches.

"Matters have moved on since we met in Aefter Yule. The King is coming north by sea and he will move against the Scots by early haerfest. The Earl is sure that his earldom will be forfeit and is taking steps to move his family. I think Lady Aethelreda is likely to go to Flanders though some of the children, Dolfin in particular, are likely to be placed in your charge. My steward, Orme, will bring those who are. The Earl's next move rather depends upon the King, but he is taking steps to protect his wealth and I have orders to leave this chest with you pending his further instruction." Hravn gestured to Godric who stepped forward with Osric to present an iron-bound oak coffer.

Elftred let out a long breath. "The King's intentions are much as I surmised. De Taillebois' letters to his daughter have implied as much. It fits with what you told me of Walthoef and I have heard that raids in Dunhelm and Richemund have encouraged the King to move by sea." He gave Hravn a knowing look.

"Hravn smiled thinly. "Mayhap, but now to our plans." He glanced at Ealdgith. "We intend destroying the Pendragons by the time the King comes north and will then secure our position in order to face whatever comes after that."

As Ealdgith pulled a sealed scroll from the inner pocket of her cloak Hravn said, "This charter confirms the grant of lands to us individually and directs how we are to manage them. It also makes provision for right of passage to your lands in Loncastre, and for Ivo de Taillebois to come north to visit his daughter.

Elftred sat forward in his chair, looked from one to the other and then eased himself back slowly, calming an obvious impulse to speak out. "He's a shrewd man, your uncle. It will be as he wishes. I shall read the charter in due course."

Ealdgith lent forward and spoke for the first time. "I am sure you will find that it is fair, My Lord, and is in line with what we told you some months ago. Now mayhap you could suggest where we might build a hall from which to control our lands."

Elftred spluttered into the tankard of ale that he had just raised to his lips. "Hah! Edie! Now that is a question, and a good one." He paused, replaced his tankard on the table and wiped his mouth with the back of his hand whilst he took a deep contemplative breath. "The lands are too spread out for you to control them from the Pendragons' hall at Mallerstang once you have taken it. I suggest two. Build another at Askum which is on the stone road that runs west over the fell tops south of Ulueswater. Both of these are on main routes and you can react quickly and move freely. Mayhap keep a small household at each, and then split your time between them.

Hravn glanced at Ealdgith, read understanding in her eyes and said, "That's sound advice Elftred." He paused, before adding to gauge Elftred's reaction, "I'm minded to build a watch tower at Tibeia too, to keep an eye on the pass and the stone road to the south." A twitch of Elftred's eye showed that the implication wasn't lost on the Cumbric lord. "Anyway, thank you My Lord, and for your ale. But we must depart now. I'll keep you informed of my progress and, if you hear from the Earl before we do, then you can send a despatch through Gunnar of Morlund."

*****

Ulf leant across to Hravn as he swung up into the saddle. "Well done. The wily fox didn't get a chance to get a word in. I could see he's not happy about us controlling the passes south."

"That's why I made the point. He was deliberately steering us away from building a hall at Ofertun or Crosebi Raveneswart, either of which would control the principle stone road over the border. We couldn't hang around though. We've two more coffers of the Earl's gold with us and I wasn't going to risk Elftred or Maldred catching sight of them. We've enough to pay our way for a year or two yet, but I don't want him knowing that."

Ulf slapped Hravn on the back, "Who's the wily one now? Come, let's set a good pace, we've fifteen or more leagues to cover yet before we get to Morlund, and Gunnar's hospitality."

*****

Hravn pushed his stool back from the long table and stood up, feeling light headed from tiredness and too much ale. He glanced across to the far end of Gunnar's hall and smiled. Behind a half-closed curtain, he could see Ealdgith already asleep, with one arm around Aebbe. The girl was, once again, Ealdgith's constant shadow. "I need some fresh air, Gunnar, I've spent so long living outdoors that I've forgotten what the smoke and fumes of a great hall can be like. Let's have a word outside." He nodded towards the hearth, his attention caught by a sudden cackle of laughter. Ulf and Eadwulf were swapping war stories watched by a heavy-eyed Tyr. "I can't see them staying awake much longer. Stopping the supply of ale was a shrewd move."

Gunnar laughed and pushed Hravn in front of him. "Aye, but you're old before your time, lad. A hall's built for warriors to drink ale in and bond over a yarn. That's how the sagas were formed."

Hravn breathed deeply as the cool, fresh air cleared his head. "From what you say, the Pendragons have started raiding again with upwards of thirty men now, mainly outlaws and refugees from across the hills or the lands to the south." He sucked air through his teeth. "That's a lot more than I expected, they out number us two to one."

Gunnar nodded, "That's about the sum of it. On top of the dozen men I've promised you, I've half a dozen men I can call on at short notice from the farms hereby and mayhap another half dozen further afield. We haven't been troubled yet but others have. Borr and his family were slain at Crosebi Raveneswart in Aefter Yule and their hall ransacked, though not burned."

Hravn looked sharply at Gunnar. "Crosebi Raveneswart! That is to be part of my land. It's at the foot of the escarpment is it not? Is the hall still empty?"

Gunnar sensed from the intensity of Hravn's questions that he had a plan forming. He nodded, "Aye, it is."

"With your dozen, we can almost face them man for man, though that's the last thing I want to do. We need to whittle them down, piecemeal. I mean to draw them out to a place of my choosing where we have the advantage of numbers and own the ground we stand on. Then we kill or take all whom Uther sends. I can't see him stirring far from Mallerstang himself, he's too canny and too frail. He'll send Nudd or Math."

"Yes!" Gunnar hit the longhouse with the side of his fist. "Yes, we could draw him out the once, and mayhap take half his force. But we'll only get the one chance. Once he knows there is a move against him he'll keep to the fastness of his hills and draw us in instead."

"I know, and I know just how we can do it." Hravn rubbed his jaw as he thought. "Let me sleep on it and speak to Edie. I'll have a firmer plan in the morning. One thing you can do is muster your men. We've three weeks left in Thrimilce. I want to be ready by Ærraliða. That will give us a month to destroy the Pendragons before the hay harvest is due. You'll need your men back for that."

Gunnar stared at Hravn, amazed at how quickly he came to a decision. He nodded, grinning. "Aye, that sounds fine to me. I'll summon them in the morning."

Hravn yawned suddenly. "And I must hit the boards before I fall over. But tell me, is Brother Patrick still at the church in the vill?"

*****

The hall was slow in rousing that morning but it gave Hravn a chance to talk his ideas over with Ealdgith. It was past noon when he sent Ole to summon Gunnar, Ulf and Eadwulf. Ulf strode in chewing a length of willow twig and settled next to Ealdgith on a bench by the hearth. She dug him in his ribs and smiled sweetly, "Ulf, that may help clean your teeth, but it does nothing for your breath. Have you left Gunnar any ale for tonight?" Ulf chuckled, blushing.

Hravn smoothed an area of ashes and began to scratch out a map of the upper valley with the tip of his spear. "You know this land as well as Edie and I, Gunnar, but Ulf and Eadwulf need to understand it. Chip in if I miss anything out." He etched a line down the left side of the ashes. "Assume we're looking south, as if we were looking at the ground from here. This is the river Eden, it rises at the edge of the Pennines, in the steep wooded valley of Mallerstang. The Pendragons stronghold is here." He pointed to the centre of the valley, near the edge of the forest. "It is a large longhouse, even larger than yours, Gunnar." Hravn laughed, teasing the Norseman, "and it is surround by a stake-wall with a gatehouse. There's a small vill outside where most of the families live, including my great aunt."

Eadwulf glanced up in surprise. "Remember, Eadwulf, these were my family's lands until Uther Pendragon took them." The cold forcefulness of Hravn's tone surprised Eadwulf. "My great aunt, Rhiannon, was a girl then and the only one of those who weren't sold into slavery whose life was sparred. I have a blood feud, and Uther Pendragon's death is the cost of settlement." Eadwulf nodded, grimly. "Aye, Lord. I've known many a blood feud. It'll only end if you wipe that family out."

Hravn continued, etching the outline of the Haugr-Gils and a river to their north. "This is the Lune. It rises behind my family's manor of Ravenstandale, flows through a high, secluded valley south of Ofertun then sweeps south at Tibeia down a steep dale straight into Ivo de Taillebois' lands. You can see why I want a watch tower there. There's an old stone fort we could mayhap use."

The three men watched, fascinated, as Hravn proceeded to shape the hearth ash into a map of the land to their south. He finished by placing a pebble. "This represents Crosebi Raveneswart. Gunnar tells me that the hall has been empty since the Pendragons raided it a few months ago. As you can see it is at the foot of the escarpment and in land that we can control."

He stood back from the hearth, a smile playing on his lips. "With Gunnar's dozen men, we can almost match the Pendragons man for man. Many are outlaws from our own lands. One or two may have been warriors in the past, but most will lack our skill and training. That said, we can be sure that they will fight hard, driven by desperation, and I won't risk facing them on equal terms. I want to draw them out and take them down step by step."

Ulf slapped his thigh, laughing. "And that is where the empty hall comes in, is it not?"

"You know me too well, Ulf. Yes, it is. I want to play to the Pendragons' greed. They don't know that we

149

are here, or what we intend. Surprise is on our side. If we dangle a big enough prize we can draw them out onto our land and hopefully destroy half their force. We only have one chance though. Uther is wily, it's how he has survived so long. My guess is that he will send one of his two grandsons. Edie and I killed the last of his sons."

Ada and Ole, listening in the background, glanced at each other, wide-eyed. Both realised that none of them could expect much mercy if things went wrong.

Hravn tapped the base of his spear on the stone-fagged floor to emphasise his next point. "I want to take this war, for a family war is what it is, stage by stage. The first stage will be to gain the advantage in numbers. I think we can have two bites at that particular fruit. We will start to rebuild the hall at Crosebi Raveneswart now and spread the word that it is being prepared for a Lady of high birth who is a refugee from Norman-held lands. That will grip Uther's attention. He may suspect that it is Edie, but he won't know. We'll put concealed patrols around the manor and once we are sure that he has taken the bait and is showing interest in the hall, we will let slip the day and route of her arrival, spreading the rumour that it is Earl Gospatric's niece and that she has been endowed with a fortune. I would place money on Uther ambushing Edie within a couple of leagues of the hall and that is when we will take them. If Uther doesn't strike then he will most certainly attack the hall. Either way we will have him.

Gunnar's loud exclamation set everyone laughing. "By Thor! Hravn, you have it. I always thought your blood was more Norse than Cumbric."

Hravn grinned, then looked sternly at them. "This will be different to our fights with the Normans, when we were forced to take no prisoners. Edie and I are agreed that our fight now is with the Pendragons, not those whom they control. Some may, like we both were, have been forced to work for them. We will take prisoners where we can. The lives of any Pendragons will be forfeit, but others will be spared if they swear to serve us. I'm happy to give any man a second chance." He watched their faces, relieved to see that Eadwulf nodded agreement. "Now, Gunnar, spread the rumour to the other manors and Edie and I will speak to Brother Patrick. Oh, and find two covered carts with which we can move Edie and her household. Ulf, I want you to accompany us to Crosebi Raveneswart tomorrow, where we will start to prepare the hall and place standing patrols the day after. Eadwulf, start to train Gunnar's men to work with ours. We'll form them into three sections of four. Gunnar can appoint the section leaders. We have three weeks until Edie's grand arrival on the first day of Ærraliða."

They started and Gunnar jumped up as Tyr flung the longhouse door open and burst in. "Fader! There is a rider come for Hravn. He is outside."

Hravn glanced at Gunnar then strode briskly to the door. "Cola! What is it?" Cola was still seated in his saddle, ashen faced with exhaustion.

Ealdgith ran to him and helped him down. "Ada! Fetch some ale, and Ole, see to the horse. It's fair lathered and close to collapse itself." She eased Cola to sit on the bench by the longhouse entrance. The men watched, concerned yet amused at the speed of Ealdgith's reaction.

Cola forced a tired smile of thanks, embarrassed by Ealdgith's solicitousness, then raised himself to his feet. "Lord, Edric has had word from Orme. The Earl has bid him take Dolfin and his other children, and all the women and children of our household, to join Elftred in Carleol. He is to be there by Ærraliða. The Earl will provide the escort. They are to remain with Elftred until the lands here are secured. Edric wants to know your orders."

Hravn glanced at the others, then looked away, rubbing his chin, thinking. He made his decision quickly. "Cola, rest here the day, then return to Edric. Tell him to close the fort and then everyone, Hrodulf and his men, with Aelf and Esma, are to come here. Bring all the ponies and carry what you can of the remaining grain, leaving only sufficient to sustain Orme's group as they pass through. If he still has ox carts, then he is to use them. It will be slow but he has time, though I would like him here within two weeks. I would rather that he brings as much food and fodder as he can. We are burden enough on Lord Gunnar's hospitality." He turned to Gunnar, "At least we will now have men to help with your harvest once we've finished with the Pendragons."

As Cola relaxed, Hravn turned to his masters-at-arms. "That will give us another ten men, and Aelf and Esma to assist Gunnar's household and refurbish the hall." He grinned, "I think we will be able to give the Pendragons quite a reception."

Ealdgith interrupted, "I think you're forgetting Elftred. If Orme is to remain there for a while, with Frida and Cyneburg, then he needs to understand the situation with Elftred and De Taillebois. Gunnar, do you have any parchment and ink?"

The Norse lord almost choked on his laugh. "What! Edie? What would I want those for? I've been schooled in the sword, not the pen."

Hravn was quick to understand Ealdgith's concern. "Brother Patrick will. I agree Edie. Can you write to the Earl and ask him to take Orme into his confidence? If you think Orme's reading is up to it, write a second letter to him and warn him to keep his counsel and listen to Elftred's household chat. If he can, he should try and get Elftred's trust by letting slip a few snippets of our plans and then find out more about his interests in the Norman lands. We also need to warn him that Elftred's daughter-in-law is Norman. We don't want Frida and Cyneburg taking against her. Tell him we need to keep our enemies closer to us than we do our friends."

Sumor

Chapter 13

"That looks to be a pretty fair ambush." Gunnar lay alongside Hravn under a flowering hawthorne just below the crest of a ridge, and slapped sharply at a mosquito that had the temerity to land on his bare forearm. A warm midday breeze blew into their faces from the east, as they watched a dozen of the Pendragons' men wait in ambush on the track below them.

Hravn nodded as he sucked the end of a long rye grass. "Both Nudd and Math have a skill that we shouldn't underestimate. That's Math down there by the look of him, he's a bit taller and slimmer than Nudd, but both have the Pendragons' black hair. He's chosen well. Edie will be around that corner and almost onto the cart before she sees it." Gunnar sensed a begrudging admiration in Hravn's tone. "And with four men on the cart and eight on ponies hidden in that fold of ground this side of the track, they'll have Edie's two carts surrounded."

"Aye, don't forget they're likely to have a similar number hidden yon side of the track. We saw the glint of their spear tips. It could be a stiff fight." Gunnar's caution was obvious.

"Hmm, more targets for Edie then." Hravn chuckled dismissively. "Look, we've your dozen men, mounted, in the wood behind us. Eadwulf has three sections in the wood on yon hill, and Edie has Edric's men and Ari's section hidden in her carts. That's two score to their one score. It's just what we want. They ambush Edie and then we ambush them, and don't forget that we have the advantage of horses against

154

their ponies. Ponies may be better suited to the fells, but horses will outrun them on this open grassland. It gives our men the advantage of height in the saddle too. Remember, I want Math dead. He's the only Pendragon down there. If we get any prisoners we'll take them to the hall and hold them in the byre until we assess them."

Sköll growled suddenly and both men turned with a start as a man crawled up behind them. "Wulf, what is it? You did well to get close without us hearing." Hravn was increasingly impressed by the new recruit's ability.

"Lady Edie is on her way. Mayhap five minutes off. It's slow going for those carts on that track.'

"Thanks, regain your mount then join Gunnar's men in the wood. Tell them to be ready. We'll be there shortly."

It had been a long morning. In the past couple of days Hravn had identified three possible ambush sites within a couple of leagues of the hall and had tasked a section to monitor each of them. His men had reported having seen Math start to position his men at first light and Hravn had then positioned his men on the higher ground either side of the ambush area, making the assumption that Math would not expect to be disturbed and would therefore be unlikely to post guards looking outwards. He had been right. Edie was taking longer than he had expected, but it was working in their favour. He could see that the Pendragon men were becoming restless. The heavy ox carts were slow and would doubtless be finding it heavy going on the hard, rutted track. He hoped that the carts' high wattle side panels would conceal the men within and give the impression that they were piled high with possessions. Hravn nudged Gunnar and started to wriggle backwards. "They're close. See the dust trail."

*****

Ealdgith cursed the track, the ox cart, the dust, and above all she cursed the constant jolting and her failure to have brought a cushion. "Don't you feel it, Ulf?" she asked, as she bounced against his side.

Ulf chuckled. "Hah! Of course, I do, Edie. It's a soldier's lot to be uncomfortable is it not? So, I just get on with it. It's the poor sods in the back that I feel sorry for. At least we can see the ruts and rocks coming; they can't."

Ealdgith smiled thinly. "I suppose you're right, though all I can see are two fat oxen and their flatulent backsides."

Ulf turned to Ealdgith and roared with laughter. "That's your best grumble yet, Edie. Wait 'til I tell Gunnar." He nudged her teasingly as he saw the faint hint of a smile.

Hati, trotting alongside the cart, gave a sudden sharp yap and turned his head towards the ridge on Ealdgith's left. She knew he sensed Sköll was nearby.

Ealdgith lent to her other side and shouted across to Godric as he rode slowly alongside the lead ox cart. "Stay close as we go around that next bend, Godric. This is one of the possible ambush sites and I want you and Osric close. I want us to be sucked in. I can't risk your sharp eyes compromising their ambush. I want to draw them in to me when they do pounce. Can you drop back and warn Edric to be ready and check that Ada is coping."

"Aye, My Lady." Godric nodded and eased to a halt whilst the second ox cart closed up.

Ealdgith turned and glanced behind the hessian cover that screened the back of the cart. "This could be it Ari, get your crossbows ready. Wait until my command and then drop the screens. Take your targets from right to left. Edric's men will work from left to right." She flashed a smile of encouragement, ducked her head back out and pulled the hood of her cloak forward over her face. Like Ulf, she wore a cloak over her armour. She couldn't risk any mail showing.

"Hah! We have them!" Ulf shouted loud enough for those in the back of the cart to hear, then turned to Ealdgith, "I'll stop just short of where they've blocked the track. That'll give Edric space to close in behind."

Ealdgith nodded. Her stomach felt suddenly knotted. The sight of Math brought back the very real fear she had experienced during her last fight with the Pendragons. She could tell that he recognised her. The cold stare of his pale blue eyes seemed to pierce her to her heart and she edged closer to Ulf.

Ulf lowered his hand and reassuringly touched Ealdgith's knee. "Don't worry, Edie. I'll have the little skita."

As Ulf slowed the cart to a halt he lowered his hooded head and sat poised to move, his eyes fixed upon Math's face.

Math urged his pony forward a few paces and stopped as Godric lowered his spear towards his chest.

Commanding Hati to stay at heel alongside the cart, Ealdgith raised her hand and spoke with a calmness that surprised her. "Let him come closer, Godric. Math, I am surprised to see you. These aren't your lands."

Math rode closer and stopped with the flank of his pony close to the cart. "Oh, Eadmund, but they are. Surely you remember that all who pass through must pay tribute." He gave a short, cold, laugh. "But you aren't Eadmund are you? You never were. Who are you and what happened to your cousin? Hravn wasn't it?"

Ealdgith held Math's gaze. Her confidence surged back now that she was committed to fight. She had him just where she wanted him. "How right you are, though I am the same Edie as I was then. I am Lady Ealdgith, niece to Earl Gospatric and in whose name, I now hold these lands. Mayhap you have heard that I have taken the manor of Crosebi Raveneswart? I am

157

here to claim it. As to Hravn, you can see that he is not here. His way was to fight Normans, mine was to return to my uncle."

Math glanced at Godric, then returned his attention to Ealdgith. "Tell your man to move back and raise his spear. He is too close for my liking, and it is you I want to talk to."

Godric obeyed as Ealdgith nodded. She could see that Math was sweating, but it wasn't caused by the heat of the day. She could sense his nervousness. As Godric moved back Math raised his hand. Ealdgith glanced quickly about as armed, mounted men crested the low ridges that lay either side of the track and slowly rode down to within ten paces of the carts.

Ulf didn't move, but flicked his eyes to the left and right to assess the situation, then cast his eyes down to the footboard and kicking plate in front of him, to where his Danish axe lay with its blade hidden under a dirty rag. He looked back up at Math, fixing him with a dark scowl.

"What is it that you want, Math? My uncle gave me land, not money, and as you see, I have only a small household.

Math's lips tightened in a thin, cruel, smile. "That is no matter. My grandfather wants you. You owe him a debt for the death of his son and grandson." His thin smile widened. "It is a debt you will pay in person, and I will take you to him now."

The underlying meaning of Math's threat was not lost on Ealdgith. "My four men are warriors, unlike your cattle hands. Don't spill more blood and invite my uncle's wrath. Now, move that cart and be sure to pass on my regards to your grandfather and brother. Oh, and to Beli if he still lives after my hound savaged his leg."

Ealdgith's taunt had the effect she desired. Math turned in the saddle and shouted to his men in

Cumbric. "Seize the two women, kill the men, then let's be gone."

Although Ealdgith only partly understood, she knew that the moment was hers. "Now!" She shouted.

As the ox carts' wattle side panels dropped outwards Ulf grasped the Danish axe with both hands. "Duck, Edie!" He bellowed. Standing up with one foot braced on the seat he swung the axe in a wide arc that just missed the pony's head and sliced into the side of Math's shoulder. The broad heavy blade cleaved through rib cage, lungs and heart, thrusting Math's body sideways out of the saddle as the pony bolted, and dragged the body with its half-severed upper torso in a bloody gallop down the track.

Math's body was still toppling from the saddle when a storm of crossbow bolts flew from the back of the two carts. The sudden thrum of their passage through the air and the thwack as they hit their targets resounded between the ridges either side of the track. Within seconds different sounds rent the still air - the screams of dying and wounded men, and harsh whinnies as ponies panicked.

"I knew this bad boy would come in handy one day." Ulf joked, half to himself, as he placed the axe down; it helped him ease the stress of sudden violence. Ealdgith gasped, took a deep breath and sat up slowly as Ulf touched her shoulder.

Every bolt had found a target and halved the size of the now leaderless force. Nine bodies lay on the ground, four were obviously dead, others writhed in pain whilst the ninth slowly pulled himself up to lie against the base of a tree. Riderless ponies circled in confusion and those outlaws who were as yet unscathed turned their mounts intending to gallop along the track after the fast disappearing, now headless, body of their leader. But they stopped, frozen, as Hravn's men crested the two ridges, to pen them as they had the people in the two carts.

"Stop! Drop your weapons and you might yet live." Hravn's clear command in Cumbric and then in English cut through the air.

As swords and spears began to drop one rider urged his pony towards the trees beyond the road block. He fell, pierced in the back by Godric's spear.

Ealdgith leant across to Ulf and kissed him on the cheek. "You're the best huscarle and friend I could ever want. Thank you." She smiled quickly, then jumped down and ran back to check on Ada. Her maid was already running towards her.

"Edie, are you alright? That was so bloody, not like those times in the dark." Ealdgith, relieved that Ada seemed unfazed, gave her a brief hug, turned and ran to Hravn, Hati at her heels.

"Math's dead. That leaves two to go, three if Beli still lives." Ealdgith shouted gleefully up at Hravn as he swung down from his saddle. She felt buoyed with a surge of adrenalin and relieved that their first battle was already over.

Hravn pulled her to him in a swift, close embrace. "Thank the gods you are safe, Edie. You did well, you all did." He kissed her and stepped back. "We have dead to bury and prisoners to herd back to the hall."

Ealdgith slowed him with her hand on his arm. "No, have the prisoners bury their dead away from the track. It will focus their minds and give you more time to think. I'll find Brother Cedd. He was riding with Eadwulf and I'll have him say a few words over the bodies."

Hravn nodded agreement. "I doubt we'll find what's left of Math's body. Let the animals scavenge it wherever it lies."

As he spoke, Eadwulf strode up to them. "That was more a slaughter than an ambush. You planned it well, Lord. There's one man of theirs that needs your attention, My Lady, his arm's been sliced by a bolt. I think he will need a tourniquet and the edges sewing back together." He gave a grim smile, "I've seen to those that had no hope of surviving."

Ealdgith's reply surprised, but impressed, the master-at-arms. "Thank you Eadwulf. It's a foul task, but the kindest way."

*****

Ealdgith had been right to involve Brother Cedd. Having cleaned and bound the wounded man's arm, she watched as Cedd and Godric supervised the ten other prisoners. Lacking shovels, some used their weapons to cut away the turf and topsoil whilst others collected boulders and broke apart a small limestone outcrop. They laid the bodies together and piled the boulders over them in a crude cairn. The men stood around the cairn whilst Cedd gave a simple blessing in English.

One turned to him as he finished. "Thank you, Brother. You showed them more respect dead than any of us have been given for many months past."

Ealdgith stepped forward. "Why so?" She asked. "I know the Pendragons. There are mayhap three or four of them and a dozen or so men from their lands that ride with them. From what I hear, there are many more of you who fled from Norman lands. If you weren't happy to work for them why didn't you ride away when you had the chance?"

The prisoner stared at Ealdgith, blinking, puzzled. His eyes flitted between Ealdgith in her shimmering mail tunic, Hati and the slim, raven-haired girl behind her wearing a leather helmet, stiff leather jerkin and leather breeks. Her cold stare and her hand resting on the hilt of the slender blade at her waist disconcerted him. He cleared his throat. "If you know the Pendragons, My Lady, you know they are cruel."

Ealdgith gave him a slight smile of encouragement. "That I do. Go on."

"Most of us who ride for them are forced to do so. We fled from the Normans to escape their cruelty, but found a worse tyranny here. Many of us brought our wives and children with us. We thought that we had found sanctuary when we reached that valley of Mallerstang. Instead, we had our families torn from us and held apart. They work in the Pendragons' kitchen or in the fields. It was made very clear to us that if we refuse to reave, or if we run, they will be killed or sold into slavery in Dyflin." The prisoner watched Ealdgith as he spoke. She was nodding slowly and he could read compassion and understanding in her eyes.

"Thank you." Ealdgith waited until she knew the man had finished speaking. "Wait here with Brother Cedd. I want my husband to talk to you." She turned to Godric. "Take the others down to the track and hold them there. I will find Hravn, there is much to our advantage here. Ada, stay here with Hati."

Ealdgith turned around and found that Hravn was already striding across to her. She signalled for him to stop until she joined him. "Before you do anything with the prisoners you need to know that many are held captive as we were. Uther holds their women and children hostage whilst they reave for him. I wondered why they didn't run when it is obvious that they outnumber the Pendragons."

Hravn sucked air through his teeth. "You're right, Edie. I should have realised that the Pendragons must have a hold over them." He paused, "though mayhap not all of them. There may be those who take pleasure in reaving."

Ealdgith nodded. "I know, that is why I wanted to speak to you out of earshot. I think the man I have just spoken to is genuine. He approached Brother Cedd first, but I think we both have his trust."

"Take me to him. If he'll work for us I'll take his guidance as to who we can trust before I speak to the other prisoners individually."

The prisoner was unremarkable to look at: of medium height with brown hair and eyes and, Hravn guessed, in his late twenties. It was the strength of his personality that impressed. He spoke with the heavy accent of the long-vanished kingdom of Elmet. "I'm Swithin, Lord. I was once a blacksmith in Ledes, before I fled from the harrying. I would serve you if I may."

Hravn paused and held Swithin's gaze for several moments. "My wife has told me of your work for the Pendragons and how they hold your families hostage. If you serve me it will be to destroy the Pendragons. We will see what happens thereafter." He paused, then decided to take Swithin into his confidence. I am Sir Hravn of Ravenstandale. I serve Earl Gospatric, my wife's uncle, and I am here to reclaim my family's lands. The Pendragons' stole them many years ago and killed all but my ealdmoder and her sister. Lady Ealdgith and I were held by them two summers ago. We fled, leaving two of them dead. That is why we understand your plight. Now, who amongst the other prisoners can we trust?"

Swithin hesitated, wide eyed with surprise, then he focused his attention on the question. "All, Lord. Uther sent those of us who have families to seize the lady who was take over the hall in Crosebi Raveneswart, knowing that we would return. His own men, and those who are committed to his business, remain at his longhouse. Some of his men are as cruel as he is and many of the single men will do whatever it takes to have food, bed and ale." Swithin stopped and drew breath, "Lord, there are women who have been widowed today, and all our families will be at risk if we do not return."

Hravn nodded and glanced around. "Ada, run and find Ulf, Eadwulf and Gunnar. I need them here, now." Turning to Ealdgith he added, "Edie, I think we have to strike tonight. Swithin could be our way into Uther's stronghold."

"I agree. Tell me Swithin, how many men does Uther now have left and just where would you expect them to be at sunset this evening?"

"Twelve of his own, My Lady, and eight who will fight for him. There are always four guarding the families, usually two sleep whilst two keep watch. They are held in a barn between the vill and the longhouse. There will be another four manning the gate to the fence around the longhouse."

"We know it," Hravn interrupted, "do they have one in the tower, one on the gate and two in the hut?"

"Aye Lord. The remaining twelve will be asleep around the hearth by then, or sinking some of Uther's ale."

"What about the Pendragons? Uther used to live in the longhouse with a younger woman to take care of him. Nudd lived in a hall in the vill with his wife and son, Belli."

"No longer Lord. All are in the longhouse. They have rooms curtained off at the back. Uther is old and frail but has an iron grip on everyone. It was Nudd and Math that controlled us directly. Belli is a cripple with a crutch and withered leg." Swithin turned and spat. "Sorry, My Lady, but he's a mean little bastard. Carries a whip and strikes anyone who gainsays him."

Ealdgith gave Swithin a thin smile, "Don't be sorry. My hound, Hati, left him with that leg. It will be a daily reminder to him of what he tried to do to me."

The speed of Hravn's next question surprised Swithin. "I want you to lead a section of your men. Choose four and tell me who can lead the other four."

Ulf arrived, panting. "The others are just coming. What is it?"

Hravn laughed. "A change of plan, Ulf." He waved his hand towards the grass. "Stretch out, we're going to be busy tonight."

As Hravn introduced Swithin and described the situation with the prisoners he was surprised and relieved to see that all were nodding in approval, Eadwulf in particular.

"We'll have them, Lord. They don't even know that we're here, let alone that we've taken half their men. I agree, we do need to rescue the families before their lives are forfeit.'

Hravn chuckled. "I'm pleased Eadwulf, well volunteered. That is the very task I have in mind for you. Take Dunstan's section and half the prisoners; Swithin has recommended that Oderic would be suitable to lead them. He is to guide you to the barn where they are held. I need it secure just before we attack the longhouse. Kill the guards silently then force entry and kill, or take, the other two. Brother Cedd and Oderic are to reassure the families. Keep the place secure until I send word that we have the longhouse.

"Gunnar, I want you to post cut-offs around the outside of the longhouse to prevent any escape. You need to be in position, quietly, just before we approach the gate, so keep an eye on the gate's watch tower and look for our approach."

He turned to Ealdgith. "I want you to take Godric, Osric and Ada and keep Rhiannon safe. Just stay with her in her house until I send word. Ask her to think about who I should appoint to run the manor once the Pendragon's are dead. Only she can tell us." He paused before adding, "You know the land around the vill and the longhouse, Edie. Lead Eadwulf and Gunnar's groups in before you go to my aunt. There is a track on the east side of the valley, at the foot of the cliffs. Take that and then cut through the woods down to the vill and longhouse."

I know it, the track we were on when Owain caught us and took us hostage. How could I forget."

"Ulf, you are with me, and bring that Danish axe with you. We'll move in two groups. Swithin and his men will go first, pretending to return from today's raid. Swithin, you simply need to bluff your way in, get the gate open and then keep it open until Ulf and I bring our other three sections and Edric's group. Our numbers will be about right in case anyone is watching and counting.

Hravn then checked with each individually to confirm their understanding before he ended his orders. "We need to move quickly if we're going to get the sections on the ox carts back in time and I want all the prisoners to swear an oath to Edie and me. They will then be released into my service before we ride to the hall. Esma should have food ready there by now and I want everyone to be fed and rested. We will move into Mallerstang an hour before dusk."

Chapter 14

The sun was dipping behind the western fells as Ealdgith led her group into the dark shadow of the jaws of Mallerstang. She felt a sense of foreboding when entering the gloomy valley with its high crag-topped sides. She raised her hand to halt the column and slid down from her saddle. Those behind her did likewise and followed as she led her horse down a small path that wound its way between the ancient oaks in the old forest.

Nearing the edge of the wood she passed her reins to Ada and signalled to Eadwulf, Gunnar and Oderic to do likewise and follow her. They halted within the shadow of the forest edge. The fields along the banks of the Eden were visible, cast in dusky shades of grey in the failing light.

Ealdgith spoke softly, just audible in case her voice carried on the still evening air. "Gunnar, the longhouse is two furlongs to the right. You can just see the turf roof above that high stake-wall. It surrounds the longhouse and its outbuildings. The only entrance is the gate on the south side. Look closely and you can pick out the top of the watch tower."

"I see it. It's closer than I expected." He glanced at Eadwulf, reluctant to suggest a change of plan to the experienced master-at-arms. "I think we should leave all the horses here, under two of my men. It's an easy point for us to return to once the light goes."

"Ealdgith and Eadwulf nodded assent, then Ealdgith continued. "Oderic, is that barn directly across from us the one that holds the families?"

He nodded. "Aye, Lady. The doors are on yon side, facing the river." The barn was barely half a furlong away.

"Where do the guards keep watch?" Eadwulf's gruff voice was louder than he intended. He felt chastened by Ealdgith's sharp glance.

"Just inside the door. One goes out periodically to walk round outside, though not often enough for you to plan on taking him out."

Ealdgith held up her hand for quiet. "Work it out once we go our own ways, though I suggest that they won't barricade themselves in. Just kick in the door and get a sword to their throats. They're there to keep women in, not men out."

The three men looked at her surprised and embarrassed. They knew she was right.

"Now, look to the left. That row of little cottages on this side of the vill is where Hravn's great aunt lives. Hers is the one on the left." She paused, glancing at them with a smile. "The light's going, we need to move now. Good luck."

*****

The six-league ride to Mallerstang tired the horses. It also gave Hravn time to think and he realised what it was that was nagging at the back of his mind: the Pendragons men had ridden ponies, they were riding horses. He cursed, though there was nothing to be done now. At least it would be almost dark when they attacked the longhouse. He raised his hand to slow, then halt, the long column and waved for Swithin to join him.

As Swithin rode up to Hravn, it was obvious that his pony was exhausted. Like the others, it had struggled to keep pace with the horses. Hravn bent forward in his saddle. "It's two summers since I was here, but if I'm right, we have half a league to go."

"Aye Lord." Swithin nodded and pointed. "Look yonder, where the track bends, it's less than two furlongs from there to the gate. The guard will have a clear view as we approach."

Hravn glanced at the setting sun and gestured for Ulf to close in. "I think we can give the men and horses a quick rest. We'll ride when the sun touches the ridge. The light will fail quickly after that." He dismounted and lay back against a tree, irritated by midges and watched the sun slowly dip whilst he mulled over their options. He stirred at last and nudged Ulf, "Come on, let's get it done."

Swithin led the other four former prisoners at a gallop, around the corner in the track and closed rapidly upon the double oak gates in the high stake-wall. They halted in a cloud of dust as Swithin shouted at the guard in the tower. "Quick, open up. Math's just behind and he's in a foul mood. The English bitch has plagued him all day. We need to get her inside."

The guard lent over the edge of the tower and laughed. "Math, plagued by a woman! She must be a feisty one...the feistier the better for what he will have in mind." He turned and shouted below. "Get the gates open."

A draw bar grated on the other side, then the gates swung open, creaking slightly. The five men urged their ponies forward and then halted inside the entrance. Swithin had decided not to use violence in case it caused the alarm to be raised. He only needed a moment. "It's been a long day and we lost men," he spat at the feet of the guard. "That bitch has a lot to answer for." He continued talking whilst the sound of galloping hooves resonated around the small courtyard in between the guard hut and the longhouse.

"There are horses out there!" The lookout yelled at the gate guard, "What ...?"

"Our prisoners." Swithin yelled at the lookout, urging his pony sideways to push the guard against the gate. The guard slipped, struggling to keep his balance and stared up wide-eyed in sudden panic. He gasped as

Swithin rammed a thin seax directly into his throat, choking his scream.

The lookout failed to notice, distracted by the rapidly closing horsemen. He yelled, "Those aren't prisoners, there are too many," and grabbed the rope hanging from the alarm bell. His last living act was to ring the large bronze bell six times before a spear ripped through the small of his back as more than a score of horses thundered through the gates.

Swithin leapt from his pony and, followed by two of his men, kicked in the guard hut door just as it was opening. The force knocked the guard inside backwards into his companion. Both fell to Swithin's sword.

As Hravn swung down from his saddle he caught sight of the iron-studded door of the longhouse. It opened, then quickly slammed shut. He knew that by the time he reached it, it would already be doubled barred from inside. Within the small courtyard, a chaotic sea of men and horses clustered noisily. Hravn knew that he had to regain control quickly and leapt up the short flight of steps to the longhouse door, where he blew his horn to still the noise and attract attention.

"Swithin, have your men hold the horses calm just outside the gate. Edric, try and break that door down, or at least keep their attention on it. Everyone else, around the back with me. There's a kitchen entrance. Ari first, followed by Hrodulf, then Cenric. Ulf, we'll need your axe." Hravn sprinted to the back of the large longhouse, past a couple of wooden outbuildings. The longhouse was set on a low stone plinth and its steep turf-clad roof sloped down almost to the ground. It was the largest building of its kind that Hravn had seen. He knew that inside there was a large central hall with high rafters, whilst the edge of the longhouse was a maze of small dark cubicles and curtained off chambers. It would be a challenge to fight through. Sköll ran ahead. The hound remembered the hall, and remembered too the kitchen entrance. He leapt at the door, scratching and barking.

Ulf skidded to a halt outside the door. The studs in his boots slid on the stone flags as he shouted at Sköll to back off, then swung the Danish axe in a wide, overhead arc. The door splinted and flew open, as the shattered lock fell to the ground.

The entrance opened onto a narrow passage, open at the top to the dark smoke-blackened rafters, but screened on either side by thick wool or hessian curtains portioning off the many storage and sleeping quarters. In front, he could see past the end of the corridor to the main room of the hall, the central hearth and, at the far end, men piling furniture against the main door. Ulf sprinted down the passageway, his Danish axe held in front of him. Hravn followed, with Ari behind. Ole strove to keep up with Hravn, guarding his back, but the speed of their attack disorientated him. He stumbled, shouldered sideways in the rush down the narrow passage and fell through a heavy curtain. He gasped as he bumped into a dishevelled boy hiding on the other side. The boy pulled away, wide-eyed in fright. "Na! Na!" He gasped.

Ole regained his balance and realised that the boy was more frightened than him. He yanked back the curtain, ripping it from its fastenings, and waved his sword towards the passageway.

Hravn crossed the threshold into the main hall, then flinched as something flashed past his eyes. He turned as Carl fell sideways, gasping, a crossbow bolt embedded in the side of his neck. Hravn threw himself forward, rolled onto his feet and crouched ready to react. An old man was stooping by the side of the hall, desperately trying to reload a crossbow. As the man looked up Hravn saw a look of pure hatred in his eyes. "Uther!" Hravn hissed through his teeth.

Before Hravn could move Sköll leapt forward and knocked Uther backwards as his fangs ripped into

171

Uther's upper arm. "Guard!" Hravn commanded Sköll to keep Uther pinned down, then he turned to join Ulf at the maelstrom by the main door.

Ulf swung the axe in a figure of eight pattern in front of him, it's blade glistening red with reflected light from the hearth. No one dared approach the flashing arc. As Ari led Paega and Tófi to his left, Ulf cleared the pile of furniture from the door with one devastating swing of the axe. Shattered wood hit the defenders whilst his second blow cleaved through the wooden cross bars that secured the door shut. Edric shouldered the door open and led his men in.

Hravn had cut around behind Ulf and Ari to where Cenric's men were fighting the last four men standing, three were shielding a fourth behind them. Two others lay dead, or dying, whilst the remaining seven were already face down whilst their hands were tied behind their backs. He caught the eye of the fourth man, "Nudd!"

Hravn read the loathing and fury in Nudd's eyes as they turned to face each other. As Nudd stepped forward, Hravn edged slowly backwards, gaining space, but also drawing Nudd away from those who had been defending him.

"So, Nudd, it is just you and me. Your men are dead and dying, or deserting you. I have your grandfather too. Beli is a cripple and of no account." Hravn goaded Nudd.

Nudd's anger needed no goading. Hravn parried a sudden sword thrust as Nudd spoke. "You little skita! I should have listed to Uther and killed you both. Urien didn't trust your clever words either, but he found you both useful."

"Hah! You should have listened to us, Nudd. Edie is my wife and she is Earl Gospatric's niece, as she claimed. He has granted her lands across the upper Eden. Oh, and I am Sir Hravn of Ravenstandale. My family's lands have been restored to me."

Hravn watched the meaning sink in. "Family?" Nudd looked confused.

"The family that Uther and his father slew when they took Ravenstandale. Well before you and I were born, Nudd. But the sins of the father fall upon the children. Your family has pillaged and plundered across my family's land for four generations Nudd, but no longer. You can choose a warrior's death in front of your men, here and now, on the tip of my blade, or we will overpower you and hang you from the gate tower."

Nudd's eyes flicked from Hravn and briefly scanned the room. His men had stopped fighting, all were watching him. He refocussed on Hravn. "Take me, if you can, but spare my wife and son."

"I'll spare your wife, if she is of a mind to cooperate, but not Belli. He has his own sins to atone for." Hravn held Nudd's eyes, feinted to his left and, as Nudd stepped to his right, Hravn lunged directly at Nudd's unprotected midriff. Nadr sliced though Nudd's woollen tunic and into his stomach. As he fell forward he seized Hravn's blade and pulled it deeper into, and across, his body. He had no desire to live.

Hravn withdrew his sword, dealt a swift cut through Nudd's chest, and then wiped the blade on the twitching corpse. He looked up at the circle of men. "Ulf, send word to Edie and have her bring Rhiannon here, they will both want to see Uther dealt with. I'll need Edie to look at our wounded too. Send Swithin and his men to Eadwulf, they can relieve him and Dunstan and then take care of their families. Ari, give me a head count please. I fear Carl took the bolt meant for me." Hravn cleared his throat. "He hasn't served me long, but he was a good soldier. I'll want Brother Cedd to say a few words over him." Then his eyes narrowed as they focussed on Uther, who was still cowering under Sköll's watchful stare. "Edric, bind that worthless excuse for a so-called Lord and drag him to the gate, and rig a noose. I want everyone to witness his hanging." He paused for breath, the reaction to his fight with Nudd beginning to tell on him. "And Hrodulf, clear the rooms at the back. We've at least two women and a cripple to find."

Feeling suddenly alone, Hravn left the hall and walked to the gate. Swithin had left two men guarding the horses. He was just about to shout for Gunnar when he saw the Norseman stride out of the shadows. "Gunnar, it's over. Bring your men in and have them relieve these two so that they can find their families."

"Aye, it is over for certain," Gunnar called back. "I have three female prisoners for you and a body."

Hravn clasped Gunner in a hug. "Thank you. Bring them to the gate and drag the body there, but first tell me how you caught them."

"Moments after we heard you go into the longhouse we saw three women and a man on a crutch slip through a concealed gate in the stake-wall. I expect you'll find a hidden door in Uther's chamber. As we closed in the man started swinging his crutch like a club. It was all we could do to take him down in a hail of spears. The women have said nothing, nor have they struggled."

Hearing the gallop of hooves, Hravn turned as Ealdgith and Osric rode up, leading two horses. "Ulf told me. He's with Godric and Ada, walking slowly with Rhiannon. She's too frail to ride."

Hravn laughed, "I should have realised," then pulled Ealdgith close to him. "It's almost over Edie. I, we, have retribution at last. I intend to hang Uther when Rhiannon arrives, then it really will be over." He felt warm tears as she hugged his neck, then heard her sniff, trying to stem their flow.

"I'm glad it's dark. Give me a couple of moments then I'll go and see to our wounded."

A little later Ealdgith stood holding Hravn's left hand as he held Rhiannon close with his right arm around her shoulders. None of them felt any compassion. Ulf hauled Uther Pendragon up the steps of the watch tower and held him whilst Eadwulf tightened a noose around his neck. There was no ceremony and no words said, as the frozen-faced old man was pushed from the tower to fall and swing, broken-necked.

Hravn stood for a while, then spoke quietly, "He deserved worse. Think only of all those whom he had killed, robbed or sold into slavery. He and his clan were evil." He pulled the two women close, then turned. "Come, we need to rest, then tomorrow we will build our new future."

*****

"I want him to hang by the gate for a full two days so that all the villagers can see him and know that the Pendragons' days have gone for ever." Hravn sat at the long trestle table in the hall, with Ealdgith, his headquarters team and section leaders. They had snatched a few hours sleep during what was left of the short mid-sumor's night, either on the hard floor of the longhouse or, for those who wanted to be away from the smell of the fight, lying on the paving outside. After a rudimentary breakfast Hravn's men cleaned their weapons and waited for his next orders. Rhiannon sat by the hearth, listening, awed by the sudden change in her life and her great nephew's strength of character. She knew instinctively that her family was once again safe on their historic lands.

"Give the Pendragon women a purse of coin and as many ponies as they need, then see them off. I don't want them to starve. They may go wherever they choose, so long as it is not on our lands."

He glanced at Brother Cedd. "Brother, after he's cut down have Uther buried with the other Pendragons; somewhere remote. Their grave is not to

175

be marked. All the others are to be buried in the vill's cemetery."

"Now, to the matter in hand." Hravn turned to a stocky bald man in late middle age. "Leolin, my aunt tells me that you have the trust of the community and have often spoken for them when dealing with the Pendragons. I want you to continue to represent the people to me. If you desire, you may move your family into the hall that Nudd once lived in, that choice is yours. I will also pay you a retainer for your service. Is that acceptable?"

Leolin's momentary look of surprise was quickly replaced by a broad smile of relief and gratitude. "Yes, Lord. I can only say that this is a day I have long hoped for, but never thought I would see. Thank you. Thank God, too." He glanced at Brother Cedd. "Christian ways have been absent from here for far too long."

Hravn's next command caused equal surprise. "Swithin. I am impressed by your honesty and support. Can I trust you to continue to work for me and do my bidding?"

"Y...Yes, Lord, of course."

"Good, then you and your family will keep this longhouse for me. I need to live in the centre of my lands and this is too remote for our regular use, though I intend to spend time here every few months. Keep the place aired and ready. You may set up a forge at the back if you wish. If you need assistance, as I am sure you will, then you may employ some of the women who were held hostage and widowed yesterday, though I want Lady Ealdgith to speak to them first to see that they are suitable. We will also see if any want to work and keep house for us at Crosebi Raveneswart. Is that acceptable?"

Hravn was reassured by the look on Swithin's face. "Certainly, Lord."

"Very well. Leolin, between you and Swithin, I want you to build a large house by the gate. Big enough for eight men-at-arms to live in with their equipment. I will have men here all the time and rotate them weekly so that all of them are familiar with the land hereabouts." Hravn was quick to reassure, "They will not be here to control the vill, but to control the pass through Mallerstang from the south and to patrol the hills. And Swithin, before I depart, I want you to brief me on exactly where the Pendragons have reaved south of the border."

"Ulf, Eadwulf, we need to rebalance the men across the sections. Speak to all who used to serve the Pendragons. If they are prepared to soldier for me, and if you are confident that they will accept your discipline, then take them into my service." He paused, looking sternly around the table.

"Today marks a change, a big change. Lady Ealdgith and I are no longer striving to regain our lands, we have them; thanks to the blood and courage of all of you and our men. Our task now is to hold our lands. We know that there is movement, and trade of sorts, between Carleol and Norman lands to the south. We need to find out exactly what is happening. This will keep our men busy, but we need to make sure that they are properly trained and that our section leaders have the confidence to act alone. I intend to make the hall at Crosebi Raveneswart our base for the time being. In the meantime, we have a harvest to get in here, and I have promised Gunnar that we will help with his."

The two masters-at arms nodded agreement and Ulf spoke. "We will recruit those whom we can, rebalance the sections, and then we can tell you how many we can field."

"Good, thank you. We can readjust them again if needs be once we know if Orme has brought men with him. Godric, once the sections are reformed take Ari's with you and go to Carleol and escort Orme and the families to Crosebi Raveneswart. Ulf, Eadwulf, I want one section left here when we go. We'll increase it to two as soon as you are ready. I will show both of you the old fort at Tibeia, and then we can work on building a section house and tower there. I will want two sections there as well." He paused, "Is there anything you want to add, Edie?"

Ealdgith smiled and shook her head slowly. "Not really, you covered everything we talked about, though you forgot Bran, Ole's prisoner." She glanced at Ulf and Eadwulf, "He's a Pendragon by birth, but was illegitimate and disowned by them. He's been their stable boy. He helped us when we were held hostage and I want him to join us. We've enough horses and ponies to keep him busy and out of mischief," she added with a laugh.

As the men left the hall, Hravn went to his great aunt and knelt beside her, taking her hand. "Are you sure you won't join us?'

The diminutive grey-haired lady smiled sweetly. "No. This is still my home. You've given me the freedom to enjoy it now. I'll be happiest here."

Chapter 15

Orme reined to a halt and turned in his saddle to watch the line of horses, pack ponies and horse-drawn waggons pass along the stone road leading down to Carleol. It was an impressive sight, the dull green cloaks of the men-at-arms escorting the convoy contrasted with the bright clothes of the women and children in his care. Although it was five days since they had left Bebbanburge he still felt daunted by his responsibility and was nervous about his forthcoming meeting with Lord Elftred.

As he watched Earl Gospatric's eldest son, Dolfin, riding alongside the leading man-at-arms, Orme recalled the Earl's parting words, 'You've done well, Orme. Few men have mastered their numbers and letters as quickly as you. My steward says that you are a credit to his profession. You're a good soldier too, and I have every confidence that you will escort my children safely to Carleol. But the art of politics and intrigue is a skill that only experience can teach. Be aware that although Elftred holds Cumbraland for me his loyalties are being pulled in another direction. He held lands of his own in Amounderness, and although he still has them, they are now held from a Norman, Roger de Poitou, a very young Norman lord whose father has considerable influence over the King. Elftred is more entangled with the Normans than I would wish as his son has a Norman wife. I trust Elftred to hold my lands and care for my children until I can join him, but take care that you don't allow Hravn and Ealdgith to be drawn into the web of intrigue that he must of necessity weave.' The Earl's concern had echoed that in Ealdgith's letter.

Orme knew that the long, slow convoy heralded the beginning of the end for Earl Gospatric's family in

Northumberland. Much of the Earl's remaining treasure was in the slow-moving carts, the rest had already been sent to Flanders by sea. The Earl remained at Bebbanburge with his constable and a small garrison pending the King's arrival in the near certain knowledge that the Earldom would then be forfeit. Of the two score men-at-arms escorting the convoy ten had been tasked to remain with Orme, as escorts for Frida and Cyneburg and the half dozen wives that were to join their husbands in Hravn's service. With a glance towards the west and the smoky miasma that hung above Carleol, Orme spurred his horse and cantered down to ride briefly alongside Frida and blow her a kiss, as she rode with Agnaar bound to her breast, before joining Dolfin at the head of the line.

*****

Maldred gave Orme a few moments to settle Frida and Cyneburg into their quarters in one of the fort's old stone buildings before taking him to meet Elftred in the main hall, where the Lord's ebullient welcome was less than reassuring.

Orme passed on the Earl's greetings and message. "My Lord, the Earl thanks you for taking his elder children by his first wife into your care. It is an uncertain time for him, and Aethelreda has already sailed to join The Atheling, Edgar, in Flanders with the younger children. She is of the House of Wessex and he does not want to risk her falling into Norman hands. He wants Dolfin, as his heir, to be schooled to govern Cumbraland. I have to tell you, my Lord, that the Earl fears that his Earldom will be forfeit once the King arrives. He has bought his way back from rebellion twice already and is sure that his name is now too closely associated with the resistance for him to be allowed to remain in the land. His intention is to join the Scot's king, but that will depend upon the outcome of William's campaign. He has also sent much of his treasure for your custody and asked me to account for it with your steward."

Orme held Elftred's eyes, determined not to flinch under the scrutiny of his gaze.

"Very well," Elftred spoke at last. "I see that you have the Earl's confidence. Does he have other orders for you?"

"Only that I am to remain here until his children are settled and his treasure secure in your care, by which time the Pendragons' lands should have been recovered. I am then to take our women and children, along with ten of the men I brought, and join Sir Hravn and Lady Ealdgith."

"Good, that will give you time to learn something of how I order affairs here. Mayhap you can then instruct your master and mistress as they have never stayed here long enough to understand my ways. I understand that you have your wife with you, and the huscarle's wife too. Join me when we eat later. You can meet my sons and their wives."

Orme's stomach tensed nervously. "My Lord, you need to know that Frida and Cyneburg suffered badly at the hands of the Normans and...", he hesitated, choosing his words carefully, "...have no love for them."

Elftred's laugh surprised Orme, "And nor do I, but I know where the future lies. The Earl no doubt told you just who my son's wife is?"

Elftred continued as Orme nodded. "Well, it may surprise to you that she has no love for either her father or the Norman court. Your women would do well to get to know her."

*****

Orme was surprised at the meal's organised informality. Elftred sat at one end of a broad oak table and his wife at the other. Orme was ushered to the centre seat on one side, flanked by two of Elftred's sons, Gilbert and Ketel, whilst Christiana sat opposite with Frida and Cyneburg by her side. It looked casual but Orme sensed that it would allow Elftred to observe the conversation and he had the uneasy sensation that he was a captive about to be questioned. Elftred didn't disappoint him. "You've had a fulsome two years by all accounts. I've heard some of it from your master and mistress, but I know my sons and Christiana will be fascinated to hear more."

"We all served in Lord Thor's household at the time of The Harrying," Orme lied, deliberately setting a scene that might give them an appearance of higher social status to avoid difficult questions. "After the manor of Hindrelag was destroyed we fled to the forest and joined Hravn's father in creating a cluster of hidden settlements for those who refused to submit to the Normans. We thought Hravn and Ealdgith had perished along with Lord Thor. Little did we know that they had fled to Westmoringaland and were entrapped by the Pendragons. The Earl heard from one of his spies that Ealdgith had escaped and was trying to reach him. Their arrival in the forest coincided with the Earl's visit. He was trying to befriend Count Alan whilst at the same time developing a resistance against him."

Whilst Orme continued with a description of the resistance Frida tried to divert the conversation, choosing the only subject that she had in common with Christiana, childbirth. She and Cyneburg relaxed in her company, surprised by her open and unassuming manner. She laughed when Frida said suddenly, "I was with Ealdgith when she and Hravn worked for Count Alan. She said that Norman men were too arrogant to live with."

"Well she might, they are!" Christiana smiled across at Ketel, "That is why I have an English husband."

Christiana sat back and looked at each girl in turn. "I heard that you have each suffered at the hands of my people. Please don't tell me how, just know that I understand. There is too much suffering in England; at times, I am ashamed of what my people do."

"Thank you." Frida said with relief, whilst Cyneburg remained silent, the slightest hint of a smile playing on her lips.

Orme was beginning to relax too. It was obvious that Ketel was genuinely impressed by the resistance. "I'm surprised at how a few organised men can pin down so many men-at-arms."

"The Normans knew us as the Silvatici, or the green men of the woods. Hravn played to the name, having the Earl equip us with the green cloaks that our men now wear, but we weren't alone. I heard that further south, beyond Euruic, the Normans are loath to leave the main routes for fear of ambush, and that merchants hire armed escorts."

"That is why I will be pleased when the Pendragons have at long last been flushed out." Elftred suddenly joined in the conversation. "It will enable me to reopen the trade routes into Loncastre."

Orme was about to stab a hunk of meat with his knife. Instead, he laid the knife down and turned to Elftred. "I can't agree, my Lord. The Earl was most emphatic that the borders must be secured, with no excuse for the Normans to cross them; as was the Scots' King." He hesitated briefly, reluctant to interfere too much, "Surely, if we

183

invite the Normans in to trade then we risk encouraging them to expand their lands even further?"

Gilbert looked across at his father, then spoke bluntly. "I agree ...."

Elftred cut him short and raised his hand as he spoke. "No. Do not forget that I have lands in Loncastre and Amounderness. We have copper and silver that we bring across the Solway from Culewen, and then there is our lead from the Caldbeck hills. We need to trade."

The conversation stopped. Orme knew that he was committed and spoke first. "I understand that, my Lord. As does the Earl." He was beginning to enjoy the role of the Earl's spokesman, and the freedom to express Hravn's policy as if it was Gospatric's. "But if precious metal is to be carted into Loncastre, who is to say that it is free from reaving there? And I cannot see that any Norman lord would permit your men to escort it across their land. Would it not be safer to continue to send it by sea to a port of your choosing?"

"Exactly! Is that not what I have been saying all along?" Gilbert's interruption surprised them all. "Through Christiana we know just who to deal with, and Ketel and I are quite capable of trading with them; as we are of selling the produce from our lands in the south. It is far easier to do that and then bring coin back home afterwards."

Elftred sat back and looked around the table. "I will think upon it."

*****

Hravn reined his fell pony to a halt, pulled off his helmet and wiped his brow. Three days of hot weather were drawing moisture out of the fells and turning the air humid. He turned and laughed as he watched Ulf ride up to him. The housecarl was finding it hard to come to terms with his pony, albeit it was the largest in the herd. "I don't know which of you is struggling the most, Ulf, though I'm sure that black beast of a stallion of yours would never cope with the slopes of the Haugr-Gills."

Ulf pulled a face in reply and stopped alongside Hravn, "Aye, happen you're right. I'll tame this one yet, though. Phew! Look at that!" He paused, momentarily distracted by the view that had opened up in front.

"It's impressive, isn't it." Hravn couldn't hide his excitement. "Edie and I used to ride up here whenever we could get away from the Pendragons for an hour or two. Little did we know that one day the land would be ours. You can see why I want our men to get to know these ridges and patrol them. Look, off to the north west you can see the high ground beyond Hep and the entrance to Ulueswater. Then there's Penrith and Gunnar's lands at Morlund."

Ulf nodded. "Aye, I see them. Is that the line of the stone road too? I can see where it leads to Crosebi Raveneswart, though the vill is hidden by the escarpment."

"You're right, Ulf. Now look to the right and you can see the stone road down from Stanmoir, and then right again there is Kircabi Stephan and, closer in, the entrance to Mallerstang."

Hravn let Ulf adsorb the panorama before them, knowing that it would be invaluable for Ulf's understanding of his plans. "When you're ready, Ulf, turn around and tell me what you see to our south."

Ulf wheeled his pony and hesitated for a long moment. "Surely those will be the Norman lands in Loncastre, I can see where the stone road continues down the wide valley from Tibeia."

Good, Ulf," Hravn encouraged him. "Loncastre is much further south, but you can see towards Sedberge, where there is a wooden castle, and beyond that to Kircabi Lauenesdale. Edie and I led the Pendragons on raids to both of them."

Ulf gave a chuckle, more out of respect than amusement. "And why doesn't that surprise me?"

"You're right about the stone road in the valley, Ulf. It leads right into Ravenstandale and over the escarpment down to Crosebi Raveneswart. That is why I want us to have a constant watch from the stone fort at Tibeia, at the top of the valley."

Ulf nodded. "I understand now. We need to get Eadwulf and all the men up here too. They've had a busy two weeks getting Gunnar's harvest in and building the watch tower. Once they have seen this they will understand the need for patrolling and keeping watch." Ulf paused, then added, "If you agree, I think they should also patrol down into the Norman lands. It would help keep them focussed, but if they get to know the people in some of the smaller vills it could keep us better informed."

"Aye, that's a sound idea. We'll need Gunnar to recruit us some Cumbric speakers too. We'll have to be careful though, Swithin confirmed that the Pendragons raided a couple of Roger de Poitou's manors, though he didn't think they had touched Ivo de Taillebois's lands. But we can start to spread the word that the Pendragons have gone and that we will give a guarantee of security. That might help gain their support."

"Mmm..." Ulf continued to stare towards the south. "I can't see any Norman lord letting raids go unanswered. I think we have to plan and train on the assumption that we will be attacked. We need a watch at the head of Mallerstang as well as Tibeia, and beacons to relay a warning."

"You're right, Ulf. Edie and I need to visit Hep and Ulueswater soon, and we need to start thinking about lead mining there. It'll mean leaving our defence here to you and Eadwulf."

Ulf wiped his forehead with a rag. "You've no worries on that score. Eadwulf understands me. He has a free rein, but I have the final say," he laughed, "after you and Edie, of course. Just give us clear orders and all will be well."

*****

Cyneburg lifted Adelind up onto the front bench of the high-sided cart and turned to take one last look at Elftred's hall and the old fort of Carleol. It surprised her that she felt a strange affection for the place, or rather, for Christiana. She had relaxed in the young woman's company and laughed at her tales of Norman male arrogance and small-mindedness. At last, she had realised that it was personality, not race, that made a person; it no longer worried her that Christiana was a Norman. As she climbed up next to the cart's driver, Cyneburg's thoughts turned to the journey ahead and reunion with Ulf. They had already been apart for far too long.

Frida, too, had fallen for the Norman woman's charm and, with Agnaar strapped to her breast, she turned in her saddle and waved a fond farewell before following Orme out of the gate.

Orme, on the other hand, was relieved to be leaving. He had enjoyed Ketel's company and found that they shared many opinions in common, but he was more circumspect about the young man's father. Elftred's self-interest and his tangled Cumbric-Norman politics were a frustration that he could do without. Godric's arrival two days earlier had been a godsend, and the prospect of re-joining Hravn and Edie and re-establishing their household drove him to reach Crosebi Raveneswart as quickly as possible.

As her cart rattled and bounced along the stone road Cyneburg forced her mind to ignore the constant jarring and, with Adelind cuddled into her side, she thought about her reunion and how she would honour Ulf with a song. One that Frida could accompany with the simple four-stringed lyre that Lady Aethelreda had given her after she had learned to play.

It was late on the second day, with the sun casting long dusky shadows from the western fells, when Godric dropped back to ride alongside Orme. You can see the smoke from the manor, we'll be there well before the sun drops. I'll send Ari ahead to warn of our arrival.

*****

"Stop and listen, men and women
that be of free English blood.
I shall tell you of a good knight.
His name is Sir Hravn, Aske's son.

And of his good-wife too,
Lady Ealdgith, Thor's daughter.
Their realm is the green wood.
Their people, the Green Men, are we.

We ride and we reave.
The Normans are our foe.
Their granaries and mills,
are burnt by our leave.

Ulf is their huscarle.
Tall and brave is he.
But none is gentler as a father,
and kind husband he is to me..."

The hall, packed in celebration of the household's reunion, fell silent. Even the hounds lay quiet, their ears pricked up to listen. Cyneburg's soft,

188

haunting voice floated on the thick smoke-hazed air, backed by the clear echoing notes of Frida's lyre. As they listened, many felt a silent tear slip down their cheek. Cyneburg remembered them all in her song, sang of their bravery and the dangers they had faced and sang too about those who had died or been left behind.

At last Cyneburg fell silent, emotionally and physically drained. Ealdgith, sensing her friend's plight stepped forward and, taking Cyneburg's hand in hers, she grasped Frida's hand and raised them both in the air. She turned and beamed at those standing around them. Hravn jumped onto the main table and led their ever-growing household in a rapturous applause.

Holding his hand up for silence, he spoke. "What can I tell you that Cyneburg hasn't. She has told our story, your story, better than any of the skalds of old. But we have a new story, one that has yet to be lived before it can be told. The days of living in the green wood, reaving, resisting and taking our revenge against the Normans are over. Edie and I have our retribution against the Pendragons and that blood feud has passed too. The lands around us are our new home, held by Edie and me from the King of the Scots, through Earl Gospatric. We are to secure the borders around the head of the vale of the Eden, prevent any reaving across them and make sure there is no excuse for the Normans to break the peace; for if they do we will be ready to bloody their noses. This is our land to farm, to raise sheep for mutton and wool and, what is more, it is land rich in lead for us to mine. That will be the story of our future. It will be a story of your loyalty and your service, and our one family."

Chapter 16

Hravn leaned forward across the trestle table he had erected outside the Crosebi Raveneswart hall, and listened intently to Ulf. He sat back at last and stretched.

"That's good Ulf. You've done well, as has Eadwulf. I've had some success too. I met Håkon of Kircabi Stephan yesterday and he's agreed to provide ten men, all Cumbric speakers, who we can employ as we see fit, on condition that we cover his duty to the Earl of securing his lands as far as Stanmoir. We will need to train them though, so I've added to your burden. With the six Cumbric speakers from Gunnar, those we recruited from the Pendragons and Orme's men, we now have fifty men-at-arms, plus Edric's men on top."

Ulf gave a low whistle. "That's some war band, not that we're looking for a war," he added quickly. "But before I start to reorganise the sections from Bebbanburge can I suggest that we hold some as a reserve?"

Hravn laughed. "I'm ahead of you Ulf. The four sections that we led into Dunholm are our real strength; they're properly trained and have been blooded. I want them here, to be under you command, as a reserve in case we need to counter a Norman threat. I want two Cumbric speakers with them too. I'll release one of their sections at any one time to take its share of patrolling the fells. That will also keep them busy and they can get to know the lie of the land along the length of the border. As to the others, for the time being, I want two sections at Mallerstang guarding the pass and patrolling the eastern Haugr-Gills, two at Tibeia guarding the stone road and patrolling the western Haugr-Gills and two covering Håkon's border.

Eadwulf is to take charge of them. Keep the rest here and train them hard, rotating them every two weeks. Once they are all trained then we'll start to patrol the lands from Tibeia north to Hep and Ulueswater."

Ulf asked, "What about Edric?"

"I was coming to that. I've agreed with him that he should be responsible for the head of Ulueswater and overseeing the mines once we get the miners there."

Ulf nodded agreement, 'That'll work, but we're short of mail hauberks and steel helms. Every man has a sword and we've enough crossbows for two per section. We're short of green cloaks too."

Ealdgith interrupted. "Mayhap Gunnar can help. His armourer made my leather helm and first padded jerkin. If Gunnar can spare him to make more for us that should give the new men sufficient protection until we can speak to Elftred and buy his armourer's services."

Hravn squeezed Ealdgith's shoulder and gave her a quick smile. "Yes! I'm sure he will. The tailor at Morlund could possibly make more waterproofed cloaks too, after all that's where we got our first two. It doesn't matter if they aren't a perfect match, just so long as they are green and weatherproofed. Can you speak to Gunner, Ulf?" Hravn turned to Ealdgith.

"Edie, I've completely lost track of how large our domestic household is. I'm sure it's bigger than I think."

Ulf laughed. "It is!"

"You're both right. I took three of those who were widowed at Mallerstang, two have children as well. Then there are the six wives that Orme brought from Bebbanburge." Ealdgith hesitated and laughed gently. "Though there are a couple who claimed to be wives without that affection being returned by their supposed husbands."

Ulf interrupted with a chortle. "I'm sure they won't have long to wait. Now that we are more established I know several of the lads are looking to become more settled and to take a wife." He smiled at Hravn's sudden look of concern. "That's life, it's inevitable."

Ealdgith glanced sharply at Ulf and raised her hand to still his enthusiastic good humour. "Hravn's right to worry. I've just gone through Orme's record keeping. My uncle has been generous, but we can't live off his treasure for ever. Maintaining a large armed household is expensive, very expensive. It is certainly more than all our manors can sustain and we will need to buy grain and increase our holding of livestock. I think we can sustain the household for a year at most. We have to start mining within six months and get lead to market within nine."

Hravn nodded. "I know, Edie, I know. I have to see Elftred and hasten those miners he promised, though I'm loath to get him too involved. I just don't trust him."

Ealdgith sat back looking intently at the two men, then spoke to Hravn. "My love, have you not forgotten Alfr? You once spent an ale-filled night talking about nothing but lead mines with him."

The bang, as Hravn thumped the trestle table with his fist, drew looks from those in the hall doorway. "By Thor, Edie! That's it! I've been so blinkered by worry about Elftred that I forgot all about Kelda. We should go there and speak to Frode and Alfr before we visit Ulueswater."

Ealdgith leant sideways and quickly kissed Hravn's cheek, "Yes, and I can see Edda again. I've a lot to tell her. Tomorrow?" Hravn new that the question was really a command. "Anyway, now that's settled I've news for you too."

Casting a quick glance at Ulf, Ealdgith continued. "Mayhap you don't yet know, Ulf, but

Cyneburg and Frida have some plans of their own. Both have time on their hands and Cyneburg wants to take charge of the dairy, just as she did at Grinton, though on a larger scale of course. We've all benefitted from Frida's skill as a seamstress and she wants to encourage some of the women to make clothes for the household. Between the two of them, and Esma as housekeeper, they will keep all the women here very gainfully employed."

"Hah!" Hravn chuckled, "What, with Ulf training the men and you keeping the women from being idle, there shouldn't be much chance of hanky-panky."

"I doubt that!" Ulf guffawed.

Ealdgith looked at the two and blushed slightly, "Be that as it may, I'm keen to see them start as soon as possible. I need to find someone to help me too. I can't be the herbalist for everyone. I'll have to find and train an assistant who can then take over. I'm going to put the word about in the vills hereabouts and see who may be interested."

"Mmm, Edie. You're right of course, but it may take a while to find the right person." Hravn agreed quietly.

*****

Hravn tested Ole's memory and ability to find a route by requiring him to lead them up the winding track from Nateby, over the high pass above Mallerstang and eastward down into the steep vale of the upper Swale. It was the reverse of the route they had taken nine months earlier when they fled to the sanctuary of Bebbanburge. Ole seized the opportunity, cantered ahead and waved to Ada to follow. Ealdgith nodded her consent. Hravn followed with Godric and Osric, both men now settled fully into their roles as housecarls.

193

Ole rose to the challenge and, if he seemed uncertain of the way ahead, Ada quietly prompted him, her sense of direction proving to be almost as good as Hravn's. They didn't falter as cold mist on the cloud-shrouded hill embraced them and Hravn found himself smiling with proud satisfaction as he watched them choose the route.

The party paused where a beck tumbled in a series of waterfalls to join the young river Swale. Ealdgith called across to Hravn. "Tarry here a while longer. I can't let Edda be faced with four hungry men without a pot on the boil. Come on Ada, I'll race you, but take care of your pony on this rough ground." She cantered off, allowing Ada to keep close behind.

Ealdgith slowed as the small cluster of tight-packed thatched cottages came into sight around the shoulder of the fellside. "Well ridden Ada, but catch your breath. We'll walk the ponies down and cool them off a bit." She was always amazed at how the small community survived in such a remote valley. Barely self-sufficient in food and wool the people clung to life and kept their freedom. Ealdgith thanked God that the Normans had yet to penetrate this far into the dales.

A small flaxen-haired girl appeared from behind a rock, struggling to carry a heavy pail back to the vill. She turned as Hati barked, dropped the pail and stood staring. "Edie!" She shouted and ran forward.

Ealdgith swung down and swept her up. "Agata, I've come to see your moder. Why don't you lead my pony and I'll carry your pail? We'll go and find her."

Edda gasped at the sight of Ealdgith in her mail tunic and Ealdgith felt suddenly self-conscious. She was about to stutter an apology when Edda ran forward and embraced her. "Edie, you always surprise me. When we first met, you were homeless and in search of your family. Last time you were a Lady fleeing with her people. Now you are a warrior, dressed as a queen. I think you have a tale to tell me."

Ealdgith laughed as she returned the hug. The two women were social opposites and Ealdgith still struggled to understand Edda's heavy upper-dales Anglo-Norse accent, but they had bonded like sisters, albeit Edda was ten years older. "I will, but first we have a meal to prepare. Hravn is on his way with his servant and two of our men at arms. We have a lot to tell and a big favour to ask, yet again."

Ada and Agata helped Edda bring the meal outside to where the Ealdgith and the men, joined by Edda's husband, Frode, and Alfr the miner, sat on the boulders and off-cut tree stumps that passed for seats. Frode had lit a fire in the outside hearth and, as the heat of the day faded, the warmth of the flames took over.

Godric stretched his legs out, took a swig of watered mead, winked at Ada and said, "Well done today Little Lady, you certainly showed Ole the way." He paused, anticipating Ole's reaction. Just as Ole jumped up, red-faced, he laughed, "You're like a fish hooked on a line, Ole. You did well, you both did. Your path-finding is far better than mine at your age."

Ole sat down, blushing but grinning with pride, as the men laughed.

Edda glanced at Godric, "And just what were you doing at that age, Godric?" The twinkle in her eye hinted at the attraction she felt for Godric. Tall, angular faced and muscular he was very different to the men of the vill, stunted by a life-long poor diet. He had a physique that a woman could admire, though Edda was too loyal to her husband to look for more.

"I was training to be a man-at-arms for the Earl, as was Osric. I would have been there now if Lady Edie hadn't run me into the ground in a race up a sand dune."

Ealdgith laughed, interrupting. "To be fair, Godric, I only had Ada over my shoulder. You were

195

cursed with Osric, and even then, you came from behind to beat me."

"What!" Edda giggled, rather coyly. "Why did you switch your allegiance from the Earl?"

"It was partly that, and the desire for a challenge. I've seen more action this past six months than in six years in the Earl's service. But it was after My Lady laid an ambush in which she slew two Normans...though to be fair to Ada, she wounded one herself first. A woman who can do that deserves my service and the protection of my sword. Whilst I serve Sir Hravn, my oath is to My Lady."

Edda was momentarily silent, her mouth agape. "Oh my!...and you Osric? Is that why you gave your oath?"

Osric shook his head and there was a sadness in his eyes as he remembered the event. "No, I was with Sir Hravn that night. I was caught in a fire in a granary trying to rescue one of my men. I failed. Later, when we got clear of the Normans, Lady Edie healed my burns. Look." He held his hands out for Edda to see. The skin, scarred with red and white wheals was firm and supple to touch. Her hands have the magic of an elven princess and she cares for us as no one else can, stitching skin together and even tearing strips from her under-shift to bind my wounds. Who else could I follow?" His eyes twinkled as he gave a cheeky smile.

"Osric!" Ealdgith laughed in mock annoyance, but with a degree of embarrassment.

Hravn slapped his thigh, laughing. "And that, Edie, is why men follow you!" he paused, letting the humour subside, "Now, perhaps we should tell you all that has happened this past nine months."

Edda and Alfr listened silently. Frode asked a few questions, but for the three of them the politics of power were beyond their understanding.

Hravn brought their story to an end, "And that is why we came today. Not just to tell you that the curse of the Pendragons has gone and that your road to the west is safe, but also to ask for your help and advice in opening up lead mines at Ulueswater."

Frode spoke first. "If ever I was to swear loyalty to any man it would be you Hravn..."

Hravn interrupted. "...Never Frode. There is no need. Bonds of friendship are enough. If ever you are under threat, send word and I will come with men. Your only danger is from the Normans at the foot of the Dale. If they venture westward, let me know."

"Thankyou. I will." Frode looked at Alfr. As headman, Frode had the final say about village affairs, but he was loath to commit Alfr to a venture a long way from home.

"Aye, Lord. I can help, so long as Frode looks after my family's needs. Just give me a week to put the mine in order and I will join you, and maybe bring a man with me. I'd like to see what Ulueswater has to offer."

Hravn and Frode spoke together. "Thank you Alfr." Then, as Hravn deferred to Frode, the headman continued. "We still send our pig lead to Carleol along the stone road. But it is an expensive port. Elftred charges high dues and it is a longer sail around the coast to the market ports in the south. There is a port at Rengles, on the west coast. I haven't been there but know that it is at the end of the high stone road that runs over the fells from Ulueswater, down to Ameleseta then over passes to the coast. It is an old port, founded by the Romans. It would be a long haul over the fells but you have more ponies than we do. It could save a day's sailing too."

Ealdgith glanced at Hravn, then asked Frode. "What markets would you sell to?"

"The Isle of Mann is close to Rengles and the seas thereabouts are safe, but they have lead of their own. The waters on the way across to Dyflin aren't to be trusted. It is safest to sail by the coast and trade through Ceaster. The Normans are building a castle there and prices are good."

Hravn gave a low whistle. "If we use Rengles and Ceaster, we would need to find a ship, an agent and a market. We would have to visit both, and that would mean putting our heads in the Norman noose at Ceaster. Moreover, we don't speak Norman and I can't rely on finding a Breton merchant in Ceaster."

"No, but Brother Cedd speaks Norman." Ealdgith was quick to see the opportunity. "Go in your own right as a Cumbric lord, taking your priest, huscarle and servant. Mayhap I could go as your lady wife. But we would need to find a ship first."

"You're right, Edie. Cedd and I should go, but I think you need to stay to take care of our lands. We can't take the risks together that we once did. Ulf should stay too, but I'm sure that Godric will be keen for adventure."

As the soldier nodded, Frode chipped in, "I would be happy to send my pig lead with yours, Hravn, and mayhap if you find a ship and a buyer we could start to send it before you produce your own. That would help test the market."

Hravn stood and offered Frode his hand. "That is a deal."

*****

Having risen early the next morning, they crested the pass with the sun still low in the east behind them. Its light caught the fells to the west and highlighted a myriad ridges and valleys. "Look, Edie. That is the backdrop to our lands. With a border like that we don't need a fortress to be secure."

He sidled his pony next to hers and pointed. "See where yon fell drops in a long spur down to a dark stretch of woodland?"

She nodded, "Yes?"

198

"Look closely and can you make out a dark line leading up the spur?"

Ealdgith narrowed her eyes, concentrating, and nodded slowly, "Mmm, I think so."

"That is the stone road that Frode mentioned. Elftred mentioned it too, if you recall. That is High Street, our road to the coast."

"In which case, the foot of Ulueswater must be just the other side of the spur?"

Hravn cheered, "You've got it Edie! One day you'll be hefted to these fells just like any Herdwick." She cheekily poked the tip of her tongue at him by way of reply, before he continued. "And that is where we are going tomorrow. I want to meet Aki Thorkelson at Bartun and Ulick at Askum to confirm who has the lands at Patrichesdale, at the head of the lake, for it is he who has the land where lead is to be found. I want to arrange a boat for a week tomorrow and have warning of our arrival sent in advance. Mayhap we can arrange to have ponies meet us. I am sure that we will have some distance to travel to where the lead is known to be."

Ealdgith threw her head back and laughed. "I don't see this year getting any quieter, do you?"

Haerfest

Chapter 17

Aelf rubbed the stubble on his chin as he studied the early morning sky. "I hope this weather holds, Lord. The corn will be ready for cutting by tomorrow."

Hravn nodded agreement. "Aye, you're right. I'm glad you'll be here to keep an eye on it. I'm just waiting for word that everyone is ready, then I will be off to Patrichesdale. Remember that you have Edric's men to give a hand. Hah!" Hravn gave an embarrassed laugh, "Albeit two of them are your sons."

Both men turned at the sound of a sudden half-choked squeal and a woman's laugh. "There, I told you they were too hot!" Esma had her arm around Bran's shoulder as he crammed a freshly baked scone into his mouth, gasping as it burnt. Releasing the boy's shoulder, she walked across to her husband and Hravn.

"He's a canny lad, Master Hravn. He's never been mothered though, and has a lot to learn. I'm glad you brought him here; he's good at heart."

"Well, there's no one better than you to mother him, Esma. It's as well the Pendragons rejected him as one of their own, else he would have been tarred with their brush"

A brisk clatter of horses' hooves drew their attention. "That's Ole with my mount. Aelf, Esma, I must go. But thank you for looking after Bran, just so long as he remembers he's a job to do in the stables."

They slowed their horses to a walk as they neared the lake. Ealdgith turned to Hravn, her eyes twinkling with delight. "It's beautiful," was all that she said, as she stared at the silver-mirror of the water, reflecting the dark green wooded slopes of the fells, grey crags and bright blue sky. She stopped and looked about at her six companions. Each was as awe-struck; the beauty of the lake spoke for itself.

Hravn shattered the spell. "I bet it is fearsome in a storm. Come, I can see Ulick's man waiting and there is a boat just off the shore."

They handed their reins to the man on the shingle strand, removed their boots and socks, rolled up their leg hose and waded knee-high in the cold water to the waiting boat. Two men steadied it with an oar apiece whilst two others helped them aboard. Ealdgith thanked the gods that she had had the foresight to insist that none of them wore mail.

The helmsman spoke first. "Welcome My Lord, and My Lady too. Torstein sends his regards and will meet you on the shore at Patrichesdale."

Hravn wondered at the design of the boat. Much smaller than the snekkja, it was pointed at both ends and broader in relation to its length than the snekkja. Its one short mast supported a yardarm from which hung a furled sail. He could see that it was less sophisticated than the Earl's snekkja: the planks of its clinker sides were more roughly finished and were held together by wooden pins rather than iron nails. Three central cross benches could take two oarsmen each, but rather than fitting through oar holes, the oars were held in place by peg-like tholes.

Hravn waited while the helmsman ordered the four crew to raise the grey sail, made from finely spun Herdwick wool, then moved aft and settled himself near the steering board. "Tell me, who builds these? The craftsmanship is outstanding." He could have added 'for a boat built in primitive conditions', but wanted to gain the man's confidence.

"We do, Lord, by the lakeshore at Patrichesdale. My father, Ragnar, and his men. His grandfather built boats over on the coast. We crossed the fells and settled here when I was a babe, but he has kept his skills alive. Many of the boats hereabouts are roughly built and flat bottomed, or still just skin stretched over a wicker frame. He's built three like this over the years. We use them for moving fleeces and grain, animals too on occasion, to market in Penrith." The helmsman was impressed by the compliment and the young lord's easy going manner.

"How easy are they to sail? Could my men be trained?"

"Aye. They are easy enough when you know how, but the lake is fickle. There are three stretches to it and each has its own mood. Here, the fells are low and the wind more constant. At yon end, as we approach Patrichesdale, the wind can rush down the valleys and take you from three sides at once. That is a challenge and takes experience and skill."

"She's sailing well now, I can feel the speed picking up."

"Aye Lord, we've a nor' westerly and so, with luck, we may just be able to use the wind both ways. She can sail pretty close thanks to the keel, that's what gives her the edge. She's a good lass, Kára. "He patted the gunwale.

"You named her for a Valkyrie?" Hravn asked, puzzled.

The helmsman roared with laughter, "No, Lord. For my daughter...though mayhap she is the Valkyrie."

He laughed again at a sudden shriek from the bows as Ole and Ada were soaked by the splash from a wave. Hravn pointed to the water flashing by the left side of the boat, it was barely a hand's breadth from the top of the gunwale and, raising an eye brow, he asked "Is that safe?"

The helmsman laughed a third time. "It depends how good your helmsman is. She heels with the cross wind and we're right on the edge of what she'll take. Better than rowing though, eh?"

"Mmm." Hravn rubbed his chin, thinking. There was a lot to learn, but once Edric and his men moved to Patrichesdale they would need at least two boats like this to serve each end of the lake, and to move supplies and pig lead, when they produced it. It was a question to add to the ever-growing list to ask Torstein.

Ealdgith sat back and enjoyed the motion and sensation of speed. The beauty of the fell sides and the colours of their reflections awed her. Above the shore line the varied greens of mixed oak, ash and birch were interspersed with bright reds of early rowan berries. Small clearings amongst the trees were pale yellow with freshly harvested hay, barley and oats, whilst the clearer fellsides above were flecked here and there with light grey dots where Herdwick sheep grazed. Occasionally smoke drifted up from the small farms clustered together on the flatter ground between the craggy spurs that dropped down towards the lake's edge. It was her idea of heaven; and it was hers.

As they passed the first of the three islands that led the way into the final stretch of the lake Ole whooped and pointed to a cormorant diving from the outstretched branch of a lone pine tree.

Hravn looked beyond the island and pointed to a high craggy peak that dominated the head of the lake. "That's a fearsome fell top, does it have a name?"

"Oh, Aye. Helvellyn." The helmsman spoke in Cumbric, giving the local name.

Hravn laughed, as he understood the meaning of the Cumbric name. "Surely not? Its neither yellow, nor moorland! From here it looks the exact opposite."

"I agree, not from this side at any rate, but it is from t'other side of the fell. Look to the right of the ridge, where it drops before Stibarro Dodd, that is Sticks Pass which runs over towards Kesewic. Most of the fells hereabouts are named; the smaller one to the right, that is Gowbarrow; behind us is Place Fell; and yonder, the crag to the left of Helvellyn is Saint Sunday, though why it is so named I do not know."

The helmsman suddenly fought with the sail and steering board as they passed the second island. "I told you the winds were fickle hereabouts," he shouted through clenched teeth then, as they swept around a small headland, he ordered the sail lowered and oars manned. After some muttered cursing the crew managed to stow the yardarm and sail lengthways between the passengers. They each then shipped an oar to row towards a broad gravel beach. Hravn glanced across the bay to several other small craft: two leather skinned coracles with fishermen and a squat raft-like boat piled with fleeces that was being poled across the shallows at the head of the lake.

A squat, ruddy faced man with long brown hair that merged with an equally long brown beard, stood on the grassy bank beyond the beach, chuckling as he watched them wade ashore then hop on the gravel to replace socks and boots. He stepped forward at last, to speak in hesitant English. "Welcome, I'm Torstein. My Lord Hravn and Lady Ealdgith?" If he was surprised by Ealdgith's clothing he didn't show it, her leather jerkin and breeks were very similar to his own. It was Ealdgith's reply in halting Cumbric that caught him unawares.

"Torstein, yes, I'm Lady Ealdgith of Hep and Ulueswater. Please, speak Cumbric. It is a tongue that I need to practice, as my husband keeps telling me." Ealdgith deferred to Hravn, who stepped forward and offered Torstein his hand.

"Pleased to meet you, Torstein. I'm part Cumbric, part Norse, and though Edie is English she is fluent in Norse and is striving to become so in Cumbric. Speak in whichever tongue you choose and we will understand. But first let me introduce our household.

Edric and Alfr in particular, for they will soon be staying here in Patrichesdale."

Torstein led the way to where ponies were tethered waiting. Mounting, they followed as he trotted away from the lakeshore, over a wide ford and up the widest of the valleys that met at the lake head.

Torstein called across to Hravn as they rode. "I hear you're after lead?" As Hravn nodded, he continued, "It seems there is a vein that runs across the valley, and it's said there is more on the tops at Stibarro. I'll show you what we know."

Hravn looked puzzled. "If you know of it why hasn't it been worked?"

Torstein shrugged. "I wish we had the skill. The vill suffered from famine a generation or more ago; two years of drought followed by a hard winter. More than half died. Any remaining knowledge of mining died too. I've men here who would be keen to learn, for it will surely bring wealth to us all. That is why I welcome your over lordship."

Hravn grinned and nodded backwards towards Ealdgith. "Not mine, these lands were granted to Lady Ealdgith by her uncle, Earl Gospatric. He knew of the lead, but didn't have the resources to mine it. The lead is my wife's but, as you say, we will all benefit."

Torstein nodded understanding, "We've a way to go yet." He clicked his tongue and urged his pony into a brisk trot. The others followed. The track lay to the right of a wide slow-flowing river in the middle of a flat valley patterned with small fields of hay and barley and pasture for cattle. Steep craggy slopes rose on either side and Hravn soon felt almost imprisoned amidst the towering fells. They were higher than any he had ever seen and, glancing back at the following riders, he realised that they were each as awed. After more than a league Torstein swung away from the main track into a valley on their right. Passing a small lake, they began to follow a narrow way through a wood, the ponies following in single file. The track led them to a small clearing and the overgrown mossy ruins of an old homestead.

Torstein swung down and, throwing the reins around the branch of a stunted rowan, he shouted, "Tether them here, we've a short way to go on foot." Then, turning to Hravn he said, "This was where the old miners lived. The vein is up the fellside."

Hravn flashed a smile at Ealdgith, "We're nearly there, at last, Edie." He looked around, "Alfr, stay close. The old workings are up the fellside. Mayhap your eyes will pick up signs of lead that none of us will see."

Any path that the old miners had used was long-since overgrown. They sweated as they scrambled up the steep fellside, occasionally grasping at the slender trunks of birch or rowan to pull themselves up. The ground began to level as they cleared the trees.

Torstein paused, gathered his breath and pointed over to their left. "There, that's where there is a line of pits."

Alfr laughed and tapped him on the shoulder. "Aye, but you've missed this." He pointed to a small level area on top of a low mound across to their right. "That's a bale site, it's where they smelted the ore. Come." He strode forward.

The top of the mound had been shaped into a low hollow, three or four paces across. Dry earth was covered in small rough-edged brown and black stones. The edge of the patch was surrounded by a collapsed wall of fire-shattered reddened rocks.

"Why is there no grass? Everything seems dead." The patch of arid ground on the verdant fellside puzzled Ealdgith.

Alfr picked up a piece of the stone and rubbed it between his fingers before passing it to Ealdgith. "Slag, My Lady. It's what's left after smelting." He kicked the hardened ground. "Just as I thought, there's charcoal too."

Realising that he had an enquiring audience, Alfr explained. "You need a windy spot, such as a hill top. Lay a clay base with a dip in the centre, surround it with a walled hearth with a small window on the windward side, build a bonfire of charcoal and wood, pile on bucket loads of ore that has been broken into small pieces and then burn it. The heat of the fire will smelt the lead and when it burns out, it will have pooled in the centre." He paused, "Though I have seen it where the molten ore can be run off down a small channel to help clear it from the rubbish that is left behind, that's a better way to do it."

Hravn nodded, fascinated. "I see, but as Edie says, why is the ground dead?"

Alfr shrugged. "I don't rightly know, but it is always the same. It must be something in the lead. The fumes when smelting it are pretty nasty."

"We're going to need a lot of wood," Edric looked around, "and there's not a lot hereabouts."

"I know, they'll have cleared the fellside over time. Those young trees we climbed through will have grown since. I'll see what other sites might be suitable, we can always take the ore down to the bale, rather than bring wood up to it, so long as we have enough wind."

"That's great Alfr, we now have a site to start smelting. Let's have a look at these pits, Torstein." Hravn strode enthusiastically across to several pits.

Alfr tugged thoughtfully at his beard as they stood around the top of the first pit. It was shallow, barely a child's height in depth. Successive pits were increasingly deeper as they progressed up the fellside. "I think this is where the vein surfaced. That'll be how it was first found. After that they've dug pits to track it back into the fellside. See how they are deeper than a man's height further up the fell." He turned to Torstein. "Is there a beck nearby?'

Torstein looked puzzled, "Aye. Just around yon corner." He gestured to a slight spur running down the fellside. "Why?"

Alfr grinned. "Digging pits is back breaking work, particularly where the vein lies deeper underground. But if we can channel water into a reservoir above the vein we can release the water in a rush and use its force to hush away the top soil and rock above the vein and cut into it more easily. Let's go further up the line of the vein and see if there is a place for a small reservoir. Mayhap we could dig a leat and channel water from the beck around into it."

Hravn could see that Alfr was enjoying himself. He hoped that this was a good sign; all their hopes and plans for the future depended upon extracting, smelting and selling lead. "So, do you think that this is going to be viable? Will we be able to extract lead and smelt it?"

The miner's weather worn face slowly cracked into a smile. "I don't see why not. I've told Frode that I can give you until winter starts to come in, after that I'm going to have to get back to Kelda. But, that's time enough to train Edric and his men and..." he glanced at Torstein, "...any you can send my way."

Hravn's relief was palpable. He beamed at Alfr and clasped his shoulders with both hands. "You're a good man, Alfr. Thank you." He turned to Torstein. "If Alfr can be back here with Edric and his men within three days can you provide them with ponies, a room and food at my expense?"

Torstein looked surprised. "Your expense Lord? Surely if these lands are now yours, or," he glanced at Ealdgith, "My Lady's, then you will expect me, as your man, to cover the cost."

Ealdgith interrupted, "No, but thank you. I don't intend to profit at the expense of my people's free labour. I haven't sunk to Norman ways. There are other ways in which you can help us too, but still at our expense. Why don't we make our way back and you can show us more of the valley and Patrichesdale?"

"What do you have in mind, Edie?" Hravn asked as they scrambled back down the fell.

Ealdgith laughed as she turned to face him. His heart missed a beat, as it always did when the sun caught her green eyes, highlighting their golden flecks. He often wondered to himself if it was her beauty more than her personality that led men to follow her.

"Why, boats of course. Surely that was why you were questioning the helmsman so much?" Ealdgith paused, then added, "But I was also thinking we should have a small house built in Patrichesdale, just for us. There's an enchantment to the head of the lake. It's more than just its natural beauty. I want us to explore it, and share it together, just the two of us, when time permits."

Hravn's sudden kiss surprised Ealdgith as much as it surprised and amused those around them. "Why not, Edie." He turned to catch up with Torstein and just caught the tail end of his conversation with Godric. The housecarl was laughing, his hand on Torstein's shoulder.

"Your young lord certainly has a way about him."

"Aye, They're a canny couple. My Lord is a rare leader, but don't be misled by My Lady's beauty and charm. She's a wildcat, normally wears the finest mail ever made. I've seen her take down a man twice her weight and kill three Norman men-at-arms. She has the gift of healing too. There's never been a lass like her, she really cares for those whom she calls her people...I guess we all follow her because we're a little bit in love with her." Godric laughed at Torstein's surprise. "I'll tell you more one day."

Hravn hung back, unwilling to intrude, but pleased that Godric saw Ealdgith as he did.

They rode back down the valley in a more light-hearted mood, no longer overawed by their surroundings. On crossing back over the ford, Torstein stopped, called across to Hravn, and pointed up towards Place Fell. "Do you see the track that cuts from left to right across the fellside, to the shoulder of the fell itself?" Hravn looked and nodded, shielding his eyes from the sun.

"That's Boredale Hause. There's a track from there onto the high stone road to Ameleseta, known hereabouts as Brethstrett. If you travel to Patrichesdale by foot or pony along Brethstrett, then you can follow that route down Boredale Hause into Patrichesdale.

"This Brethstrett, what's it like, Torstein?" Hravn asked. "I'm minded to send the pig-lead to Rengles and ship it from there rather than Carleol. Would that track be sensible to use?"

Torstein pursed his lips and nodded. "I don't see why not, so long as the ponies are up to it. It's a high route and generally firm under foot, but very exposed in bad weather. Brethstrett gives good going once on it, but there's a better route from here. If we aren't sending fleeces by boat down the lake to market in Penrith, we send them by pony to Ameleseta. We use a pass to the south of here at Kirkstein. It's another ancient stone road and far more sheltered than Brethstrett.

Godric interrupted hesitantly, "Forgive me Lord, but if we're going to use these stone roads perhaps we should base a section or two to patrol and control them."

Hravn turned, "Just what I was beginning to think too. Well said, Godric. Bartun is close Brethstrett, is it not, Torstein?"

"Aye, Lord."

"Edie, we'll stop and speak to Aki Thorkelson on our way back. When we have the time we'll also take a look at the Kirkstein pass. Now, Torstein, I fancy a dip in the lake; which means that we will all have one. Is there a secluded bay close by?"

Ealdgith collapsed in the saddle in a fit of giggles at the shock on the faces around her. Torstein laughed too. "Lord, excuse me if I don't join you, but yes, the bay at Blowick will suit. I'll show you."

Ealdgith smiled at Ada's look of horror. "You and me too. We'll find somewhere even more secluded. It's a habit brother Oswin introduced us to. You'll enjoy it."

Chapter 18

Hravn's loud whoop was whipped away on the wind as he galloped along the high stone road. Its sound mingled with that of the call of a curlew, a buzzard and a few bleating sheep. He felt literally on top of the world. The ground fell away gradually on either side whilst all around him ridge upon ridge of high fells stretched out towards a distant purple-blue horizon. He was sure that at this moment a buzzard had no more freedom than him. The road changed from stone to firm grass, then narrowed as it ran along a ridge. Hravn slowed, halted and waited for Godric, Ole and Cedd to catch up.

Godric gave Hravn a wry smile as he rode up to join him. "Your horse will throw a shoe or break a fetlock if you're not careful, Lord. It would be a long walk back for one of us."

Hravn laughed back, but felt embarrassed. "You're right, Godric, and Ole needs no encouragement, least of all from me."

Godric smiled sheepishly, "The freedom up here makes your heart sing. I admit I was hot on your heels until I saw your horse's back hoof skid on a rock."

"I was concentrating too much to notice," Hravn chuckled, then spoke seriously. "You were right to suggest basing a section at Bartun. This really is a backdoor route into all our lands. We have to patrol it to own it, and all our jagger trips will need to be escorted. There'll be plenty of spots for an ambush."

"I think you'll need to employ a team of locals too. Men who really know the routes and these fells." Godric pointed ahead of them. "Just look at that, Lord. You could lose a whole packhorse team over there if they were caught in the cloud or rain."

Hravn whistled quietly. He hadn't noticed that the ridge narrowed to a point where the ground fell away steeply on both sides in a series of craggy cliffs. As they rode slowly forward flecks of light glinted off black waters in the valley bottoms.

"Look! What's that?" Ole shouted, pointing down towards one of the small dark lakes.

"An eagle, I think. It'll have an eyrie somewhere on those crags." They were coming to understand that Cedd's knowledge of wildlife was extensive. "The king of the birds, mightier even than the raven." He joked with a sideways glance at Hravn.

Hravn laughed, "Mightier maybe, Cedd, but certainly not as clever." He hesitated, suddenly noticing that Ole was studying the route ahead with a look of trepidation. "Come, I want to be in Ameleseta well before dark. We'll ride the horses slowly over this next stretch. Ole, you follow me.

Once the old road, known by Torstein as Brethstrett, widened again Hravn increased the pace and gave his horse its head. He thought back over everything they had achieved in the month since their visit to Patrichesdale. Torstein had delivered all that he had promised: ten of his men now worked alongside Alfr; the helmsman and his four men now served Hravn, running trips up and down the lake; and construction had started on the first of two boats. Ulf had recruited a few more men from local vills and last week they had scraped together a section of better trained men to base in one of Aki Thorkelson's barns at Bartun. Hravn decided that once his trip to Ceaster was over he would bring Godric with him and lead the Bartun section up onto Brethstrett to start patrolling and really get to know the fells along its route.

The nature of the fells began to change and, as they followed a long spur down into a wide valley he saw a lake with a large vill by the shore. He was sure that it must be Ameleseta. In the middle distance, to his right, he could also see the faint line of a track as it wound up a valley. Maybe it was the route over Kirkstein and from there towards Patrichesdale. It would be good to have more than one option.

A black and white chequered sign board drew them to the inn. The keeper was very obviously nervous, but intrigued, by the sudden arrival of a priest and three men wearing mail. He relaxed as Hravn explained that he was Earl Gospatric's man, tasked with securing the borders to his east, and that he should expect more trade when he started to use the stone road as a jagger route. Hravn was in turn delighted when the inn keeper suggested that his brother, who held land around the old stone fort by the lakeshore, would be able to provide stabling for the pack ponies. The inn keeper also confirmed Hravn's suspicion that the Normans now controlled all the low-lying land immediately south of the fells, but hadn't dared venture into the valleys. His warning that on the western coast the River Esk marked the northern edge of the Norman controlled lands worried him. The little harbour of Rengles was at the mouth of the Esk and, from what the inn keeper knew, the stone road lay immediately to the north of the river.

*****

The next day was just as challenging. They rose early and continued to follow the stone road as it wound over one steep pass and then another. The sun was past its zenith when they crested the second of the high ridges.

"The sea!" Ole's shout stunned them all. "Look, and an island too."

Hravn glanced at Cedd, as if seeking confirmation, then said, "That must be the Isle of Mann and...", he paused to shield his eyes with his hand, "...

214

and the merest hint of hills beyond, right on the skyline, they must the mountains of Ériúland."

They crested another slight rise and suddenly found themselves staring at the high stone walls of a long-abandoned fort. Godric's jaw dropped in awe as he halted outside the cold grey towers of the gatehouse. He turned to Hravn, "What a place. What men must have served here? Can you not sense their presence?"

Hravn nodded, equally impressed. "Aye, I can that, Godric, and a hellish place it must have been in the winter. We can't dally, but I want to check if we could use this place to break the journey. Those jaggering the lead would be at the extent of a day's ride from Ameleseta by the time they reach here."

They crossed a large flat area and rode in through the eastern gate. The fort was similar to those at Chesterholm and Bincastre, built in a rectangular pattern with a central crossroads between large stone-built buildings and enclosed courtyards. Most of the walls were still standing, though the roofs had long since collapsed and the rafters rotted.

Hravn turned to the other three. "What do you think? It would give shelter from the wind at least. It's not as if we're going to find an inn or a farm hereabouts."

"Aye, Lord. It'll do. I'm sure we could rig an awning to shelter under, and the ponies are hardy enough." Godric had already assumed that he would be leading the first of the trips across.

Their descent to the coast was easy and uneventful as the rocky moorland gave way to woods and then strips of fields, some of which were being worked by men gathering a late harvest. They kept a close eye on the land to the south, across the valley of the Esk, but saw nothing. Glances of surprise rather than fear were cast towards them as they passed the first of the farms lying outside Rengles. It was such a peaceful remote place that Hravn supposed that men-at-arms were a rare sight and he hoped that was the case on the Norman side of the border too. Ole's sudden grumble that he was hungry was enough of a reminder that it was late and, rather than head immediately to the estuary, Hravn looked for the first sign of an inn.

Leaving Ole to tend to their horses and Godric to sound out the innkeeper, Hravn took Cedd and Sköll and walked down to the harbour or rather to the seafront as he discovered that Rengles sat next to an enclosed bay, not a man-made port, from which the sea drained completely at low water. It was busier than he expected. Two large tub-like boats that he recognised as knörrs were getting under way to catch the tide before it fell and a third was nosing its way in, the setting sun silhouetting it against the red horizon.

Hravn waited on a low wooden jetty, one of several that protruded from the shore into the shallow bay, caught the line that the bows-man threw and wound it quickly around a hefty wooden post. The helmsman brought the knörr alongside the jetty, where at low tide the small cargo vessel would settle on the firm gravel strand. The helmsman lent on the gunwale and cast a quizzical look at the warrior and priest.

Although Hravn had never seen the sea, let alone a boat, a year ago, he was beginning to feel something of an expert. The knörr was noticeably shorter and wider than the snekkja at Bebbanburge, but much bigger than Torstein's boat at Ulueswater. Built in the same clinker style it had covered half-decks fore and aft, each with a couple of oar holes. The middle of the vessel was open and full of boxes and bales of wool laid upon brushwood mats and stacked around a single central mast. The crew seemed to be just the helmsman and five. If they were to go to Ceaster, Hravn guessed that it would be in something like this. He swallowed hard as he recalled his first trip in the snekkja. He could tell from the way the knörr had rolled in the cross-current on its way in, that by contrast a trip in a snekkja would be luxurious.

"Where are you bound? Are you the master?" Hravn shouted to the helmsman, speaking in Cumbric in the hope that the crew were local.

"Ceaster, and aye, I am. Who's asking?" The helmsman called back. A short man with a powerful upper body from a lifetime spent hauling on oars and handling cargo, his distrust of strangers was very apparent.

Hravn came straight to the point, either the helmsmen would be interested in their trade or he wouldn't. "Sir Hravn, I'm a Cumbric lord. I'm looking for a passage to Ceaster."

"Ceaster!" The helmsmen laughed back. "What in the name of the gods for? There are bastard Normans everywhere there," he shouted, adding, with an apologetic look towards Cedd, 'sorry Father.'

"I've pig lead to sell and have it on good authority that Ceaster is the best market on this coast. Can I come on-board and talk about it, rather than shouting to you?"

"Aye, 'appen it would be best to come aboard."

Leaving Cedd with Sköll, Hravn reached for the knörr's gunwale and stepped across nimbly to the aft half-deck.

The helmsman picked up the conversation. "I'm known as Phelip. I'll take you to Ceaster if you want, but if you've pig lead to sell you be better trading through here. Finán the Manxman and his sons control all the trade here and have their contacts in Doolish, Dyflin and Carleol, as well as Ceaster."

Hravn's jaw dropped and he rocked back on his heels "What!" Life would be so much simpler for them all if he had an agent in Rengles. "Where can I find him...and is he reliable?"

Phelip shrugged, then spat over the side. "He's a merchant. They're all bastard crooks, but he's better than most. He's generally straight with me and he won't blindside you if he thinks he'll lose out by it."

Hravn had a sudden thought, and asked, "Do you ship lead from Carleol for Lord Elftred?"

"Aye, I do from time to time. Finán is his agent too. Though I gather that Lord Elftred prefers to send his lead overland down the stone roads."

Hravn offered Phelip his hand. "I think you've saved me a trip to Ceaster." He chucked, "My sea legs probably weren't up to it anyway."

Phelip looked Hravn up and down disparagingly. "You're probably right there, Lord. His is the stone house at the end of the harbour. You'll see him down here in the morning. Bald head and large gold rings on his fat fingers. Looks as if he wears half his wealth."

Hravn pulled a face. "Mmm...that tells me something, but thanks."

"Tell him I sent you." Phelip called after Hravn as he clambered back onto the quayside.

Hravn explained their good luck to Cedd as they walked back to the inn. Cedd nodded thoughtfully before he stopped Hravn with a hand on his wrist. "We must tread carefully, Lord. We don't know the market and the Manxman will be after a good profit. I know their kind."

"I agree, though my connection to the Earl, and Elftred, strengthens our hand. I'll tell him that I expect the same price as Elftred and bluff that I know what his rate is."

Cedd chuckled, "And I could make mention of my connections within the higher church. They might not hold much sway in Cumbric lands but they could do in Ceaster. It would be a threat, anyway."

They were in a buoyant mood and in need of a drink by the time they returned to the inn.

*****

218

Ealdgith missed Hravn. They hadn't been parted for long since the fateful first day of the harrying more than two and half years ago. It wasn't that she was worried for him, or for herself. They were more secure now than at any time. She missed his companionship, his wit, the warmth of his body in bed, and the certainty that if she didn't know what to do, he would. Cyneburg sensed it first and came to sit by her as she stared into the hearth embers.

"This isn't like you Edie, you've normally more energy than all of us together." She placed her hand gently on Ealdgith's thigh. "I felt the same when Ulf was with you on the raids. I just couldn't bring myself to do anything, other than sing with your aunt."

Ealdgith turned and smiled, "Thank you Cyneburg. I'm sorry, though I feared you would miss each other. I know Ulf did, he would talk to me about you." Ealdgith giggled at Cyneburg's sudden look of surprise and embarrassment. "Only to me, mind. He wouldn't open up that hard exterior to anyone else, but don't forget I've known him since...well, for ever. But now it's my turn. We've always been close together, Hravn and me. Even as children I knew that if I didn't play with him one day, I would the next."

Cyneburg gave Ealdgith a very secretive smile. "There's something else, Edie." She paused, watching slow realisation dawn on her friend's face.

"Are you?"

"I am, least I think so. It happened as soon as I joined you all from Carleol. Ulf took me for a walk up the hill, there is a place above the escarpment where you can see everywhere but can't be seen. We-"

Ealdgith placed her forefinger on her friend's lips and laughed. "Enough."

Cynburg giggled, blushing.

Then Ealdgith threw her arms around Cyneburg and hugged her close. "Does Ulf know?"

"Not yet. I want to be sure before I tell him. This will be so special for us both."

Ealdgith nodded. She knew just how important this would be to them. In a rare act of love, Ulf had adopted baby Adelind as his own after Cyneburg's rape by Normans. Their own child would be even more special.

Cyneburg asked, with slight embarrassment, "Can you look at my tummy and tell me if I am?"

Ealdgith took Cyneburg's hand gently in hers. "I can't tell by touching you, not for a long while yet, but tell me how you have been feeling. That is the surest way."

The sudden clatter of hooves shattered their peace. Ealdgith squeezed Cyneburg's hand and got up. She had barely turned towards the door when Eadwulf burst in.

He hardly looked at Cyneburg. "My Lady, we've just stopped a merchant on the stone road south of Ofertun, heading south towards Tibeia. He has a string of packponies laden with pig lead and an escort of men-at-arms. It's just because we out number them that we managed to force a halt."

Ealdgith knew that Eadwulf's unasked question was what should he do? She knew instinctively. The men were Elftred's; he and they, had to be stopped. Turning to Cyneburg she asked, "Please Cyneburg, find Ada, I think she's in the stables. I'll want her to dress me in my mail and then ready my horse."

Then, turning back to Eadwulf, she said, "Ulf is away with two of the reserve sections. Ready the other two and call Osric. A show of force now might just stop Elftred from meddling further. He knows my uncle's orders".

A grin spread slowly across Eadwulf's face. Ealdgith was doing just what he would have done; his respect for her now was such that he wouldn't consider acting without her authority. "Aye, My Lady, they'll be ready as soon as you are. I warned Osric on my way in."

As Ada tightened the buckles on Ealdgith's mail hauberk she asked, "Will we be alright? Hravn, Ulf and Godric aren't here?"

Ealdgith realised at once that, despite her outward self-confidence, Ada was more dependent upon the key men around her than she liked to show those that loved and protected her. She gave a forced laugh, "Don't worry. There'll be no fighting, I promise. Stay close behind me, this is our chance to prove that women can lead and command men's obedience. Anyway, we have Eadwulf. He and I understand each other now."

Fifteen minutes later, with Ada riding behind her, Hati running in front and Eadwulf by her side, Ealdgith led the ten men-at-arms at a gallop up the hill towards Ofertun. Her master at arms shouted across to her as they rode.

"One section was on the fells above Tibeia when they saw the jagger train in the distance. They rode via the fort and gathered the four men there. They blocked the road and sent one man to warn me in Ofertun. There are three men-at-arms with the jaggers, facing our eight. I suggest we bring the whole lot back here and wait 'til Sir Hravn returns."

Ealdgith shouted back, "No. He could be another week or two yet if he gets a boat to Ceaster. I intend a strong show of force and then I will send an equally strong letter to Elftred. The pen can be as mighty as the sword at times. He will certainly feel my wrath." She heard Eadwulf's loud laugh, as it was whipped away by the wind.

As they crested the hill beyond Ofertun, Ealdgith could see the jagger train standing along the road side. A dozen packponies were in line, roped together; every fourth one had a rider. Three mounted men-at-arms were at the head of the column facing eight mounted men who blocked the road in a semi-circle around the head of the column.

Ealdgith led her party at a gallop past the line of ponies, causing them to shy and rear up in confusion. She wheeled her horse and slid to a halt in front of the three men-at-arms.

She waited patiently, staring at the three escorts whilst her men-at-arms spread out to surround them. Eadwulf sat on his horse slightly to one side, watching Ealdgith and the three men. He read cold anger in her face; the flash of green behind the eye guards of her tan helmet emphasised the intensity of her emotion. Ealdgith used her knees to gently move her horse from side to side. She knew that the sun would reflect off her hauberk and cause the mail to shimmer. It would be a sign of ostentation and authority. She drew her sword in a slow deliberate movement and held it above her, pointing skyward. Again, the reflected sun sent patterns of blue and brown along the silver-grey blade. Judging her moment, she spoke in Cumbric.

"I am happy to fight, as are my men, but..." she paused whilst she sheathed her sword with a dramatic flourish, "...I see no need for fighting today, for there can only be one outcome. Who is in charge?"

"I am." A heftily built man, wearing mail and seated on a roan stallion, spoke in a flat tone, lacking any respect.

"I am, 'My Lady'." Ealdgith corrected him. "Now, just who do you think I am?"

The man stared back for a moment, holding Ealdgith's eyes. She didn't blink. "Lady Ealdgith, My Lady," he said at last.

"...of Hep and Ulueswater," she added, "remember that too, for it means that these are my lands, and you pass and trade across them with my permission."

Ealdgith looked across to Eadwulf and now spoke in English, assuming that the surly man-at-arms probably understood. "Where could we hold them, Eadwulf? There is a cave deep in Mallerstang that I know of. Would that suffice?"

Eadwulf gave a grim smile, but his eyes twinkled. He was enjoying Ealdgith's game. "Mayhap My Lady, but too comfortable for my liking."

Ealdgith turned her gaze back to the man. "I assume that you understood my English?" He nodded. "I assume too that Lord Elftred sent you, and that he told you to ignore any controls on this road. Am I correct?" The man dropped his eyes. She could tell that he was uncertain.

"He did, My Lady. We are to escort the jaggers into Amounderness, then hand them to a Norman escort."

"Did he, indeed." Ealdgith said icily. "Did Elftred..." Ealdgith deliberately avoided calling him Lord, "...tell you that I hold these lands, with my husband, Sir Hravn, on the authority of my uncle Earl Gospatric and, through him, from the King of the Scots?"

"N...No, My Lady."

"Elftred is the Earl's man, nothing more. I am the Earl's blood kin." She let the implication sink in. "The Earl wants this border sealed. He wants no movement across it and no excuse for friction with the Normans. I know that Elftred's daughter-in-law is Norman, and that he holds property within Norman lands. The Earl has given a dispensation for him to access his land and for Christiana to travel to her family, but that is all. Does this trade in lead comply?"

The man shook his head. "It does not, My Lady."

"I take it that we are agreed that you will return the lead to Elftred?"

"Yes, My Lady." The man's relief was palpable.

223

"Good. Now, what is your name? We will return to my manor. You must have ridden close by. I will write to Elftred and you will deliver my letter in person. Understood?

"I'm Howel. Yes, I understand My Lady, and thank you."

Ealdgith smiled slowly. She was enjoying the game of words and appreciated that the man-at-arms was no doubt a good soldier, loyal to his lord, but pragmatic enough to understand the politics of power. If she earned his respect, it could well serve their advantage. "Come, the sun is dropping. Join me and my master-at-arms for a meal. Your men can eat with mine. We will stable the ponies overnight then, at first light, you can ride to remind your master that this border is closed to trade."

*****

"My Love!"

Ealdgith spun around, her mouth agape. "Hravn!" She stood, momentarily frozen in the dairy's door way, before throwing herself forward into his embrace. As their lips parted, she said, "But you've been gone barely a week. Why aren't you in Ceaster?"

Hravn held her at arm's length. "Hah! It's been quite a journey, but we don't need to worry about Ceaster. I have an agent at Rengles now and he will pay us the same as he pays Elftred."

Hravn felt Ealdgith tense at the mentioned of Elftred.

"What is it my love, something's happened, hasn't it?"

Ealdgith took Hravn's hand, leading him away from the dairy. His expression gradually changed from concern to amusement as she explained the events of the previous afternoon. Then, squeezing her hand, he burst out laughing.

"Oh, to see his face when he gets your letter. That's very well done, Edie, and far better that you did it then me. He won't like it of course, but he can't gainsay the Earl's niece when she speaks on his behalf. I think he will be shame-faced whenever next we meet him. But for now, let's get some of our lead to market."

"No, for now, come with me." Ealdgith took Hravn's hand. "First of all, you're going to get changed out of that mail, then I'm taking you for a walk to a special place I have heard of."

Chapter 19

Hravn studied the sky as he rode, it was cloudless. The summer weather had been very average; cool, wet at times, sunny at others, and nothing like the moisture sucking heat of the year before. Now, the still warm air was unusual for the start of the tenth month.

"I hope this lasts until we get to Rengles and back," he called across to Godric riding alongside.

Godric pulled a face, looked skyward and shrugged. "Once we get onto those high fells, anything could happen."

Hravn patted his pony on its neck then glanced back. Behind him two of Dunstan's men led a line of twelve packponies ridden by Sigurd and two other Askham men provided by Ulick. Dunstan and his fourth man brought up the rear. Ulick had assured him that the men knew Brethstrett, the high stone road, intimately and, with the harvest gathered, could be spared for the best part of Winterfylleth. They had joined Hravn five days ago, led the packponies to Kelda to collect Frode's lead and were now making their way up the long rise from Askham, along Brethstrett. It was time to confirm that the Manxman's money was as good as his word.

The packponies plodded their way slowly up the inclines, but could be encouraged to a faster pace once on the high tops. Hravn soon realised that they wouldn't arrive in Ameleseta until shortly before dusk and sent Godric and Ole ahead to warn the inn keeper and his brother of their arrival.

Ole's eyes lit up at the opportunity, "Do you mean you trust me to scout for you too?"

Hravn laughed, "Don't chance your luck, but you're big enough and ugly enough."

Ole pretended to look serious, "Not as big and ugly as some..." then flinched and laughed as Godric gave him a playful prod with his spear butt.

"There'll be another if you dally, come on."

*****

Two days later, as they led the jagger train down the still-quiet stone road from the old fell-top fort to Rengles, Hravn took Ole and rode ahead to find Finán the Manxman, telling Godric, "Go straight to the harbour. I'll meet you there. I would rather sell the lead today than hold onto it overnight. We could all do with a night in the inn without the worry of guarding it."

To Hravn's relief and slight surprise, Finán kept his promise of a fair price. He took the lead into his storehouse after he had weighed the first of the pigs and then, keeping it to one side, used it to check that all the other heavy ingots were the same weight. Hravn, impressed at Finán's methodological approach, asked casually, "What do you think of the quality then?"

"Hah! Better than most. This has been well smelted, I'll give you that. As often as not there is too much slag left in it."

Hravn nodded in interest, "Mmm, I suppose you need to check that they're all of the same quality too. You have to trust me as much as I do you."

"Oh aye, Lord. Believe you me, I'll be the same with every load you bring. But, if they are all as good as this, we'll do a good trade, you and me."

Hravn relaxed and began to feel that Finán could be trusted, but realised that Alfr had set a high standard for Edric to maintain."

The return trip began uneventfully. Having anticipated problems with Finán, Hravn felt a sense of anti-climax as they rode back up to the old fort, with the gentle southern breeze and unseasonably warm sun cocooning them. All changed the following morning.

Hravn sensed the change when Snorri roused the camp just after first light. A freshening south westerly wind blew in the scent of the sea and high wispy-tailed clouds were forming above them. As Hravn looked up he could almost see the clouds growing in number. Sigurd, the oldest of the three Askham jaggers, strode over.

"Lord, we should move quickly today. Have you seen?" he jerked his thumb skyward.

"Aye," Hravn nodded, glumly, "I've seen that pattern before, it heralds change, and not for the better. How long do you think we have?"

The jagger squinted at the clouds and rubbed the grey stubble on his chin. "Maybe a day at best. Less if the wind picks up more."

"Mmm, that's much as I feared. We'll make Ameleseta in time, but as for tomorrow? That's up to the Norns to decide."

The wind stayed at their backs all the way to Ameleseta but it didn't strengthen. The following day broke with a sultry grey dawn, and a sheet of cloud with an undulating pattern, similar in appearance to fish scales, hung over them.

"A mackerel sky, we know what's coming," Sigurd grumbled to Hravn as he gnawed on a hunk of bread whilst adjusting his pony's harness. "We should give it a go though."

Hravn looked at Godric. He nodded. "I agree, I'd rather get wet than be stuck in this valley for days."

So be it, let's go and make best speed." Hravn made his decision with a heavy sense of foreboding.

The packponies, no longer burdened with lead ingots, moved quickly. Those carrying the men were slower on the steep track out of Ameleseta. As they gradually climbed up the fellside the mist lowered slowly onto the tops in front, whilst a wall of black rain-laden clouds loomed over the western fells behind them.

"Hel's teeth!" Hravn cursed as the first heavy drops of rain blew past and shreds of ever-thicker mist began to whirl around them. Within moments the stoney track blended into the greens and greys of the fellside. He stopped the column, rode back to the lead jagger and gestured to Dunstan to join them. "Dunstan, Have the men share the ponies with the jaggers. It'll be easier if we all lead one or two apiece." Then, shouting to be heard over the increasing force of the wind and rain thrumming in their ears, he turned to Sigurd, "Pass all your ponies across. I want you to lead and I'll follow closely. You know these fells better than any of us. When these clouds really close in, it'll be your eyes that keep us from blundering over the edge."

"Aye, Lord." Sigurd nodded grimly. His long black hair was already plastered to his head in a thick mat as water dripped from his nose and chin onto his rain blackened leather jerkin.

They rode, heads down, as fast as Sigurd felt able to lead. He paused whenever the terrain changed, the ridge branched onto a spur or they crossed broken ground with no discernible marks. Sometimes he dismounted, passed his reins to Hravn and walked forward peering at the ground for signs of the way ahead. Once, he disappeared completely and Hravn was about to move the group forward in a desperate bid to stay in contact with him when he reappeared and nodded to Hravn with a twist of the lips that Hravn took to be a sign of relief. Sleet now filled crevices and plastered their clothes.

Freezing water soaked into their clothes and ran down necks, backs and thighs, even into their leather boots. Their lanolin proofed woollen cloaks were sodden and no lingered any insulation. Hravn felt cold and turned back to Ole to mouth "Alright?"

Ole pulled the weakest of smiles in reply. Then, in the mist behind Ole, Hravn saw a rider slump forward and slide from his saddle. He yelled to Sigurd to stop, leapt from his saddle and led his pony to Ole to hold the reins. As he did so he noticed with a shock that Ole's fingers were blue and his cheeks ashen grey. He reached up to touch his face and asked, "Ole, are you cold?" Without waiting for a reply, he ran back to the fallen man.

It was one of the jaggers. As Hravn approached the man tried to stand then collapsed again, trembling. Sigurd staggered across to them, buffeted by the wind. He rubbed the man's face. "Danr! Danr, can you stand?" Danr stared back blankly.

Hravn glanced at Sigurd then pulled open Danr's sodden wool jacket. There was only a saturated thin linen shirt underneath. Placing his hand inside to feel Danr's chest he touched chilled clammy skin. He leant forward and shouted in Sigurd's ear, "He has no warmth at all. We have to get him off the fells. I've heard there's a way into Patrichesdale by Boredale Hause."

Sigurd nodded, "Aye, there is, beyond the narrows above Riggindale but," he hesitated, "it's too far. We'd be better dropping straight down into Hartsop. It's steep mind, but the ponies will find a way."

"How far?"

"Three leagues at least Lord, but there's a farm in the bottom."

Hravn didn't hesitate. "Good, we'll lift him up and tie him on to his pony. Ole can lead it." Then, remembering the awning they had sheltered under in the fort he added, "Wait with him. I'll fetch the awning, we can wrap him in that first. At least it will keep in whatever warmth he has left."

As Hravn ran back along the line of ponies he took Godric with him and checked each rider in turn. "I know you're wet, but keep moving and keep warm. We're going down into Patrichesdale. It'll be steep. Let your pony find its own way and stay close behind each other. Keep an eye on the man behind, stop if you lose sight of him, that way we'll all stop. Unleash the jagger ponies, they'll follow." He left Godric at the back of the column, "Keep them closed up as best you can. I can see a couple are almost as bad as Danr."

Ole bit his lip and concentrated on staying in the middle of the track as he followed Hravn along the narrow ridge above Riggindale. Dark grey clouds swirled around the group, wraith-like in the poor light, and his entire world had shrunk to a short stretch of rain and sleet-battered grassy track. He remembered the vertiginous crags, deep cwms and cold dark lakes into which he had looked down on their way across and knew that they were somewhere below.

The narrow ridge broadened suddenly. Ole fretted as Sigurd stayed close to the very left of the plateau and led them to the top of a small mound. Sigurd waited for Hravn to close in to him. "We left the stone road at the end of the narrows. This is the start of the descent to Hartsop. It's steep and we have to keep the crags on our left, then cut below them. Warn the men that if anyone goes further to the left than me, then they will go over the edge...it's a very long drop."

Hravn waved for the men to come close then spoke to each in turn. He leaned close to shout against the force of the wind. As he turned back to rejoin Sigurd he froze. The swirling cloud suddenly ripped apart to form a window through which he saw a long green spur above a steep-sided valley. The dark grey waters of a lake lay beyond. A second later, the window closed as swiftly as it had opened. He gasped in awe, then relaxed. The breaking cloud meant that they were close to its lower edge. With luck, they would soon be out of it. He turned, saw looks of fear and puzzlement on the faces around him and grinned, shouting, "Take that as a sign from the gods. We're in the right place and almost out of this murk. Take care and follow."

The ponies descended slowly, zig-zagging their way down the steep grassy slope. Mist swirled, thinned, then cleared and lifted as soft light flooded in to dispel the gloom. Most of the men shuddered as they saw how close to the crags they were and instinctively urged their ponies to the safety of the ground on their right. The force of the wind diminished and the rain stopped as they dropped into the rain shadow of the eastern fells.

Sigurd kept edging around to his left and gradually, as he descended ever lower, the wet grey-black rocks loomed above them. He stopped after a further couple of furlongs, turned to Hravn and pointed into the valley bottom. "That's Eithr's lake, we're going to cut across to the far right-hand end of it, then follow a track down into Hartsop. It's not as steep from here on."

It was barely a league to the scattered buildings that huddled in the dale; and not long before they lowered Danr from his pony, removed the thick wrap of the awning and carried him into a small farm to lie in front of the hearth.

Hravn laughed when the young farmer's wife blocked the door, arms on her hips, as the other men tried to push inside to claim the warmth of the fire. She jabbed her finger against Tófi's broad chest as he towered over her. "Yes, I know I have the prettiest lips, every lad in the dale has told me that, but you aren't having any favours. Make a fire behind the stable, there's kindling there too, but keep out of the barn. I'm not having our harvest ruined by wet bodies or a careless flame".

"Keep a close eye on Danr for me, good-wife, and I'll see if I can split my men up and share them around the other farms." As he looked around Hravn began to recognise the small vill from his visit with Torstein two months earlier. He realised that the lead vein was on the fellside across the valley. "Is there a miner called Alfr staying nearby, or another known as Edric?"

The farmer's wife nodded, "Aye, down by the ford...are you Lord Hravn?" She asked, flustered, as she realised why armed men were riding with jaggers.

She blushed and stood to one side as he gave a slow, amused, smile, "My Lord, come in please. Our home is yours, my husband ..."

Hravn stopped her with a touch to her arm. "No. As I said, caring for my man is enough, but...perhaps you could warm some milk for my servant. I'll leave him to watch Danr."

Taking Godric, Hravn went in search of Alfr. He found him, along with Edric and his men, in a large barn made from newly cut wood and with a thick thatch of reeds. Smoke from a small fire in the hearth billowed up into the rafters and out through a hole at one end of the roof. Half a dozen ponies were penned in makeshift stalls at the other. There was a warm fruity smell to the place. "Smells homely," Hravn joked as he clasped Alfr on the shoulder.

"Aye, Lord," Alfr chuckled. "A warm pony is a happy one, just like a warm miner, but what brings you here?"

"I can't argue with that," Hravn agreed, "but it's your lead that brings me here. I've just taken a load from Kelda to Rengles, and got a good price for it. You were commended on its quality by the way," he added with a wink.

Alfr laughed, "I had no doubt as to its quality, Lord, but you're both looking a bit bedraggled. It's not a day for being on the fells."

"Aye, you're right there. We were headed back over the high stone road from Ameleseta when the weather broke. I knew it was going to, but I hadn't reckoned on this. One of the jaggers collapsed and we brought him down ..."

"And a right challenge it was too," Godric interrupted, "I've a lot more respect for these fells now."

"So, we'll be joining you for the night. I'll be back with Ole once I've got the men settled into farms. Then you can tell me how we're getting on." Hravn called Sköll to heel and headed back to the farm.

Having settled the men across the three farms in the valley Hravn returned to Alfr with Godric and Ole, the latter now fully warmed through after being spoilt by the young farmer's wife. Ole ducked swiftly to one side as he dodged Godric's half-playful cuff to his ear, "Ole, if you don't stop bleating about how many bread cakes you've eaten, I'll tell Ada that you've eyes for another, and a married woman at that!"

Ole grinned and licked his lips in reply.

Leaving Ole to help Cola and Dudda make a meal, Hravn followed Alfr and Edric around to the back of the barn. He gave a low whistle of surprise.

"That, is impressive. How many pigs of lead are there?"

"Only half a dozen at the moment, but it's a rich vein...so far at any rate. You never know when they are going to give out, or start again further in. We've shifted a lot of rock to get this much." Alfr stood back and stretched his shoulders, as if to emphasise his point.

"By the gods, Alfr, you've worked hard." Hravn's gratitude was obvious, "How are...?" He jerked his head towards the others.

"Grand lads, all of them. Edric has a good team there. They're keen to get stuck in and learn quickly, as do the local fellows. I can't see that you'll have a problem when I leave."

Hravn called Edric across to join them. "I want you to keep going through the winter, as best as you can. When the weather closes in give Torstein a hand with the boats or in the vill. The more you can fit in with the locals the more help we'll get next year. I can see that Edie and I will be spending a fair bit of time here." He tapped a pig of lead with his foot. "Let me know when you have a shipment ready. After today's excitement, I'm not going to move any more until Lencten, but if we have enough I might have the lads do two trips back to back. Before then, I'm going to take a look at Kirkstein, a pass that Torstein once mentioned, somewhere at the head of this dale. Now, let's see how Dudda and Cola are going to tempt Godric's appetite. Something has to stop his stomach rumbling." He turned, and joined the three young men by the hearth.

*****

It was in the cold, clear early evening two days later that Hravn returned to the hall. Low clouds had hugged the fell tops all around Patrichesdale and enclosed the valley in a world of its own. He had waited until the weather faired, not wanting to risk another near-disaster on Brethstrett.

A large full moon that heralded the start of winter rose early in the eastern sky. Hravn paused on top of the low hill overlooking the vill and told Godric to lead the men down. Ole thought twice about interrupting and sat in his saddle watching Hravn as be obviously wrestled with a problem. Then, coming to a decision, Hravn called, "Come on Ole, stop dallying, I'm sure Ada is missing you and you have lots to confess." Calling Sköll to heel he led off at a gallop.

The men's arrival had forewarned Ealdgith and she was already outside waiting for Hravn, a concerned frown on her face.

Hravn laughed as he swung down from his pony, kissed her lips and said, "Come Edie, let me show you what I think we need to do next. It's cramped in the hall and will get worse when the men can't ride out in the winter. If we start now we can build a hall at the end, at an angle, so that the men have their space and we have ours."

Ealdgith laughed, relieved that Hravn's delay was due to nothing more than another of his plans. "Yes, we could," she enthused, "and the air might smell a little sweeter too."

Hravn agreed, enjoying her tease. "We would have to use green wood, so it might not last as long, but it will do for now. Once we have money coming in we could look to build in stone as at Morlund, and perhaps add a tower."

He pulled her close, his arm around her waist. "Let's go inside."

Winter

Chapter 20

Hravn sat at the long table in the hall with Ulf and Eadwulf opposite and Orme to one side. He glanced upward as smoke from a blazing log fire in the hearth billowed up, spread out below the rafters, then out through a covered hole in the roof.

He broke a chunk off a crusty loaf and played with it in his fingers before eating it. "So, what you're saying is that no matter how many men we recruit, there is always a need for more."

Ulf chuckled and nodded, whilst Eadwulf spoke. "Not quite, Lord. We can recruit as many lads as we want. They're looking for excitement, and coin of course. We could always do with more, particularly with building underway and Edric and his lads away, but we have all the patrols covered."

"And how are they doing?"

Eadwulf glanced at Ulf and continued. "They're good. Not of the same standard as the lads we brought with us, but they ride well, move fast, understand how to use the lie of the land to cover their movement and are better than many with the spear and sword. I'd not pit them against trained men-at-arms, but we have the Bebbanburge lads in the reserve for that."

A clatter of hooves in the courtyard interrupted further discussion. Ole was about to open the heavy oak door when Ketel walked in, his face flushed from a long ride in the cold. "Ye gods! It's bitter out there," he exclaimed and made straight for the fire, his hands outstretched. He stopped before reaching the hearth and offered his hand to Hravn. "I'm sorry. I was forgetting that my father didn't introduce us properly when you came to Carleol. I got to know Orme so well that I feel as if I know you too."

Hravn returned a firm handshake but didn't smile, unsure as to the reason for Ketel's visit, as he introduced his masters-at-arms.

"I broke my journey with your friend, Gunnar of Morlund." Ketel was speaking quickly and Hravn realised that he was nervous. He took a breath, slowing himself down, as he held his hands towards the hearth. "I need to visit some of my father's lands near Sedberge and to arrange the sale of their produce locally...do you want to come with me? It would be a chance for us to get to know each other and for you to see something of the lands to our south."

Hravn's eyebrows twitched in surprise, then he turned to Ketel with a broad smile and a laugh. "Yes, why not. Though I know the lie of the land beyond Sedberge fairly well. Edie and I reaved it with the Pendragons two years past."

It was Ketel's turn to stare in surprise. "What?"

"It was after we escaped the harrying and fled into Mallerstang. Uther Pendragon caught us, took us hostage and demanded a ransom from the Earl. I suggested that we could scout out manors for him to reave whilst we waited for the Earl's reply, and gave him my oath that we wouldn't run, which of course we did."

"Hah, Hravn, and therein lie many tales, no doubt." As Ketel relaxed Hravn called to Ole to bring horns of ale and heat them with a poker.

"How many men have you, Ketel?"

"Just two, I thought that if you joined us we could take more of yours."

"I agree." Hravn, already thinking through the opportunities presented by a trip into Norman lands, added, "We'll take two sections of the reserve, plus Godric and Ole. That's fourteen with you and me. That'll make an impression when we call on the

238

castellan at Sedberge. Who is it now?" He turned to Ulf before Ketel replied. "Keep charge here whilst we are away and, Eadwulf, take care of the patrolling."

"Roger of Poitou holds the land now, from his father, Roger of Montgomery. Montgomery is a favourite of the king, or so my wife says. The son is young though, twelve, fourteen at the most, and I think Hugh of Cholet acts for him." Ketel's enthusiasm showed in his wide smile and the twinkle in his brown eyes, "I hadn't intended calling on him, but come to think of it a strong first impression would do my father's interests no harm at all."

Hravn took a horn of ale from Ole and passed it to Ketel, before taking one for himself. "I think we'll make it fifteen. I've a mind to take Edie's priest, Brother Cedd, with us. He speaks Norman French and a second pair of ears won't go amiss," adding as an afterthought, "and of course if there are any Bretons our Cumbric will see us by too."

As Ketel nodded agreement, Hravn turned to his masters-at-arms. "Ketel and I have a lot to discuss, can you leave us please and stand the men by for tomorrow. Ole, find Edie, this involves her too."

Ketel spoke quickly, keen to still the storm that Howel's clash with Ealdgith had provoked. "Before Edie joins us, let me tell you that my father's a fool. I counselled him against sending Howel with the jagger train, but pride and greed got the better of him. The truth be known, he resents being told what to do, just as he resents Norman control of our southern lands. I'd warned him that you would have no choice about stopping him. You are the Earl's man after all."

Hravn let Ketel talk. He could see that the young man was an ally and was trying to make amends.

Ketel chuckled suddenly, "My father wasn't prepared for Lady Edie though, and nor was Howel. She certainly has Howel's loyalty now, and that is not easily won. I was there when he reported to my father that her presence alone is enough to quell a fight. He went as red as those embers when he read her letter, before throwing it in the fire. He didn't say what she wrote, but it was enough for him to say that the matter is at an end...mayhap it is that he has more respect for a woman that can write as well as fight. One thing's for certain, there won't be any more jagger trains over your lands, we'll send everything by sea from now."

"That's all I need to hear. Thank you, Ketel." Hravn made no mention of his dealings with Finán.

*****

They left the next morning as dawn broke over the rim of the eastern fells and rode at a brisk canter along the stone road past Tibeia and south into Norman lands. Their horses' hooves clattered on the frost hardened ground. Hravn hoped to cover the dozen leagues to Sedberge by midday.

As they drew near to Sedberge, Hravn recalled how he and Ealdgith had cautiously approached the vill on their first visit two summers earlier, and how a storm had forced them to take sanctuary with Elfreda who ran a pie stall in the market. "Hey, Ole!" He gestured for his servant to join him as they paused on the side of the hill overlooking Sedberge from the north, "There's a lady down there with a pie with your name on it, and one for Sköll too. We'll call on her when our business at the castle is finished."

Turning to Ketel, who had ridden up alongside, he said, "The castle's just this side of the vill. They'd just finished building it when Edie and I were here two summers back. It looks like there's an outer bailey now, with a stake wall around it." He pointed to a high wooden palisade that stretched from a castle atop a rounded earthen motte, down towards the vill. "From what we heard the labour of building it half-killed the people."

Ketel nodded. "Aye, I see it. That blue and yellow pennant flying from the pole, I'm sure those are Roger of Poitou's colours."

*****

Hravn left Cenric and Ari with their sections to water their horses at the stables within the baily. He joined Ketel to follow the Constable up the steps to the hall on the first floor of the castle.

"Leave your swords with your servant...and that hound." The Constable spoke to Ketel in French and glanced at Ole to reinforce his point whilst he pointed to Sköll with his toe. Cedd translated quickly. Hravn nodded imperceptibly, accepting that this was Ketel's visit.

With a gruff, "My Lord Roger will see you now," the Constable ushered Ketel, Hravn, Godric and Cedd into the great hall. Despite his resolve not to show any emotion Hravn could not fail to be impressed. The hall's outer walls, made from freshly cut wood, were hung with embroidered tapestries. The inner walls, which were of white-washed wattle and daub, reflected light from the small windows and a fire in a brazier set upon flags in the middle of the room. Wood smoke drifted up to blacken the roof beams and the top of the whitewashed walls, before escaping through vents in the roof.

"Ketel, welcome." A blond youth, taller but no older than Ole, held out his hand in greeting. Hravn was immediately amazed at the paleness of his blue eyes.

"My Lord, Roger." Ketel replied in Norman French and stooped in a slight bow as he grasped the youth's hand.

Releasing Ketel's hand, Roger turned to a tall bald man on his right. The man, who wore a leather tunic and scarlet cloak, had been staring at Hravn since

241

they entered. His narrow-set, sunken brown eyes and hooked nose gave him a distinctly hawk-like look. "My counsellor, Hugh Fitzgibbon, will speak for me. I have arrived here but recently. Hugh is my father's trusted confidant and knows the affairs of my lands better than I do."

Hugh gave an upwards nod towards Ketel and spoke in a reedy voice that further emphasised his bird-like appearance. "We haven't met, though I have dealt with your father. Who are these others with you?"

Ketel ignored Hugh's arrogant manner and replied courteously, "My good friend and neighbour, Sir Hravn of Ravenstandale, his huscarle and priest. His priest understands Norman French and will speak for Sir Hravn."

"Ah...Sir Hravn. Before I talk of business with Ketel there is a matter upon which we need to be clear." Hugh gave a slight pause, barely long enough for Cedd to translate, but long enough to underline the menace in his voice. "My sources tell me that you have closed our border with Westmoringaland. Is that so?"

"It is." Hravn held Hugh's eyes, refusing to be intimidated by the cold stare and concealing his surprise that the Norman was so well informed.

"Why?"

Hravn spoke bluntly and slowly, to allow Cedd time to translate, and to emphasise each point. "By order of my King, the King of the Scots. Cumbraland and Westmoringaland are his. The border has for long been a lawless place. Lords and merchants have long suffered from reaving by a family known as the Pendragons. Our orders were clear when the lands were bestowed upon me and my wife, Lady Ealdgith of Hep and Ulueswater. We are to hold the border secure, with no scope for friction between your people and ours. The first task is complete, the Pendragons are dead. As Ketel will tell you, the border is now closed to trade, even to his own family. The only passage across it is for Lord Elftred to access his lands nearby and in Amounderness, and for Ketel and Lady Christiana to visit her father who, as you know, is Ivo de Taillebois."

Hugh's tight thin smile chilled those looking at him. "The King of the Scots does not have that right, for he has given homage to King William."

Cedd hesitated, as he translated, the implications of the Norman's statement were immediately obvious. The hesitation forewarned Hravn and he made sure that he showed no reaction as Cedd spoke. If Malcolm had given homage it meant that William's campaign into Lothian had succeeded and that Gospatric's earldom was probably already forfeit.

Hravn strove to look unperturbed, "Really? I had not heard that. Until my King directs me otherwise his last orders to me must stand. I will bear in mind what you say and seek clarification, but until I hear otherwise the border is closed."

Hugh's eyes narrowed. "And just which border do you mean? I have it on good authority from Bishop Stigand, a man with a sound knowledge of English affairs and who was until late the Archbishop of Canterbury. He has said that the border is the line of the Eamont and Ulueswater. The English King Athelstan agreed this in a treaty with the Cumbrians and the Scots many years ago."

Hravn's face froze. He knew that Hugh was correct. He also knew that the treaty had lapsed long ago, but was wary of Norman ability to twist facts to suit their ends. The bastard King William's distorted excuse for claiming the English throne was testament to that.

Hravn suddenly slapped his thigh and laughed. "Aye, and the Romans once held this land too. Don't twist my people's history to suit your ends. Mayhap everything north of the wall from the Solway to the Tyne should be claimed by the Scots? What would your

King say to that? I know these lands and I know their borders!" He paused, starring hard at the bird-faced man. "Until I hear otherwise from my King there is little more to say. I understand that you have business to discuss with Ketel. I will take my leave now."

Hravn looked at Ketel with a hint of a smile and spoke in Cumbric, "Sorry, but we had to clear that up. I'll take one section and leave you the other for your protection. We'll wait in the market place." He then turned to Cedd, "Please tell the lad, Roger, that I appreciate his hospitality and mean him no offence, but the orders from my King cannot be gainsaid. Please stay with Ketel, as my ears and for his protection."

Hravn turned on his heel and left the room. Godric followed.

"What a revolting little weasel skitta," Godric muttered under his breath as they buckled on their swords in the outer chamber.

"I agree. He got my message alright, but I fear he won't heed it. We will need to have a tighter hold on the border, that's for certain. In the meantime, let's get Ole that pie."

*****

"Where is everyone?" Hravn leaned from his saddle as he spoke to the only man in the market place. The small, rough-cobbled, square was empty, devoid of stalls.

The man, roughly dressed in threadbare clothes, flinched instinctively before speaking. "You're not Norman, Lord?"

Hravn smiled reassuringly, "No, Cumbric. Be assured I have no more liking for the Normans than you, or any good Englishman. But, where is everyone?

"Three days in seven we must give free labour to the...bastard." He glanced fearfully at the castle. The market has collapsed, no one has money to spend nor goods to barter anymore."

Hravn swung down from the saddle, dipped his hand into his waist pouch and passed the man a few coins. "These might help. I feared life might have got worse. Is the goodwife Elfreda nearby? She once gave me shelter and I would repay the favour."

The man stared in surprise, then nodded. "You mean the widow Elfreda. Aelnod died last winter."

Hravn grimaced, "I see. Where will I find her?"

"At home, her lads will be in the fields 'til dusk. She clings on like the rest of us." The man glanced about and saw that the seven armed men were beginning to draw attention. "I must go Lord."

Hravn nodded, "Thank you." He turned to Godric and Ole. "Godric come with me, it's only a short walk. Ole, take the horses and stay with Ari. I need to find our pie woman." He led off across the market place and entered a small lane of narrow timber-framed cottages. Towards the end, Hravn rapped sharply on a half-open door. It swung back slowly.

Hravn stepped back from the door as he realised that he was blocking what little light there was. The single room was gloomy and felt cold, the few pieces of kindling in the hearth were unlit. As he moved Hravn heard a gasp from across the room.

"What? Who...is that Sköll?" Hravn followed as the hound ran in.

"Elfreda, sorry, I didn't mean to frighten you. Yes, its Sköll and Hravn. My friend, Godric, too." He smiled reassuringly as he spoke to a stocky dark-haired middle-aged woman. Even in the gloom of the unlit house he could see that she had lost weight and turned greyer in the last two years.

"How can it be? You're dressed as a man of war and," Elfreda looked nervously at Godric as she reached down to stroke Sköll's head, "you have a warrior with you. Are you in the pay of the Normans?"

Hravn laughed as he touched her arm gently. "No, but they might pay to have my head on a pike. Shall we sit whilst Godric puts a flame to that kindling of yours?" As Elfreda sat backwards onto a milking stool, Hravn pulled another towards him and sat beside her.

"There is a lot to tell, more than we have time for now. Suffice to say, fate has been kind. Edie, who I introduced as my cousin Eadmund is my wife, Ealdgith. We felt it safer for her to appear to be a boy. She is niece to Earl Gospatric and, through him, we now have lands across the border in Westmoringaland. I am here with Lord Ketel, a friend who has land on both sides and must perforce deal with that creature in the tower." He jerked his thumb in the direction of the castle.

Elfreda had a slight twinkle in her otherwise sad eyes as she interrupted. "I did wonder about Edie. There are things a woman can tell."

Hravn nodded with a secretive smile. "Mmm, be that as it may. I've heard about Aelnod and I can see what life here has become for you. There is nothing I can do to change that, but I can offer you a new life as a free woman. Your sons too. But you would need to leave tonight and leave all behind."

Elfreda gasped. "We'd be flogged and branded, or worse. Fitzgibbon is a harsh lord."

Hravn squeezed Elfreda's hand. "I have his measure already. I'm sure he would if he could, but he won't. I have a dozen men with me, all armed as Godric."

Elreda's jaw dropped. Hravn couldn't tell if it was in fear or with relief, then he saw tears in her eyes. "Join us, Edie has a place for a cook as good as you, and your lads will be welcome to serve with my men or to farm. There is land to spare. We will leave as soon as the light fades then ride over night. It will be slow as I don't have spare mounts."

Elfreda sobbed, nodding, "Yes, thank you, we are dying here. We all are."

Hravn smiled, still holding Elfreda's hand. "Good. You helped Edie and me once. It is nothing but a debt repaid. Now, pack what food you have and prepare a sack of clothes each. Say nothing outside the house and be ready come nightfall. Godric will fetch you."

As Hravn arrived back in the square and remounted he saw Ketel riding to join them. "He's a hard, mean bastard, that Fitzgibbon. I need to visit my estates to see what other markets there are for their produce. It will take longer than I planned."

Hravn laughed, leant across in his saddle and spoke quietly. "I'll leave you to it. I have just settled a debt and will relieve young Roger of four of his tenants tonight. I'll return home with Brother Cedd and Ari's section. Keep Cenric's section with you. A little show of force never goes amiss.

Hravn smiled cheekily as he watched Ketel's face. His friend's jaw dropped in surprise then broke into a grin as he realised just what Hravn intended.

*****

It was over a week later, with snow threatening, when Ketel returned to Hravn's hall. He left Cenric's men to feed and water the horses whilst he joined Hravn by the hearth. "I can see from your face that matters haven't gone well." Hravn said, as he pulled forward a stool for Ketel.

Ketel took a deep breath and shook his head slowly, "No they haven't. All the Norman manors are as ground down as Sedberge. They insist on wheat being grown instead of barley, at least where it can be, and prices have been forced down by the use of free labour. Any surpluses that our lands produce will have to be sent back to Cumbraland to fetch a fair price."

Hravn nodded and scratched his teeth with his forefinger whilst he thought. "I rather feared that after what I saw last week and from what Elfreda has told me. I can't open the Tibeia road for trade though. It would give Fitzgibbon and his like free rein to start to interfere on our lands."

"I know, that's what I thought. I'm minded to cart grain from our lands nearer the coast in Amounderness, up to Rengles and then load it on ships that have taken lead from Carleol to Ceaster."

Hravn's face creased in a frown as he realised that he would have to be open with Ketel and explain his own plans for shipping his lead from Rengles; cooperation was better than secrecy. He smiled again, "I agree. I have my own interest in Rengles, of which I'll tell you later. But there is a back way in from your more easterly lands; up the lake to Ameleseta, then over the high stone road down to Askham and join the road to Carleol. My men patrol it already."

Ketel laughed. "You're full of surprises, Hravn. Yes, that could work." Hravn stilled him with a flick of his hand and a cheeky grin.

"There is a price to pay. I have a desperate need for an armourer and a blacksmith. I have tried to employ my own man, but he is a woodcutter by trade. The number of men I'm now keeping in the field need their weapons and equipment properly looking after. Can you spare Cenhelm and Gamel?"

Ketel bit his lip, sucking air. "Mmm …. yes. I think I can persuade my father, particularly now that we can be more open about trade yet keep the border closed." He held out his hand, "We have a deal."

Chapter 21

Hravn pulled Ealdgith to him in a tight embrace, kissed her warmly, then as he stepped back said, "We'll be back the day after tomorrow. Orme has to understand the working of the manors at Askham and Bartun, and I can't see Fitzgibbon trying anything on in this weather." He raised his eyes towards the low yellow-grey clouds to emphasise his point then, placing his toe into his stirrup, he mounted and turned away, urging his horse to a trot. Orme followed with Osric and Ole.

Ealdgith watched the men ride out of sight then turned with a toss of her head; her news for Hravn would have to wait. She walked around to the back of the hall and entered the kitchen to look for Elfreda. The woman looked up as Ealdgith walked in. "Aha! Elfreda! Making pies again. Hravn will never forgive you if the men end up too fat to ride," Ealdgith teased her, "though I'm glad you're settling in. How about your lads?"

Elfreda smiled and tossed a scrap of meat to Hati. "Well, My Lady. They're changed men, thanks to you and Sir Hravn. Aesc, the eldest, is training with Eadwulf; Tata is helping as a stable lad; and Wemba seems determined to work lead with Edric at Patrichesdale. I've never known them so full of life. I just wish my Aelnod had lived to see it." A wistful look crossed her face and Ealdgith turned away with an understanding smile.

*****

Ealdgith dozed, half aware of the sound of the household, and woke as the grey half-light of early dawn filtered through the shutters of her chamber. A sudden clatter of hooves startled her and, jumping from her bed and grabbing a gown, she ran into the hall just as Eadwulf burst through the door.

"Bastard Normans, My Lady! We need to ready the men." He spoke, breathless, stopping as Ulf and Godric ran in rubbing bleary eyes and pulling on clothes.

"Come, sit, all of you. Ada, fetch some small beer." Ealdgith pulled a stool from the beside the table and sat by the newly lit fire in the hearth. Now, Eadwulf, tell us all, but slowly."

"Our men at Tibeia lit the beacon in the night and sent a rider to warn me. They saw light from a fire a league down river last night. Two went to look and heard Norman voices. They can't be sure but there were at least a dozen men-at-arms there, with horses. The men at Ofertun are stood by. I've given orders for the Tibeia beacon to be relit if there is any movement towards us."

Ealdgith sensed her men were waiting for her to take a lead. "Good. Hravn said that he expected some sort of reaction to our closing the border after he had words with Hugh Fitzgibbon at Sedberge, but he thought this threat of snow would deter anything for the time being. They're up to something, but whether it's looking for our outposts, checking our reactions, probing, or something more sinister, I can't say."

She came to a decision. "Eadwulf, move the Ofertun men to the high ground overlooking Tibeia. Have them follow any movement and send a rider back to keep us informed. They are to keep the Normans in sight but are to keep their distance and not get engaged in a fight. Ulf, ready the reserve and move them to Ofertun. You, Godric and I will go with them. Brother Cedd too, as he speaks Norman." As they nodded agreement Ealdgith turned to Ada. "I want you to warn Hravn. He will be at Askham or Bartun. You know where they are, don't you?" Ada nodded whilst Ealdgith continued, "Take Hati and Aesc, Elfrida's son. He's not trained to fight a battle yet, but he can handle himself well enough to protect you. Go now. Tell Hravn what my orders to Ulf and Eadwulf are, and ask him to return immediately."

Ealdgith looked at the three men. "If they move into our lands we have no option other than to fight. It is a move not only against us but, after Hravn's warning to Fitzgibbon, it is also a challenge to the authority of the Scots' King. Do you agree?"

"Aye, we do, Edie." Ulf spoke for his deputies, then briefed Eadwulf. "Return to Ofertun now and I'll bring up the reserve within the hour. Have your cook get some sort of meal ready for us. We all fight better on a full stomach." He banged the table with his fist. "If we give Fitzgibbon a hard lesson now, it will save us lives in the future."

"Yes, Ulf," Ealdgith cautioned, standing up with a stern look around the table, "but make sure the men know that fighting Norman men-at-arms is not the same as the Pendragons."

Ealdgith stood alongside Ulf and Godric, watching the men of the four reserve sections finish a quick meal, and adjust and clean their weapons and equipment in the small fort at Ofertun. It was dull and gloomy with no indication that the day would get any brighter. "I wish it would snow," Ealdgith looked up at the clouds. "If it did, the Normans wouldn't risk being cut off and vulnerable to us following their tracks."

"Aye, My Lady, but if anything, it'll rain. Just so long as the mist doesn't clag-in we'll be able to keep our eyes on them." Godric shrugged then paused and pointed. "Look, who's that riding in, and why's he leading a spare pony?"

The man wheeled and halted, to dismount by Eadwulf who directed him to Ealdgith and Ulf. "They're coming, My Lady, north on the stone road. They passed the other side of the river from the stone fort and …

251

Sigmund is dead. We were trying to get close enough to count them and he went forward leaving his pony with me. Their scouts spotted him and rode him down, they ... hacked him to death. I've come straight here, but I know where his body is and will recover it." Ealdgith slowed him with a touch on his arm. "It's hard to count them, but I think there are a half dozen checking the route then mayhap up to a score following half a league behind. What we can see is that their shields are blue with a yellow flash."

Ealdgith looked from Ulf to Eadwulf. "Roger of Poitou's colours. That confirms what we thought."

"Aye, and the bastards want a fight. They mean to have you and Hravn, there's no doubting that now that they have slain one of ours." Ulf's bluntness shook Ealdgith. She turned back to the rider.

"How fast are they moving?"

"We've not long, My Lady. Mayhap a quarter of an hour."

"What!" Ealdgith looked aghast.

Ulf took charge. "We ride, now. If they are on the stone road they will be heading for the manor at Crosebi Raveneswart. Edie, this has to be an attack against you and Hravn."

"Yes, agreed. We have to ambush them, we can't fight in the open, not against those numbers and with just the reserve. But we need time."

Eadwulf spoke. "The ford on this side of the manor is the place. Its wooded all around and they'll be channelled into the valley where it narrows.

"You're right, Eadwulf. Ulf and I can take the main party, but you will need to get ahead and block the scouts. If they are moving half a league ahead they could be almost at the manor before the main party cross the ford, though I would expect them to stop short of the manor and wait. Go now and take Dunstan's section. Warn those in the manor to run for the woods to the south. Get your men into the woods on the ridge to the west of the road. Ambush them if you can, otherwise charge down into them if they threaten the manor or wait until you hear our ambush, then take them from behind when they return to investigate. Are you clear on that?

"Yes, My Lady. We'll see the bastards dead before the day is done."

"Ulf, we need to get to the ford. When we get there, you take the south bank with Ari, I'll take the crossing with Cenric, and Godric, you are to take the north bank with Hrodulf. We'll talk again when we are in position. Cedd, stay with me."

Ulf interrupted, "Aye, agreed Edie, but the men based here need to get out now and then block the road to any who flee back from our ambush. I'll warn them."

They ran to their respective sections, shouted orders, quenched the hearth fires and were gone within five minutes.

Ealdgith's mind raced as she galloped northward along the stone road. She tried to work out just how much time they had. Four leagues was a long gallop, but if they covered it in half an hour they would have bought as much time again. Was it enough for the horses to recover and for them all to get into position for an ambush? She hoped so. She hoped also that the Norman advance party wouldn't see them on the long straight road, but realised with relief that if she couldn't see more than three furlongs in the gloom and mist, then nor could the Normans.

When Ealdgith arrived at the ford, Ulf was already dismounted and directing Ari's section into ambush positions in the trees overlooking the stone road just to the other side of the ford. He called across to her, "We'll tether the horses behind the wood. It's too dense for them within the trees."

"You're right. At least the Normans would have to dismount to pursue us into the trees, and I can't see them doing that, though it means we will lose time if

253

we have to regain our horses and remount to pursue them."

Godric overheard and shouted, "There's a field behind the strip of trees in which I've placed my men, My Lady. Tether your horses there and you'll be able to get to them fast enough. It's screened from the road so they won't be seen by the advance party."

Ealdgith smiled her appreciation and ran to position her own section where they could cover the ford. Once she was satisfied, she called for Ulf and Godric to join her.

"What do you think, Ulf? Should we hit horses or men first?"

"First hit the horses, Edie, then the men. That should cause enough chaos, prevent immediate escape and give us static targets on the ground. The men have enough bolts each to keep up a steady rate for two to three minutes."

"Good. Ulf, I want your men to hit the first four just as they are about to leave the ambush site. That will be the signal for us all, and that way we should have drawn most of them into the killing area before we strike. Godric, you'll have to be prepared to deal with any who try and work their way around behind or try to escape."

Godric grinned, "You've no worry there, My Lady. This is what we've trained for."

She smiled appreciatively. "Let's get settled then. Their advance party can't be far away."

Ealdgith listened as the woods along the riverbank and roadside returned to normal. Bird song rang out and trees dripped in an atmosphere of winter stillness.

The rapid clack of hooves on the stone road heralded the arrival of the Norman scouts. They moved in pairs, keeping each other in sight about a furlong apart on the straight track, but bunched closer together as they made their way slowly across the ford. The leading pair moved cautiously into the muddied water and Ealdgith felt a momentary panic: had they noticed footprints and hoof marks? Then the leading man-at-arms looked backwards and waved the next group forward before spurring his horse onward towards the next bend in the road.

Meanwhile, Eadwulf had sent Dunstan to warn the household in the manor and then positioned his section of men behind a line of trees on a long spur, west of the vill, that overlooked the route half a furlong below.

Time dragged as he watched. The land didn't lend itself to the sort of close-in ambush for which they had trained. The road was beyond effective crossbow range and he knew that if they attacked the Normans it would have to be in a downhill charge into their flank. Speed and surprise were their only advantages. The road curved around the hillside below to rise slowly towards the limit of his view, barely two furlongs away. He stilled and clicked his fingers to attract Dunstan's attention. Two men had come into view and paused as they saw the vill and manor house in the valley below. Two more joined them, then moments later another two.

The men sat on their horses, studying the buildings, then wheeled and moved back a short distance. Eadwulf realised that they were watching the manor from dead ground, so that they could see without being seen. They were obviously well trained. It was obvious also that they were waiting for the main party and Eadwulf realised that he would either have to wait until the main party was ambushed, and then react to whatever the scouting party did, or move his men so that they could regain the advantage of higher ground, and then attack; albeit with the risk that their movement would give them away. He was about to move when he heard a distant scream. The six Normans turned and looked back towards the ford.

*****

Ealdgith stood behind one of the many oak trees in the small forest, her bow poised, an arrow fitted to the string, her eyes measuring the distance to the various aiming marks within her allotted arc. Twelve more arrows were lined up in front of her. She breathed slowly, to calm herself, and listened for any sound of the approaching Normans or the first clash of Eadwulf's attack on the scouts.

A slight movement to her right caught her attention and she saw Godric adjust one of his men's positions so that he could better cover their right flank. She nodded approval, worried that when Ulf engaged the leading riders the tail of the column would not be within Godric's killing area. Godric glanced quickly to his right them returned swiftly to his own position, flashing an upturned thumb towards Ealdgith.

The Normans arrived at a brisk trot, riding in pairs twenty paces apart. Ealdgith knew immediately that, unless the men-at-arms bunched when crossing the ford, the column was longer than the front she had allocated. She pushed her left arm forward to draw her bow and tracked the riders as they began to cross the ford. She let six riders past, then focussed on the seventh. Knowing that her bow lacked the strength to shoot an arrow through mail at that range, she concentrated on his horse's neck.

The sudden thwack of arrow and bolt heads against metal and flesh signalled the attack. Horse after horse squealed and reared in pain and shock. Some threw their riders, others bolted. Ealdgith's target sank to its knees and blocked the middle of the ford.

Ealdgith could shoot arrows quicker than her men could reload their crossbows, and concentrated on hitting the horses in front of her. As she shot, she watched men-at-arms tumble, writhing. Two ran towards the edge of the trees, swords drawn, but were hit and thrown backwards by the impact of heavy bolts ripping into their chests. She saw too that there was a gap between Ulf's killing area and her own. The third pair of riders spurred their horses and galloped forward, hunched low over their mounts, to escape the ambush.

Godric watched the riders pass with trepidation, he knew some would escape the killing zone. As Ulf's attack shattered the woodland peace, he saw that the last pair were too distant to engage. He shouted to Wulf who was next in line on his left. "The last but one pair. Take the nearest, I'll take the other." Both horses reared as bolts stabbed into them. One horse bolted, dragging its rider by the leg, the other sank down and rolled onto the man on the ground.

Godric placed the toe of his boot into his crossbow stirrup, pulled back on the stave to re-cock the bow, then reloaded as he ran. He joined Hrodgar over to his right. As he moved he saw the last two men-at-arms wheel their horses and climb the bank through the trees past where their own mounts were tethered. "Hrodgar, get ready. They'll try and take us from our flank," he yelled as he braced himself by a tree on the edge of their open flank. The two men-at-arms dismounted and ran forward, certain that their way was clear. Godric waited. He was keen to retain the advantage of surprise and knew that he would have just the one shot. Hrodgar followed the housecarl's lead. As Godric squeezed the trigger he was confident that the bolt would find its mark. He barely waited to see the Norman jerk and fall, his chest and lungs ripped apart, before he turned and ran, shouting for Hrodgar to reload and follow.

Ulf cursed as the two Normans charged past him, escaping the killing area and intent on joining the six scouts. He shot one more bolt then paused to see if any Normans still stood. None did. "Hold!" He shouted loudly. His voice reverberated through the trees. "Hold! Ari, take your men forward and check the bodies. I want mail and weapons recovered. Edie, Godric, we need to mount and give chase. There are still eight of the bastards mounted and out there. I'll meet you above the woods." He turned and clambered up through the trees to regain his tethered horse.

Ealdgith called across the ford. "Cedd, stay here. See to any who live and check who we may have killed. It's possible that Fitzgibbon led them. I doubt that he would have allowed Roger of Poitou to be involved." She ran across to where Godric was already checking that Hrodulf and Cenric's sections were mounted. He glanced at her to make sure that she was ready, then wheeled his horse to face up the hill. "We'll lead, My Lady, Cenric and Hrodulf will follow on either flank." As they sped across the firm turf, Ulf joined from their right.

*****

Eadwulf was very aware that the six Normans would cover the half league back to the ford within five minutes and that they could take Ealdgith's party either in the flank, or whilst they were dismounted checking the bodies in the killing area. Yelling at Dunstan and his section to follow, he urged them on. "Catch the bastards. Take them in the rear before they get to the ford." He galloped across the turf, trying to keep the Normans in sight as he followed the curve of the hillside up and around in an attempt to gain height and cut the corner.

Eadwulf lashed his horse hard and gradually drew ahead of the rest of his men. As the side of the hillside straightened he saw that the Norman scouts were only fifty paces ahead and fifty feet below him. Calculating that he could intercept them several furlongs before they reached the wood and the ford,

Eadwulf aimed at a point a hundred paces in front of the Normans. He glanced over his shoulder, Dunstan was over a hundred paces behind. Eadwulf readied his spear in his hand and prepared his final charge.

Suddenly, with no warning, the rear two Normans wheeled around and split apart. Within seconds they were behind Eadwulf. Swinging sharply to his right, he flung his spear at the Norman above him with a growl of anger, then started to draw his sword. Sensing movement behind him, he slashed backwards with the blade, then jerked forward with a gasp of shock and pain as the second Norman's spear stabbed into the small of his back. As Eadwulf pitched forward the first Norman sliced his sword viciously down, cutting through mail and leather into Eadwulf's bowels.

The two men turned again and, as Eadwulf slid to the ground, galloped off striving to catch their compatriots.

Dunstan saw Eadwulf fall and screamed in anger and anguish. He had barely time to look down at Eadwulf's bleeding body before he closed with the nearest Norman and thrust his spear at the horse's hind quarters. The embedded spear was ripped from his hand as the galloping animal bucked, then tripped and rolled forward taking its rider with it, crushing him. Dunstan left the man for his men to deal with and slashed forward with his sword at the second Norman as he turned to face him. The Norman blocked the blow with his shield and pushed Dunstan's sword back against his chest, whilst drawing his own weapon. The blade slid from its scabbard, but was then flung into the air as Snorri's spear thrust into his side with sufficient force to throw him from the saddle.

Dunstan's heart leapt as he looked past the fleeing Normans to see a mass of riders swarming over the edge of the hillside above the woods pursuing two horsemen who had just joined the remaining four scouts. "Stay with Eadwulf, Snorri. We'll give chase."

As Ealdgith galloped over the crest of the spur, she saw strung out groups of horsemen racing towards her. She saw two close with their pursuer and one man fall, and then a second fight in which two more bodies fell, but in the misty gloom she couldn't tell them apart. Suddenly, she could see the blue and yellow of the Norman shields and she identified their enemy.

As Ulf and Godric screamed at the men on their flanks to close in, Ealdgith eased her horse back so that she fitted in behind them, in the apex of an arrowhead of charging horses, hard steel and spear points.

The clash came quickly. The strung-out Normans lacked the mass to stop the armed phalanx as it crashed into them. Ealdgith gasped as Norman horses and men fell away on either side. Seconds later, Godric and Ulf peeled apart, breaking the phalanx as they wheeled the sections around to deal with any Normans still fighting. Two were, mounted either side of a man with a thin hawk-like face. He dropped his shield and sword and yielded to Ulf as men hacked his compatriots from their saddles.

Ealdgith continued forward, feeling suddenly lonely and exposed she realised just how much she had come to depend on Ada riding behind her and Hati at her side. As she neared the fallen bodies she could tell that two were Norman, but the furthest away had carried a black and red shield that now lay beside him. She saw, too, that Snorri was bent over him gently easing his helmet from his head. "Eadwulf!" She gasped to herself.

Dropping quickly from her horse Ealdgith ran to the stricken warrior, catching Snorri's expression as he looked up and slowly shook his head. Eadwulf lay on his back. Thick sticky blood pooled on the grass beneath him.

When Ealdgith saw the chalk-white face and blue tinged lips she knew that Eadwulf could not be saved. She pulled off her gloves and placed her hands gently against his cheeks.

"Edie, you came." Eadwulf spoke softly. His breath rasped. "I should never have doubted you when I met you, My Lady."

Ealdgith stopped him with a touch of her fingers to his lips. "That is past, Eadwulf. I know I had to prove myself to you, it is only right. And you have proved yourself to me, time and time again, as a strong and courageous master-at-arms."

He smiled faintly, then winced. "I'm cold. T..There's so much pain."

Ealdgith lent close to Eadwulf and held his eyes with hers. "I can't save you. You know that. But I can ease your passing if you want me to. A warrior's death, but painless." She watched, tears dripping, as Eadwulf nodded slowly.

"Snorri, there is a leather roll in my rear saddle bag. Quickly please." Ealdgith kept her face close to Eadwulf's, smiling gently, until Snorri returned. She deftly undid the fastening and removed a small packet of folded linen containing coarse-ground black seeds. Without being asked Snorri passed her his leather water flagon.

Ealdgith looked again at Eadwulf. "Sleep now," and gently kissed Eadwulf's forehead. As Eadwulf opened his lips she dropped the powder into his mouth and poured a trickle of water slowly from the flagon.

Eadwulf forced a weak smile, murmured "Thank you," then closed his eyes. Ealdgith sat by him, her fingers gently feeling the pulse in Eadwulf's neck until moments later she turned a tear stricken face to Snorri. "He's gone."

He nodded, his hand on Ealdgith's shoulder, tears in his eyes, until the sound of hooves drumming across the turf drew their attention.

Godric arrived in haste. "Quickly, My Lady. We've taken their leader alive. He wants to yield to Ulf, but Ulf will have none of it, saying only you can take his surrender...What! No! It can't be." Godric saw that the body was Eadwulf. He dropped from his saddle and knelt by him, biting his lip.

"Stay with him Godric and say your farewells. Snorri, go to the hall and fetch blankets to wrap Eadwulf in and, if anyone is there, tell them it is safe for all to return." Ealdgith mounted and rode slowly across to where Ulf held his sword to the throat of a tall hawk-faced man. She needed a moment to regain her composure and to decide how to handle him. "Fetch Brother Cedd from the ford," she shouted to Cenric.

"He's on his way, My Lady," Cenric called back.

Ealdgith removed her helmet and hung it from her pommel, shook her hair free, and dismounted slowly. As she looked around she could see the bodies of six Normans and one of her own lying on the grass. A seventh Norman sat up, blood streaming from a head wound. Bondi stood behind him, his hand clutched to his arm trying to stem blood from a deep sword slash. Sword in hand, she strode purposefully towards Ulf and his prisoner just as Cedd came galloping up the hill.

"He's Hugh Fitzgibbon, My Lady. Just as you suspected. I recognise him."

"Thank you, Cedd." Ealdgith stopped in front of the Norman, her hands resting on the pommel of her sword as she held it point down. "You can lower your sword now, Ulf. You were right to refuse his surrender, though mayhap it would have been easier if he were dead." Fitzgibbon's arrogant stare failed to intimidate her. She felt only cold anger buoyed by adrenaline.

Ealdgith spoke through Brother Cedd and could tell from the intonation of his voice that he translated the sentiment as well as the message of her words.

As Fitzgibbon folded his arms and raised his chin imperiously Ealdgith snapped at him icily. "Don't presume to relax in front of me Fitzgibbon! I know who you are and why you came." She stared into his eyes and sensed the hint of a smirk as he appreciated her feminine beauty and the quality of her armour. She could also read his arrogance and the contempt in which he held women; why did men's eyes always give them away?

Ulf flicked his sword point up in line with Fitzgibbon's eyes until the Norman pulled himself into a more respectable stance.

"Three of my men are dead, including my loyal and trusted master-at-arms, and another has wounds that I would rather attend to than spend time talking to you."

Ealdgith held his gaze. "I know your type, Fitzgibbon. I could block you in a cave and let you rot, or mayhap let my men have their revenge upon your body. That right is mine after your attempt on my life. But if you yield to me, as a Lady, I will have a duty to you. I'll remind you though that this is not Norman land. English women have rights of ownership here that you now deny on the lands you have stolen, just as my land in Ghellinges-scir was stolen. Deal with me, as is my right, on my land, and I will deal with you as is your right as my prisoner. Otherwise..." She let the implication hang in the air and watched his face as Cedd translated. Fitzgibbon lowered his gaze and looked straight at Ealdgith.

Just then, Ealdgith heard a low whine and felt a dog nuzzle her hip. Hati! She dropped a hand to her side and felt his soft warm tongue gently lick her fingers. As fresh confidence surged through her, she realised that Hravn must be back too. She turned her attention back to the prisoner.

"You have one chance, Fitzgibbon. Chose the right answer now and you will not be harmed. One word will suffice. Do you yield to me?"

Fitzgibbon stared at Ealdgith and took a deep breath as if to argue, but then nodded his head. "Yes, I do. I yield to you, Lady Ealdgith." He lowered his chin and looked straight at Ealdgith. "May I ask, Lady Ealdgith, why it is that your men serve a woman so readily?"

Ealdgith gave a surprised laugh, but she did not smile. "Ulf. You have known me since I was a child. Tell him."

Ulf hesitated, embarrassed, but proud to have been asked. "My Lady. You respect the value of our lives, you take risks that we would not, you are not afraid to face a man sword to sword, you place our welfare, and that of all your people, before your own and...you tend to our wounds. There is barely a man who can better you."

Ealdgith gave Ulf a gracious smile. "Thank you, Ulf. Now, Fitzgibbon, there you have it. Leadership by example. It's not something I've seen in many of your country men." She paused, waiting for a response. Fitzgibbon stood, stern-faced, silent.

"I know full well that my husband explained to you clearly why we have closed this border in the name of the King of the Scots, and yet you chose to flout that ruling and came here to threaten our safety. I care not for the reason why. You clearly transgressed and your men paid a high price for your arrogance. However, it has potentially drawn your Lord, Roger of Poitou, and through him his father, into conflict with me and my King. Remember, those lords are my equals, not you. I have the blood of an English queen in my veins and carry her sword. I suggest that you think on that."

Ealdgith knew she was stretching the truth, but Fitzgibbon wasn't to know and she wanted to emphasise her point. "This is the end of the matter between you and me as far as I am concerned. I can, however, only release you to return to your master if you give me your sworn undertaking, witnessed by my priest..." Ealdgith gestured to Cedd with her hand, "...that you will ensure that there are no further transgressions. Oh, and be certain that I will ensure that my King knows of all that has happened. Do you so swear?"

"I swear that there will be no further transgression over your borders, Lady Ealdgith." Fitzgibbon spoke reluctantly.

Ealdgith turned at the noise of movement behind her. "Hravn!"

Hravn stepped forward, "I arrived a few moments ago, just in time to hear your words. The day is yours, Edie, and you ended it well." He gave Ealdgith the warmest of smiles then stood square in front of the Norman.

"Fitzgibbon. An oath to my wife is an oath to me too. Now, there is daylight left. Our men will escort you to the edge of our land. Where you go thereafter is your concern, but do not return here." He turned to Ulf. "Have one of the sections escort him now. We have more important matters to attend to. Our men need our attention and we have dead to bury."

"One thing more." Ealdgith interrupted. Your wounded will stay here whilst I tend to them. Those who recover will be free to return to you, should they so choose.

Fitzgibbon frowned. "Choice? They have no choice. Returning is their duty."

"No, Fitzgibbon, you misunderstand me." Ealdgith's tone was icy, "I will accept the service of any man who swears to me. I will offer them that choice. Wait and see."

*****

265

Two mornings later Hravn and Ealdgith lay late in bed. As Hravn started to get up Ealdgith pulled him back down and took his hand. Placing it on her stomach she whispered quietly. "You might not feel new life there just yet, but soon, very soon, you will."

Aere Yule 1073

Chapter 22

"Here, Ada, take Little Bear. He's grizzling but at five months he's too young to be teething. Let him suck on you little finger whilst I join Hravn in his council."

Ada took the baby gently into her arms. "His eyes are the spit of Hravn's father, I can see why he is his namesake."

As Ealdgith passed her baby son to Ada, she kissed him gently on his head, then left the chamber and entered the hall.

"Take a seat, Edie." Hravn welcomed her as Godric stood and pulled back the chair next to Hravn. "We were just saying that it is a year to the day since Fitzgibbon's raid and that the peace seems to have held."

"Thank goodness for that," Ealdgith agreed, "so much else has happened that we couldn't have coped with more conflict. Orme told me that at last we are able to replenish my uncle's treasure chests. The lead is finally turning a profit."

"It is that." Hravn looked around the table. "You all need to know that Edric has now opened a new mine across the valley from the first, it is near Hartsop. It seems to be an extension of the same vein. With luck, we'll soon be sending twice as much lead to Rengles. Now, you might be wondering why I have asked Leolin to join us from Mallerstang. I'll let him explain."

Leolin stood, obviously embarrassed by the attention. "Well, as you know Lord, we had a good harvest. The best for years without the yoke of the Pendragons to hold us back. But, more than that, the men have had time to explore what they long thought was a vein of lead. I'm please to say now that we definitely have lead in Mallerstang too, and mayhap some coal, for we have found traces of that as well."

"Thank you Leolin. You've done well, you all have. Be sure to pass my appreciation on." Hravn looked around the table with a sparkle in his eye. "When Lencten comes, I'll ask Frode and our friends in Kelda to help us out once more. If there really is lead in Mallerstang we can spread the wealth from three mines right across our estates and continue to support enough men to keep the border and our jagger routes secure. Ketel certainly appreciates the service that our escorts provide."

Hravn turned to Ealdgith. "Edie, I think we need to share the contents of the letter you received from Lord Elftred."

She nodded. "In fact, I have two letters. One from Lord Elftred, as Hravn says, and a second from my uncle, the Earl, passed to me by Brother Patrick. There is much to tell. My uncle has flouted the terms of the two kings' agreement and has left Flanders for Scotland. It would appear that he has King Malcolm's blessing and has been granted lands in Dunbar that border those he was forced to forfeit last year. His health isn't good though and, although Lord Elftred doesn't say as much, reading between the lines of my uncle's letter, I fear that he may not live long. His children by his first marriage are now all at Carleol, from where Dolfin will rule us all, under Lord Elftred's guidance. Walthoef has also been given the lordship of Allerdale in his own right. That places the port of Rengles in his hands, although as he is still but a child, control will again rest with Elftred. Both Elftred and my uncle infer that King Malcolm's hold on Cumbraland is now very weak. It really is all down to Dolphin and Elftred now, and us of course."

Hravn took charge of the meeting again. "Thanks Edie. At least we now know where we stand, and I'm glad to say that I am getting on with Lord Elftred much better now that we have a proper understanding. I can't see that changing. Ulf, how are the border patrols?"

"Good, Lord. We've recovered from our losses a year ago and created a fifth section in the reserve. Escorting the jaggers and Lord Ketel's journeys south of Ameleseta are keeping them well occupied. The lads doing the patrols are on top of things too. We've developed good relations with many of the outlying farms and small vills south of the border. They keep us well informed. It helps that we pay our way with them though, and I sense that the Normans are loathe to push too far into the valleys. They stick to the manors where they feel safe and can tax."

"And what of the two Bretons whose wounds I attended?" Ealdgith asked.

"Ah, both are good soldiers, Edie. It seems their love of the Normans is no more than ours. Both were pleased to escape Fitzgibbon's service and have given good advice about Norman tactics. They are in the reserve now."

Hravn pushed his chair back, smiling, "We can all take pride in a good year's work. It was a hard struggle at times to get here, and there will doubtless be struggles ahead. Before we get ready for Yuletide there is one last undertaking for us all."

Hravn looked around the table. "Before we left Bebbanburge the Earl told me about a local custom on a fell top above Kircabi Stephan. It's called Standards Rigg, and since well into the days of the old gods those who hold land hereabouts have built their cairn on its summit. Please honour Edie and me and join us tomorrow with a rock in your hand. We will build the biggest cairn yet.

~~~~~

Whatever the future holds for Hravn and Ealdgith,
it will always be uncertain. The North rebelled again
in 1080, and then in 1092 the new English King,
William Rufus, invaded Cumberland and
Westmorland. Hravn and Ealdgith may yet return.

Glossary

Aefter Yule. After Yule. January; the month after the Yuletide festival that became Christmas.

Aere Yule. Before Yule. December.

Ærraliða and Æfteraliða. See Liða.

Atheling. Old English. A royal prince eligible to be king. Here, specifically, Edgar the Atheling, who was elected King of England by the Witenagemot in 1066, but never crowned.

Blōtmonath. November. The month of blood sacrifices.

Breeks. Breeches. From Old English, brec. Northern dialect.

Burh. A Saxon fortified settlement. Typically a timber-faced bank and ditch with a palisade on top, enclosing a manor house and community.

Castle. A European innovation, castles originated in the 9th and 10th centuries. Many castles were built originally from earth and timber, but had their defences replaced later by stone. The motte and bailey castle was introduced to England by the Normans. It consisted of a circular moat surrounding an earth mound (motte) upon which a wooden keep (tower) was built. The baily was a wooden palisade inside the moat that encompassed the motte and flat land upon which the castle's domestic buildings were built.

Dale. Old English and Norse for a valley.

Ealdfader. Grandfather.

Ealdmoder. Grandmother.

Earl. An Earl is a member of the nobility. The title is Anglo-Saxon, akin to the Scandinavian form: Jarl.

Ēostre. Easter

Eostremonath. April. After, Eostre, goddess of spring and fertility.

Fader. Father.

Fell. Norse for a mountain or high moorland.

Freyja. Norse. Goddess of love, fertility, and battle.

Furlong. Old English. An eighth of a statute mile or 200 metres.

Haerfest. Harvest. Autumn.

Hāligmonath. September. Holy month.

Hall. Old English: Heall, a large house.

Hefted. The instinctive ability of some breeds of sheep, including Cumbrian herdwicks, to know intimately the land where they live and to which they return if moved from their heft.

Hel. Queen of Helheim, the Norse underworld.

Hlafmaesse Day. Lammas Day, or loaf-mass day. Traditionally the first of August, when the first grain from the harvest would be used to bake bread.

Holmganga. Norse: "going to an island", a special place for a duel governed by rules of combat.

Hrēðmonath. March. Hreða, or Rheda's month. A Germanic fertility goddess.

Humbre. River Humber.

Hundred. Most of the English shires were divided into 'Hundreds;' groups of 100 'Hides'.

Jagger. Northern English. Someone who controls a team of packhorses. A Jagger way = a packhorse trail. Jagger train = a line of packhorses led by one rider.

League. A league is a classical unit of length. The word originally meant the distance a person could walk in an hour. Its distance has been defined variously as between one and a half and three miles. I have used the Roman league which is 7,500 feet or one and a half miles.

Lencten. Spring.

Liða. June and July were together known as Liða, an Old English word meaning "mild" or "gentle," which referred to the period of warm, seasonable weather either side of Midsummer. To differentiate between the two, June was sometimes known as Ærraliða, or "before-mild," and July was Æfteraliða, or "after-mild."

Logi. Norse god of fire.

Longhouse. A Viking equivalent of the English manor house, typically 5 to 7 metres wide and anywhere from 15 to 75 metres long, depending on the wealth and social position of the owner.

Mǣresēa. River Mersey. Old English. Mǣres: boundary; ēa: river.

Manor. An estate of land. The manor is often described as the basic feudal unit of tenure. A manor was akin to the modern firm or business. It was a productive unit, which required physical capital, in the form of land, buildings, equipment and draught animals such as ploughing oxen and labour in the form of direction, day-to-day management and a workforce. Its ownership could be transferred, by the overlord. In many cases this was ultimately the King.

Moder. Mother.

Nadr. Norse. Viper or adder.

Norns. Norse. The Norns were female beings who ruled upon the destiny of gods and men. They roughly correspond to other controllers of humans' destiny, the Fates, elsewhere in European mythology. (See Wyrd.)

Reave. To plunder or rob. Reaver: a raider. From Old English: reafian. Also: reive.

Reeve. An administrative officer who generally ranked lower than the ealdorman or earl. Different types of reeves were attested, including high-reeve, town-reeve, port-reeve, shire-reeve (predecessor to the sheriff), reeve of the hundred, and the reeve of a manor.

Seax. The seax is a type of sword or dagger typical of the Germanic peoples of the Early Middle Ages, especially the Saxons. The smallest were knives, the longest would have a blade over 50 cm long.

Shire. Groups of hundreds were combined to form shires, with each shire under the control of an earl.

Silvatici. Norman term for the 'men of the woods' or the green men.

Sōlmōnath. February. The month of cakes, possibly referring to the cakes' sandy, gritty texture.

Skíta. Old Norse: shit.

Snekke. Or snekkja, meaning 'thin and projecting' was typically the smallest long ship used in warfare, with at least 20 rowing benches. Typically, 17 m long and 2.5 m wide with a draught of only 0.5 m. It would carry a crew of around 41 men (40 oarsmen and one coxswain or master).

Staddle Stone. Supporting bases for granaries, hayricks, game larders, etc. The staddle stones lifted the granaries above the ground thereby protecting the stored grain from vermin and water seepage.

Sumor. Summer.

Thegn. A member of several Norse and Saxon aristocratic classes of men, ranking between earls and ordinary freemen, and granted lands by the king, or by lords, for military service. The minimum qualifying holding of land was five Hides.

Thrimilce. May. "The month of three milkings," when livestock were often so well fed on fresh spring grass that they could be milked three times a day.

Vill. Medieval English term to describe a land unit which might otherwise be described as a parish, manor or tithing.

Weodmonath. August. Plant month.

Winterfylleth. October. The winter full moon.

Wyrd. Norse and Anglo-Saxon. Fate or personal destiny.

Yule. Aere Yule ('Ere Yule or Before Yule) is December and Aefter Yule (After Yule) is January.

Historical Notes

The background to the main historical characters and events is told within the narrative of the story. Whilst Hravn and Ealdgith, and their wider household, friends and associates, are fictional the principle characters other than Maldred and Hugh Fitzgibbon are real. Earl Gospatric, to whom this book is dedicated, is my many times great grandfather through the Curwen line. Elftred's family also feature within that same family line.

As the Harry of the North Series has evolved I have developed Ealdgith's character to reflect that of a young English noblewoman of the pre-invasion period. She would have been educated alongside her brothers and schooled to support her husband in the management of his estates. This would often have been in the role of 'peace-weaver', enabling disputes to be resolved diplomatically rather than force. Some women in Anglo-Saxon society had a special role in their community. They were wise women, people trained in the art of healing and spiritual guidance. Ealdgith has grown to fill both these roles.

Whilst it was unusual for a woman to lead men into battle, it was not unheard of in medieval European societies. Aethelflaed, the Lady of the Mercians, has a particularly significance in English history. The significance of having her as a forebear would not have been lost on Ealdgith.

Following the Harrying of the North in the winter of early 1070 the Normans imposed a firm grip upon the region, impoverishing many, dispossessing most of the English nobility and closely controlling those who were able to retain their lands. Durham became the preserve of the church.

In 1072, with his position again secure, King William came north with an army and a fleet. King Malcolm 3rd of Scotland met William at Abernethy and, in the words of the Anglo-Saxon Chronicle "became his man," handed over his eldest son Duncan as a hostage and arranged peace between William and The Atheling, Edgar. Accepting the overlordship of the king of the English meant little, as previous kings had done so without result. A condition of 'the peace' was that Gospatric would not be permitted to take exile in Scotland, hence his consequent flight to Flanders following his expulsion from the Earldom of Northumberland. Earl Walthoef, Gospatric's cousin, was appointed in his place.

In the years that followed the Conquest, as the Norman expropriation of English lands intensified, large numbers of English thegns fled overseas. Other thegns, plus the vast majority of common English people did not have this option, and stayed in England. Most submitted and some took to the woods. The Anglo-Norman monk Orderic Vitalis tells us that the Normans called these 'resistance fighters' silvatici – the men of the woods. The English, it is said, called them the same thing in their own language: green men. A tradition of resistance and rebellion against unwanted masters that lies at the heart of the later Robin Hood legend. Whilst the Normans were able to retain control of productive low-lying arable lands and communication routes, their grip on remote forested valleys and uplands was tenuous. These were the preserve of those who lived outside the law. Who is to say that the actions of Hravn and Ealdgith were not the basis for some of the 'green man' stories of that time? Theirs was certainly a means by which a resistance could have been continued.

Forteviot was the ancient capital of the Pictish kingdom of Fortrenn. Built on the site of a Neolithic settlement and Roman fort it was an early medieval palace and favourite residence of early Scottish monarchs including Kenneth MacAlpin and Malcolm Canmore.

There is no Highland Dance older or better known than the Sword Dance, or 'Ghillie Callum'. The Sword Dance is the ancient war dance of the Scottish Gael and is said to date back to King Malcolm Canmore. Tradition says the original Ghillie Callum was a Scot's prince who was a hero of mortal combat against one of MacBeth's Chiefs at the Battle of Dunsinane in 1054. He is said to have taken his own bloody claymore (the two-handed broadsword of Scotland) and crossed it over the bloodier sword of the defeated Chief and danced over them both in exultation.

High Street, or Brethstrett, is an ancient high-level route that follows a series of connected ridges at heights up to 800 metres to link the Eden valley to the Windermere valley at Ambleside. Its construction is unlike that of other Roman roads and it probably dates back to the Bronze Age. It would have enabled the quick movement of marching troops between the Roman forts that controlled the central Cumbrian fells.

Pendragon Castle is a stone-built early medieval castle in the valley of Mallerstang. According to legend an earlier version is supposed to have been built by Uther Pendragon, father of King Arthur. Whether there is any substance to these old tales will probably never be settled, and there is no evidence from the limited archaeological investigations for any building here before the Norman castle built in the reign of King William Rufus. The name and the location provide an excellent basis for the violent, reaving, "Pendragon' family.

The ancient road to the east of the River Eden in Mallerstang is known as "Lady Anne's Highway" in memory of Lady Anne Clifford, the Countess of Pembroke, who often travelled along this track while moving between her many castles. It is, however, much older than this and was used by the Romans as a route between Wensleydale and their forts along what is now the A66 across Stainmore. It would have provided an excellent 'back door' into the land of the upper Eden valley.

The upper Eden valley is known to be rich in various minerals, though not now to a commercially viable extent. Lead and coal have both been extracted in small quantities from Mallerstang in the past.

Lead has been mined across the North of England since Roman and Norse times. Although the archaeological evidence is limited this is because extensive extraction in the past three hundred years has obliterated much of the earlier workings. The head of Ullswater was a particularly productive source and Greenside Mines at Glenridding, near Patterdale, were in production until the mid-20th century. Hravn and Ealdgith were fortunate indeed to be granted these lands

Printed in Poland
by Amazon Fulfillment
Poland Sp. z o.o., Wrocław

50630571R00174